MURDERS IN VOLUME 2

MURDERS
IN VOLUME 2

Elizabeth Daly

FELONY & MAYHEM PRESS • NEW YORK

All the characters and events portrayed in this work are fictitious

MURDERS IN VOLUME 2

A Felony & Mayhem mystery

PRINTING HISTORY
First U.S. edition: 1941
First UK edition: 1943
Felony & Mayhem edition: July 2005

ISBN: 978-1-933397-01-6

Manufactured in the United States of America

Printed on 100% recycled paper

CONTENTS

The icon above says you're holding a copy of a book in the Felony & Mayhem "Vintage" category. These books were originally published prior to about 1965, and feature the kind of twisty, ingenious puzzles beloved by fans of Agatha Christie and John Dickson Carr. If you enjoy this book, you may well like other "Vintage" titles from Felony & Mayhem Press.

For more about these books, and other Felony & Mayhem titles, or to place an order, please visit our website at:

www.FelonyAndMayhem.com

MURDERS IN VOLUME 2

Volume I

*Invective by
Lord Byron*

CHAPTER ONE

Fourth Dimensional

ON WEDNESDAY AFTERNOON, June fifth, 1940, the sun made one of its rare appearances during that cold, wet spring. It poured through the windows of Mr. Henry Gamadge's library, made him shift his typewriter, and persuaded him that summer had come at last, and that he needed a rest. The branches of the big ailanthus tree that screened him from the backs of the opposite houses were in full leaf; a pleasant smell came in on a warm breeze, reminding him that New York was a seaport; he sighed.

Theodore, his old colored servant, came in with a card on a tray.

"Lady to see you, Mr. Gamadge; she say she have no appointment, but Mrs. Harrison Barclay tell her you ain't stiff about things like that. I wanted to say you ain't stiff enough about anything."

"The wonder is you didn't turn her away." Gamadge took the card, and read what was on it.

"She ain't anybody to turn away, Mr. Gamadge. Nice lady, not as young as she was any more; came in a nice little car with a chow dog in it, young lady drivin'—you don't see many young ladies like her around this town."

"Glad you approve of the outfit. Quite a nice name on the card, too," said Gamadge.

"You goin' to see this lady?"

"Of course I am. Nobody turns down a Vauregard."

He got up and went along the hall to his bedroom at the front of the house. He freshened himself a trifle, gazing without interest into the mirror. It reflected a tallish, well-made figure in the process of being ruined by long stooping over manuscripts, and the rather colorless face of a man in his middle thirties. Its features were blunt, its expression amiable, and its eyes a hard green-gray.

He went downstairs to his office, which had once, in his parents' time, been a drawing room. It retained its marble chimney piece and its molded ceiling, but was now furnished with a steel filing cabinet and a roll-top desk, besides several comfortable chairs; and it was walled with reference books. A lady got out of one of the chairs.

"I'm in luck," she said.

"I hope so, Miss Vauregard." Gamadge's first impression of this member of an old and once important family was pleasant. Miss Vauregard was probably between fifty and sixty years of age, slim, straight-backed, with very dark eyes and hair, a sallow-ivory face, and an engaging smile. Her plain black suit had been cut by an excellent tailor, but not recently. It was a trifle out of date, even shabby, but she wore it with elegance. She began with a rush:

"I must warn you first, the whole thing is completely crazy; you may not want to have anything to do with it. I shouldn't blame you. You'll have to hear how silly it is before I even sit down. Perhaps you won't listen to another word."

"That sounds ominous. Try me." Gamadge smiled at her.

"Mr. Gamadge, do you believe in the fourth dimension?"

After a moment's pause, Gamadge replied calmly and with gravity:

"Do I believe in it as a mathematical speculation, Miss Vauregard?"

"No; I mean about people or things going into it, and then perhaps coming out again."

"Oh. There was a lot of that kind of talk about twenty years ago. As a boy, I was fascinated. The proof would have to be watertight to convince me, Miss Vauregard."

"I knew you'd say so. Uncle Imbrie is convinced, though; he thinks somebody went into the fourth dimension, and then came out again. We want you to take the case."

"Is there a case?" Gamadge, studying her anxious face, concealed his amusement.

"Yes. It's a business matter. We want you to charge your usual fee."

"But I'm not a detective, you know; I don't charge fees for detecting. It wouldn't be proper."

"I know; but this case is in your line, really it is. When I tell you about it, you'll realize, as we do, that you are probably the only living soul who could help us out of this mess. I mean it—the only one."

"You can't be serious."

"Indeed I am. You'll know what I mean in a moment if you decide to come to our rescue."

"And send in a bill. All right, Miss Vauregard, I shall, if I find that I can do anything to help you. Make yourself comfortable, do. You look tired." He pulled up a chair for her and sat down himself.

"I feel better already." She sank back, and Gamadge offered her a cigarette. "No, thanks, not just now. Oh, what a relief to see what you're like! I might have trusted Lulu Barclay— she's critical."

"I'm much obliged to her," said Gamadge, laughing.

"She said you were easy to talk to, besides. I know Uncle Imbrie will like you!"

"I'm to meet Mr. Imbrie Vauregard? I think I did, once—very casually. My father knew him a little, too."

"That's the point! He knows all about you, and would like to see you again, and show you his books. I can take you there. He doesn't receive many people, now, he's so old."

"I wasn't aware that Mr. Vauregard cared especially about books; he was looking at furniture when I met him at that auction."

"But not buying any. He likes to look at furniture, and then go home and look at his, and decide that nothing anywhere else is so good. His interest in books—his books—only developed a few years ago, when he retired from business. He was a great sportsman, like most of the family, you know. Horses, mostly."

"His business was real estate, wasn't it?"

"Yes, the Vauregard property. He managed to hang on to his share of it, which is more than any of the rest of us has done. Well, I talked to him about you, and he thought it would be nice for you to see the old Vauregard library, and tell him if it's worth a real catalogue. I don't believe it is; like everything else in the old house, its principal value is in having always been there."

"I remember him as a perfectly charming old gentleman. How old is he, anyhow?"

"He's eighty."

"Is he really? I hope the dear old thing hasn't been getting himself into trouble connected with the fourth dimension in space?"

"He doesn't know it, but I'm afraid he has—serious trouble." Miss Vauregard's smile had vanished, and her clever face had fallen into aging lines of anxiety. Indeed, there was something almost of horror in the look she gave him. After a moment she said, more lightly: "You will think the whole thing is grotesque, and perhaps you'll laugh; but at least you won't tell! That's reason number three why you're our only hope. One: Uncle will be delighted to see you. Two: You know queer things about old books. Three: We can trust you."

"Did Mrs. Barclay say so?" smiled Gamadge.

"I flatter myself that I can see that kind of thing for myself."

"Dangerous conviction, but I hope justified in this case."

"We don't dare to breathe a word to the police, and we couldn't possibly engage a private detective. It isn't only that we mind the publicity; but to be perfectly frank with you, Uncle would be very angry, and might cut us all out of his will. He isn't out of his mind, no matter what delusions he has; and he'd never forgive us for interfering, or meddling with his affairs behind his back. Do you think me very sordid?"

"Very sensible. I respect your candor."

"But we can't see his money go to criminals."

"I should hope not."

"We must investigate."

"By 'we,' I suppose you mean the rest of the family. Who are they?"

"Well, not many. You know who my sister is: Angela Morton. She married Tom Duncannon, five or six years ago, and retired from the stage; but she's Mrs. Morton still, to everybody but Tom."

"Of course I know Mrs. Morton—as a delightful actress."

"The whole crowd of us live with her in her Seventy-fourth Street house—she takes care of us all: Dick Vauregard, my brother's only child; Clara Dawson, my niece—her parents are dead, too—and myself. Dick is twenty-six; he's a lawyer. Clara's twenty. They haven't any money of their own, and neither have I, now. Uncle Imbrie gives us allowances—he's a darling, so generous. He gave Dickie and Clara cars for Christmas. But of course he wouldn't have us living with him in that sacred old house, the one on Traders Row."

"Never married, did he?"

"Uncle Imbrie married? Goodness, no!"

"Is it true that he's leaving the old Vauregard house to the city?"

"It's to be a museum, and he's endowing it."

"Oldest in New York, isn't it?"

"One of the oldest. It was built in 1827, and it's just as it always was, inside; outside, too, for that matter, except that there are no grounds left—only the side passage and the back garden."

"I've seen it, of course."

"Most people have. How he does hate the sightseeing busses! Luckily for him, they can't actually get into Traders Row. They used to try, but it doesn't lead anywhere, and they could hardly turn around, and the cobblestones were too much for them. Very few cabs come in now."

"That endowment business sounds as if your uncle had a considerable fortune to dispose of."

"Practically all the Vauregard money that's left. The rest of us weren't businesslike, I'm afraid. Angela made a good deal during her great days on the stage, but she is not a saver. I don't know what she has now. Her expenses must be frightful, with that great house and all. Tom doesn't contribute much, I should think—he's been unlucky in his plays lately. You know he's an actor."

"Yes, indeed. I've often seen him."

"Angela has always been perfectly wonderful. Girls in her circumstances didn't go on the stage much in the Nineties; but she took the bit in her teeth. Father was dead by that time, luckily for them both! Mother never did get over it. Angela was always so brave; I couldn't have done it. But then," said Miss Vauregard, cheerfully, "I never could do anything. I'm perfectly useless. Ever since my money finally went, about 1932, I've simply hung on to poor Angie. I do odd jobs for her, run the house, take Clara around—that sort of thing. I haven't the brains for real work of any sort."

"I imagine most people would consider a job like yours real work, Miss Vauregard."

"Well, I don't get fat on it, but it's not too much for me, yet. We go along quite happily, and Uncle Imbrie has promised us all his money when he dies. I do wish Angie had left well enough alone, and not suddenly had this horrid idea of going back on the stage."

"Horrid? It sounds delightful. What a comedian she used to be!"

"That's just it, Mr. Gamadge; she's a comedian. But this theater group—what do they call themselves? The Mermaid Group—they want to put on a most frightful old play, *The White Devil*."

"No!" Gamadge whistled. "That's exciting."

"Oh, do you know it? They want Angela to play the woman— the white devil. Did you ever hear anything so—"

"Angela Morton as Vittoria Corombona! I hope I shall live to see it."

"Don't say that, Mr. Gamadge! You can't remember the thing! I had to type out the part for Angie, so that she could study it while she was having her hair done, and being massaged, and so on. I can't type well at all, my typing is awful, but it's a tremendous secret, so she made me do it for her. I never read such a horrible play in my whole life, and I've read and seen a good many. Why do they say we're getting brutal in literature, Mr. Gamadge? As far as I can make out—of course I know nothing about the drama—I should say we'd improved."

"Have they done any more of the casting, if I may ask? Who's going to play the duke—Brachiano?"

"The wretched creature who kills his wife in order to marry Vittoria? Angela wants Tom to play it."

"Hm. Not quite the type, perhaps; rather modern. Still, I don't know."

"Angela is working on Bridge, the director of the group. She insists on Tom."

"What a comeback she's staging for herself! How far have the proceedings gone?"

"Not far at all, I'm glad to say. They can't find anybody with money to back them, and it's going to be very expensive. Angie can't possibly do it, Mr. Gamadge. She'll make such a fool of herself—I can't bear it."

"She's done some extremely dramatic plays in her day; I'm not at all sure she couldn't pull this off."

"But she's sixty, Mr. Gamadge, and the play describes Vittoria as the most beautiful young creature in the world. I can't bear to have people laughing at her."

"Well—think of Bernhardt, and Ellen Terry, and so on. They got away with murder." He rose, and walked over to a stand piled with foreign newspapers. From among them he extracted a London *Observer* several weeks old, looked through it, and finally cut a fragment from the middle of a column. Miss Vauregard, watching him absently, objected:

"But Angela isn't Bernhardt, or Ellen Terry, and so on." She added, as Gamadge came towards her, the fragment in his hand, "She isn't even Mrs. Patrick Campbell. I don't know anything about acting, of course, but—"

Gamadge looked at her, looked at the clipping, seemed to reconsider showing it to her, and put it into his wallet. He said, with a half smile: "Let's assume that you know nothing about anything, Miss Vauregard, and let it go at that. Anyhow, your family has entrusted you with the delicate task of employing a private investigator. But exactly what for? Aren't you going to explain?"

Miss Vauregard did not speak for some moments. At last she said: "I've been putting it off. I can hardly bear to tell you the story, it sounds so mad. But Uncle isn't mad. I want you to see him as soon as possible—this afternoon, if you'll come— and then meet the family, and talk it over."

"Talk what over, Miss Vauregard?"

"I'm just going to tell—oh, what a lovely cat. Here, kitty, kitty—Ouch! Take away your horrid pet, Mr. Gamadge; he has bitten me."

"I hope he didn't break the skin? No? Good." Gamadge clasped the big orange cat about the middle, and swung him in a low arc out of the doorway and into the hall. He trotted angrily away. "I'm frightfully sorry. Most peculiar cat, Miss Vauregard. He will lie on your lap for hours, if you'll let him, rubbing his head against your hand. But if you rub his head, it's all off. He wants to do all the petting himself."

Harold, Gamadge's assistant, a short, dark young man, came silently through a door which led to the laboratory. A white blouse covered his apple-green slack suit, and he held a glass slide between a finger and thumb. Gamadge said: "I'm in conference."

"You wanted this as soon as I had a report on it."

"Is it late eighteenth-century paper?"

"Yes, it is."

"Then don't bother me. Write and tell the client so."

"The ink ain't. Somebody got some old paper and wrote the letter on it; not so very long ago, either."

"Oh, the devil. Excuse me, Miss Vauregard. All right, I'll look into it later. Tell the client to hold everything."

Harold dematerialized, and Miss Vauregard said: "He looks most intelligent, but very young. Where did you get him?"

"I didn't get him; he turned up on the doorstep one day, like Martin the cat. But he works for his keep, which is more than Martin does. And he hasn't bitten me—not yet."

"You mean you don't know anything about him?"

"Not a thing, except that he's going to be good in more than one branch of science, and his taste in dress is awful, and he won't eat decent food, and I'd trust him with my last cent, and with my life. He doesn't know that, though."

"Is he good at detective work, too?"

"Oh yes, he loves it."

Miss Vauregard looked melancholy and thoughtful. Presently she said: "I suppose he might help you.".

"But what at, Miss Vauregard? What at?"

"I'll just have to get it over with, Mr. Gamadge. Do you know what the old Vauregard house is like?"

CHAPTER TWO

The Vauregard Legend

GAMADGE CONSIDERED for a few moments before he answered. "I've never been inside it; I remember the outside of it quite well. It's a nice, plain, flat-faced affair; red brick with white trim—early nineteenth-century Classical Revival, I believe. There's a white portico with columns, a white door, fanlight, side lights, white marble steps. There are two windows on each side of the door, five above, five below the flat roof. A high brick wall with a double iron gate in it, surmounted by a lantern, extends from the left-hand front corner of the house to the property next door. I shouldn't be surprised if it surrounded the whole Vauregard place—what's left of it."

"It does."

"When I was in Traders Row the gates were hospitably open. I stood and looked in. There's an old brick-paved driveway, with a three-foot grass border on either side of it. It goes straight back past the house, and ends nowhere. There's a latticed side door—kitchen, I suppose—towards the rear. A border—when I saw it there were pansies, candytuft and verbena in it, and I wondered again at the apparently spotless virtue of the neighborhood—a flourishing and well-kept flower border runs along beside the house, and stops short when it reaches what looked like a very nice little garden. I think I observed a fountain, and beyond it a sort of summerhouse, with vines on it."

"The arbor."

"I suppose that driveway used to go to the stables?"

"Yes. They're all gone, of course. Uncle keeps his car in a garage on the next street."

"I believe I noticed a background of rather tall trees."

"Yes, the yards behind Uncle's house are quite pretty, and the upper stories of those little houses in the rear are all studios. Uncle isn't overlooked at all, the north lights in the studios are too high."

"He isn't much overlooked from the front, either; not as I remember Traders Row."

"No, but it's too bad those great warehouses, or powerhouses, or whatever they are, were put opposite him."

"New York didn't begin to conserve its beauty spots until rather late in the day. Traders Row is a cul-de-sac, isn't it? I remember that it ends in a little park and a railing. The Vauregard mansion is on the south side, about the middle of the block, and the other houses are smallish brick affairs, most of them walk-up apartments."

"Uncle couldn't buy up any of that property."

"Rival landowner? Too bad. Anything else about the Row? Let's see; it has the biggest and bumpiest cobblestones I ever saw this side of Europe, and narrow, uneven brick sidewalks."

"Yes. That garden of Uncle's—" Miss Vauregard began the sentence briskly enough, but broke off in the middle of it. She remained silent for so long that Gamadge, watching her, said at last: "You look tired, Miss Vauregard, you really do. How about adjourning to my library and having some tea? My servants were Bermuda trained, and they bring it in every afternoon, whether I want it or not."

"I should love tea, but if we go to Uncle Imbrie's he'll give us coffee; he won't like it if we refuse any."

"Well, let's make ourselves comfortable, anyhow."

A little automatic lift carried them to the second floor. Gamadge ushered Miss Vauregard into the big, high-ceilinged room, installed her on the davenport, and provided her with cigarettes. Then, glancing at her again, and noting her strained and tense expression, he said: "You're feeling very low; let's have a mint julep—Theodore makes extremely good ones."

"You're much too nice to me. How restful this is."

She continued, when Gamadge had given his order and come back again: "Books, books, books. You'll laugh at Uncle's library. He only has what was always in the house, you know…I was going to tell you about the garden, Mr. Gamadge. Uncle adores it. There's a tree or two, shrubs, little flower borders— Uncle says they're planted just as they used to be—the fountain (somebody brought it from Italy once) and the arbor.

It's the original arbor, you know, and it's made of iron-work, painted white. There's a big wisteria vine on it. It's a tiny little place, with a seat just big enough for two."

"Does Mr. Vauregard take his ease there—and his coffee?"

"He never sits there—nobody does. Nobody has, so far as we know, for over a hundred years."

"Really?"

"Nobody even goes into it, except the gardener, and painters, and so on. But the family hasn't been inside it," said Miss Vauregard, trying to assume a brisk, informative tone, "since May the third, 1840."

"Dear me." Gamadge studied her, half amused, half curious.

"I'll tell you who were living in the house at that time."

"But look here, I don't think I can stand the suspense. Why hasn't anybody sat in the arbor since May the third, 1840?"

"I want to tell it properly, from the beginning, or you'll

keep interrupting me with questions, and I shan't get it right at all. In 1840, Uncle Imbrie's grandfather—Angela's and my great-grandfather—lived in Traders Row with his wife, his brother Charles, and his three children—a boy and two girls. The boy—Uncle Imbrie's father—was the eldest. He was about nine. It was through him that most of the details came down to the rest of us, but by some miracle the story never got outside the immediate family. He isn't supposed to have said anything to a soul until he grew up and got married.

"What happened was this: Sometime during the year 1839 the Vauregard relatives in England sent over a governess for the children in Traders Row; a girl of very good family, army people, all of them dead. You know the sort of thing. Her name was Miss Lydia Wagoneur. The English Vauregards knew all about her. They shipped her over on a boat called *The Pride of Whitby*. She was a perfect treasure; a pretty girl, too—regular English beauty. Blond, fair skin, blue eyes. She was quiet and reserved, but romantic—in a ladylike sort of way. Read poetry."

"I get her, absolutely."

"She was highly accomplished, poor thing. Couldn't teach the children much of anything, but was good at watercolor painting, music, and fine needlework. What made her such an absolute treasure was that she didn't seem flirtatious at all; I can hear my grandmother telling the story: 'She never cared for gentlemen'."

"Or so she said, unfortunate Miss Wagoneur."

"Well, it made her a great pet with all the eagle-eyed matrons in the Vauregard circle. All went well, until on May the third, 1840, at half past five in the afternoon, she went out to the arbor with a book. She usually strolled out there for a while after the children had had their tea, and she had had her supper with them, and they were off her hands for the day. After dinner the family sometimes had her into the drawing room to play the piano, or whatever a piano was called then."

"It was called a piano."

"Was it? On this particular afternoon she took a book with

her, to read in the arbor. It was the second volume of a set of Byron's poems."

"This kind of detail is very satisfactory to the antiquarian."

"She was wearing a cornflower-blue silk dress with a white ruffle around the neck, and a white silk scarf. The coachman saw her go into the arbor; and from that moment, she was never seen again."

"Good heavens."

"She had disappeared off the face of the earth, and all that she took with her was the volume of Byron. It has never been seen again, either. Nothing was left to tell the tale but a gap on the shelf between Volume I and Volume III. For some queer reason, the gap was allowed to remain. It remained for a hundred years, and it was as much a part of the old house as the walls and ceiling were."

"No queer reason at all, Miss Vauregard—integral part of a family legend, and I must say a rather eerie one. There never was any solution to the mystery?"

"Never."

"Did nobody suggest that Miss Wagoneur might have found some gentleman to her liking at last?"

"Plenty of people suggested it, but the family wouldn't hear of such a thing. They told everybody that she had gone back to England, sudden crisis in her affairs, that sort of story. The English Vauregards never seem to have heard a word about it all."

"Are you telling me that your great-grandparents made no effort to find this young woman?"

"None whatever. They argued that she must have vanished of her own free will, and that it was none of their business. They wished to hear no more of her."

"They didn't ask themselves whether this friendless being might not have wandered off in some kind of seizure?"

"Evidently not. We have thought of that since, but if they did, they didn't say so."

"Good heavens."

Miss Vauregard gave him a cynical smile. "You don't understand, Mr. Gamadge! Think of the dear children! Any scandal about their governess might have reflected somehow upon them, the poor innocents. But the boy was old enough to refuse to swallow any such story. He didn't believe that his Miss Wagoneur had gone off to England without her bags and her boxes, without even her hat; and without saying good-bye to her dear little charges, either. He listened at keyholes, he hung over the banisters; but all he ever found out was that she had gone into the arbor with the Byron, and had never been seen again."

"I suspect your Great-granduncle Charles. Was he a bachelor?"

"Yes, and quite a rake, I believe, but he wasn't even in the city at the time."

"Never mind, I suspect him."

"Not a breath of suspicion has ever attached to Great-granduncle Charles or to anybody else. The servants were blacks, faithful and responsible, and of course they never talked outside the family, but it was certainly through them that the idea originated—the idea that there was something wrong with the arbor. The children were forbidden by their mammies to enter it, and gradually the older people began to feel that it was just as well to keep out of it. The arbor lent a kind of fearful fascination to calls on Uncle Imbrie, and even he always seemed to view it with respect and awe."

"Quite extraordinary that such an unusual bit of family superstition never leaked out into somebody's memoirs."

"There was a ban on talking about it, too. I think we always had a sneaking sense of shame about Miss Wagoneur."

"Well," and Gamadge smiled at her, "the trail is rather cold. I suppose you don't want Harold and me to start on it now? I think you said Miss Wagoneur's relations were all dead. Their descendants are not likely to bring charges of criminal neglect against the Vauregards at this time of day."

"Don't laugh; it's too awful. Uncle Imbrie thinks she's come back."

Gamadge sat up in his chair and looked at Miss Vauregard.

"Just a hundred years afterwards, you know—on May the third, 1940. Don't laugh; it's too awful."

"I'm not laughing."

"He says she appeared in the doorway of the arbor at half past five in the afternoon, wearing a cornflower-blue silk dress with a white ruffle, and carrying a white silk scarf."

"Mr. Vauregard told you this?"

"Yes, and he isn't insane. Of course, he's always been interested in what he calls occultism; he thinks he's psychic. It's nothing connected with religion, you know, and it's not spiritualism. He calls it New Soul."

"He's addled his head with New Soul, the poor old boy!"

"Well, he has some excuse, Mr. Gamadge; when she came back, she brought the book with her."

"Book?"

"The Byron, Volume II."

"The Byron, Volume II," repeated Gamadge, staring.

"The gap in the bookshelf is filled at last. You'll see Volume II when you go into the library—the binding is fresher. He's so proud of it all, he'll probably find some excuse to show it to you."

Gamadge leaned back and lighted a cigarette. "I never heard such a story in my life."

"The book matches, Mr. Gamadge; it's out of a set of ten. You see why we want you so dreadfully? You absolutely must come and look at it."

"I shall certainly come and look at it. A collector's item, by Jove, if ever there was one!"

"And now he's dropped New Soul completely, and hasn't been near the Chandors since."

"Are they the New Soul merchants?"

"Yes. Angela introduced him, as a matter of fact—she's

always been amused by that kind of thing. So many theater people are."

"And business people."

"Then she got worried about it, he seemed so engrossed by them. Now he's dropped the Chandors."

"Doesn't need any more instruction in the occult; I see. Have you been introduced to Miss Wagoneur since she escaped from the fourth dimension?"

"Yes, but not for nearly a month after she came. However, I heard of her on May the fourth. Uncle telephoned me quite early that morning—it was a Saturday, I remember—and asked me to do some shopping for him. I often do, I'm always delighted.

"He startled me with a most extraordinary story. He said that the daughter of some very old friends of his—English— had been caught somewhere in Europe when the Germans came, and was only just able to escape to the coast. Her family was all dead, she had no friends nearer than England, and as the only boat she could find was coming to America, she thought of Uncle, whom she had often heard spoken of by her people, and embarked."

"What did he say she had been doing on the continent of Europe?"

"She was a governess in some noble family. He explained that she had lost all her luggage, and had even had to borrow a hat."

"How did she manage about papers?"

"Kind officials got her off as a refugee."

"Not a bad story at all."

"I swallowed it whole, and couldn't imagine what poor Uncle would do with the girl, or how he could stand such an upset. He then said that he wanted me to buy a complete outfit for her; the sort of thing Clara would wear, the best to be had. She was older than Clara, though—about twenty-five. She'd given him measurements, and I could tell that she was very slim, and quite tall. He said she was a blonde, and liked blue."

Gamadge closed his eyes, and murmured: "Good heavens."

"He said no formal evening things, nothing but the simplest clothes—she was quite shattered by her experiences, and couldn't stand meeting anybody for a long time. He said I wasn't to tell a soul, not until he gave me permission.

"I went straight out and did the shopping; it took me all morning, until lunchtime. Old John—that's the butler; he and his wife Eliza have taken care of Uncle for years, the nicest English couple—John met me at the door, looking bewildered, and took in the parcels. I didn't pump him, of course; but I did ask how the young lady was getting on, and he said she was resting, and hadn't come down yet. I asked after Uncle, and he said Uncle was 'a little shaken, Madam, but quite happy making plans for the young lady.' I wasn't at all surprised to hear that he was shaken. A refugee in Traders Row!

"John was evidently dying to say more—we're very thick —but neither of us quite dared. John and Eliza simply worship Uncle; they're absolutely loyal to him. I heard nothing more until last Sunday. Uncle Imbrie telephoned and asked me to coffee—that always means five o'clock. When I arrived there was nobody in the library, and I wandered around as I always do, glancing at the books and things. I had my first shock when I saw Volume II of the Byron staring at me from the shelf; that gap in the set is such an institution that it was like seeing the Winged Victory with a head, or the Venus of Milo with arms. I could hardly believe my eyes. I stood and gaped at it, and I saw that it looked quite fresh and brown—the others are faded almost to gray.

"Uncle came in while I stared, and it gave him a perfect opening. You cannot imagine the excitement and pride with which he told me that gruesome story. I wouldn't have hurt him for anything, so I didn't laugh hysterically; but I did have to sit down and drink a glass of sherry."

"I should have called for a pony of brandy."

"John always brings sherry when women have the vapors.

When I felt strong enough to listen to the rest of it, he told me how dazed, and lost, and frightened she had been, gazing around her and up at the high buildings; and how he had helped her into the house by the garden door, and how she had fainted in the hall. He called John and Eliza, hastily told them the refugee tale (he'd just been listening to the radio, poor darling) and Eliza got her to bed. It's their rest hour, between coffee and sherry time, and Eliza was upstairs in her room, and John was in their sitting room. They hadn't seen a thing."

"Neat timing."

"Yes, I realized that, and I was in a fury. Poor Uncle! I really didn't see how I could behave decently to the creature when he brought her in, but luckily I pulled myself together. He introduced her as Miss Smith. He had implored me not to refer to anything 'extra-normal,' as he called it; I was to pretend that she was really a refugee. I assure you, I feel ten years older since that afternoon."

"Quite a strain for you. Does she feel the strain, do you think? It must be terrific, for her."

"She didn't show it. A quiet, well-bred young woman, very pretty, rather stiff and formal, old-fashioned manners, you know. I could have shaken her! Sitting there knowing that we must humor Uncle! Perhaps she really is English—I don't know. I poured the coffee, and she drank a cup, and ate cakes. Uncle's story had confused me so that, to tell you the truth, I hardly regarded her as human. She's very pale."

"Don't forget that she's putting something tremendous over, or trying to."

"I tried not to remember it. Uncle was pleased with me; he told me afterwards, when she left the room, that I had been most tactful. I was to break it to the family under seal of secrecy, and they were to come and meet her by relays."

"The family ghost."

"He needn't worry about our telling people! I don't know what we should do if the papers got hold of it! Well, she's installed there; for good, so far as we know. Uncle said it would be a long time before she would be able to take up normal life again. He said it was a miracle she had kept her senses, and that he had a sacred responsibility. Dick met her on Monday— he's furious. Being a lawyer, he spends his time trying to think what we can do about it without a scandal, and without annoying Uncle. Angela refused to go—says she couldn't trust herself; she sent Tom Duncannon in her place. Uncle didn't like it at first—he thought Angie shouldn't have told anyone outside the family—but that's absurd, of course she told her own husband. Tom seems to feel as if she must be a victim, in some way. He's not as down on her as we are, I suppose because Uncle Imbrie is no relation to him. Mr. Gamadge, you will help us? May I take you there this afternoon?"

"Nothing short of violence could keep me away from the place; but what exactly do you want me to do?"

"Find out who she is, of course, and get some proof of it that we can show Uncle Imbrie."

"Let us discuss it intelligently over the juleps. Theodore has taken his time with them, but I see they're frosted."

CHAPTER THREE

Something to Be Afraid Of

"**N**OW FOR IT," said Gamadge. "Feel better?"

"Ever so much better. It was just what I wanted."

"Then let's go over the general situation. You must realize, of course, that if you took the thing into court Miss Smith would hardly last through the first day's proceedings. No, I understand that you don't care to take it into court; but your nephew, who is a lawyer, must know that there are private proceedings, in which a delicate family matter like this can be adjusted before a referee, or in judges' chambers, or something. The refugee story would be knocked into a cocked hat, and your Uncle Imbrie clapped into a sanatorium for life, if you wanted him there."

"We shouldn't for one moment consider putting him into an asylum. He isn't insane."

"But credulous, Miss Vauregard—extremely credulous. Lots of aged persons have been judged incompetent on less evidence than this preposterous arbor story."

"I won't have him put in a sanatorium. And if he isn't put in one, he'll be so annoyed at us for interfering that he'll cut us out of his will. We'll lose all his money, instead of just whatever he means to give Miss Smith."

"The financial end of it is interesting, but complicated. How will he convey property to Miss Smith, do you think?"

"In his will—he'll make a new one. Or he'll create a trust."

"Wills can be broken, and this will could certainly be broken. Don't forget that Miss Smith will never go into court with either of her stories. Trust ditto. She wouldn't put faith in one or the other."

"She'll persuade him to give her the money outright."

"Unless he really is insane on this one subject, a businessman like Mr. Vauregard wouldn't hand over cash or its equivalent—not any amount that would repay Miss Smith for all her trouble—in a lump sum, and for the asking. I suppose she and her backers—she really must have backers—can't be out after something in the house, can they? Something of great value?"

"There isn't anything in the house worth such a conspiracy. Even the silver wouldn't be worth it. I suppose she must be a member of a gang, mustn't she? And poor Uncle's alone in the house with her, except for the servants! I can't bear it. We must get rid of her somehow."

"You're not sufficiently afraid of her to risk publicity, and your uncle's annoyance, though."

"Risk! If we put him in the papers—oh, it doesn't bear thinking of. And besides, he simply dotes on the woman! I'm only afraid that the shock of finding she's an impostor will kill him."

"Perhaps nothing could shake his faith in her. Nothing will, if it's an obsession."

"But he's so perfectly sensible on every other subject. He's very shrewd about money. He would loathe having been made a fool of. If we could convince him, by degrees…"

"Delicate job. I suppose he guards her like a dragon?"

"She needn't meet anybody, unless she chooses. She certainly wouldn't see you, unless she thought you had just come to look at the books. She hasn't been off the place since she came, and I never get a moment alone with her."

"Well, let's see. What about catching her out, in some way? The clothes she came in; could we get hold of them? One single modern hook or eye, you know "

"Mr. Gamadge, it's too maddening! She burned them up."

"Burned them up!"

"Uncle told me so. He said she hated the sight of them. He was telling me the refugee story, and he said that she had worn the things for weeks, and asked permission to burn them."

"I suppose she told him that they awakened sad memories of the fourth dimension. Miss Smith is very clever."

"It's a gang—a gang of swindlers."

"How about these Chandors—the New Soul people? It sounds a little like the kind of game an occultist outfit might think up."

"We did discuss them, but Angela says they're most respectable, have a lot of important clients, dine out, make loads of money. She doesn't think they'd risk a thing like this."

"Well, we have three bets left. Miss Smith may give herself away; she can't know all the habits and customs, to say nothing of the phraseology, peculiar to England and America in the early part of the nineteenth century."

"Uncle wouldn't know enough to ask her the proper questions, or catch her if she made a mistake; and he wouldn't let anybody else ask her anything at all. I don't see how she can keep it up forever, though—playing such a part. And living in seclusion like that I should think would drive her mad."

"I'm afraid she doesn't mean to keep it up forever. Our second chance is to identify her with somebody. Would Mr. Vauregard let me take a picture of her, I wonder?"

"I can see her letting you take her picture!"

"If I brought a jolly little miniature candid camera along,

Mr. Vauregard might think it a charming idea; and she couldn't do anything about it, short of flying from the room."

"She'd fly from the room, and say she felt ill, or something."

"I can't try it out today, because I have no such camera, and can't use one effectively, anyway. Harold will have to teach me. He does all the photographing around here, mostly in the laboratory. The only trouble is, one can't do much, secretly, with a photograph. The police—"

"Please don't talk about the police, Mr. Gamadge. Angie has a fit if you mention them."

"They can be discreet."

"We can't risk it."

"Our last hope, then—the Byron."

"And that's where you come in, Mr. Gamadge! If you could just show Uncle that it doesn't belong to his set!"

"If I only could. I suppose you don't know the edition, or anything?"

"I got a minute to myself on Sunday, and copied the card in his file."

"Miss Vauregard, you are worth working with, and for."

She took a slip of paper from her handbag, and gave it to him. He read:

Byron (Lord).
THE POETICAL WORKS OF LORD BYRON,
complete in 10 Volumes.
Published by R. W. Pomeroy, No. 3 Minor Street,
Philadelphia, 1830.
Small octavo, brown cloth gilt.
Engraved frontispieces, and notes.
Fair condition, engravings foxed, bindings faded.
(Volume II missing).

"Volume II missing," repeated Gamadge, looking up at Miss Vauregard. "Gives one quite a chill."

"I had a chill when I saw it back on the shelf!"

"I suppose he hasn't remembered to erase that phrase from the card. You say Volume II is much fresher than the Vauregard set?"

"Much. It's a kind of purplish brown."

"What they called puce, I suppose. It must have been in a dry, dark place all these years."

Miss Vauregard shuddered.

"I imagine that your uncle wouldn't allow me to borrow it?"

"He'd almost sooner lend you Miss Smith, I should say."

"I never heard of this little Byron, but I'm sure it can't have much, if any, market value."

"They picked it up somewhere."

"Yes. I'm pretty well convinced that this whole remarkable scheme was hatched on the day when someone found Volume II somewhere, and remembered the Vauregard legend."

"I have thought all along that Uncle must have told the arbor story to the Chandors or some of their clients. They'd all talk about psychic experiences, and so on, I suppose."

"I really must meet the Chandors, and find out exactly what they do go in for."

"Angie will introduce you, perhaps. You'll have to have an introduction, you know—they're very particular."

"Well, have you any other suggestion, Miss Vauregard?"

"I wondered why you didn't think it queer that she was able to get to the house without being noticed. She was in costume."

Gamadge looked at her ironically. "I'll show you something," he said. He got up, went to a bookcase, opened it, and after a minute's search took out a couple of books bound in tree calf. He brought them to a table beside her, opened them, and turned the pages of one and then the other.

"Here we are," he said. "*Old Curiosity Shop*, published in 1841, and *Oliver Twist*, published in 1838. Fashions didn't change as often then as they do now, so we may take those pictures as representing styles in 1840. Look at Miss Rose Maylie, Nancy, Barbara, even Little Nell. Discount the scoop bonnets and let Little Nell's dress down an inch or so, and what do we find? We find tight bodices, with a ruffle or a wide collar at the neck; long, full skirts, without any crinoline; short sleeves; rather low-heeled slippers, with or without straps. The hair is parted in the middle, and worn high, or loose on the neck."

Miss Vauregard studied the illustrations with surprise.

"Now, tell me," said Gamadge. "If you saw a young woman dressed like that on a New York street, late in the afternoon of May the third, would you stop and stare?"

"No, I shouldn't. If she wore a long skirt, she wouldn't be wearing a hat, either."

"The puffs on those sleeves seem inclined to bloom at the elbow; that doesn't look right to me," and Gamadge frowned. "Would the scarf hide them?"

"Of course it would. Mr. Gamadge, she could have walked blocks to Uncle's!"

"And she's banking on the fact that the family won't consult the police, and let them ask whether anybody saw her, or even circulate a description."

"How I wish I could consult the police!" exclaimed Miss Vauregard, in a rage.

"Which brings us to the summing up." Gamadge closed the books, and leaned forward to look his client firmly in the eye. "You don't get all the implications of this affair."

"Don't we?"

"No, you do not. Just go over these points with me: Miss Smith can't face court proceedings—all she is out for, we suppose, is a free gift, made during your uncle's lifetime. But it's absurd to suppose that the gift could be a small one. Think of the elaborate preparations, the trouble, the huge risk. She didn't merely have to assemble that costume; she has had to learn a long and difficult part, and act it many hours a day.

"Every hour of her sojourn in that house, especially since last Sunday, when the family was taken into Mr. Vauregard's confidence, is fraught with danger to her now. Seven persons, including myself, know the arbor story—a lot of people to keep a secret—the whole business may leak out at any time. We have agreed that she wants publicity less even than you do. Why is she staying in that house? To get what she went for, of course; the moment she got it, she would disappear. But how could she be sure of getting it in time to go while the going was good? The more I think of it, the less can I see Miss Smith as a professional swindler, the member of a mob."

"But she's there, Mr. Gamadge, and it all happened."

Gamadge sat back, and gave his client an odd, rather helpless look. He said: "You still don't see the grave implications."

Miss Vauregard seemed frightened. "There's something more to be afraid of? Mr. Gamadge—surely she has no motive for harming Uncle?"

"My point is that we don't know what her motives are, or what she really wants. Look here—I must see your uncle and Miss Smith, if possible, and talk to the rest of your family, before I take this job."

Theodore came in. "Young lady calling in a car," he said. "Wants her aunt. Says not to disturb yourselves, she can wait."

"That's Clara. She's going to drive us down to Traders Row." Miss Vauregard rose, looking perplexed and uneasy. Gamadge went down with her, picking up his hat from the hall table as they left the house. Theodore saw them out of the front door, but did not immediately close it—he was evidently much interested in the neat little sedan that waited at the curb.

CHAPTER FOUR

"From a Friend"

THE OCCUPANT OF THE CAR was a large golden-red chow, which stood on the front seat with his head and shoulders out of the window. A young woman in riding clothes had taken up an easy position on the curb, and leaned against the car beside him, rubbing his head.

"Well, darling," said Miss Vauregard. "Did you see Ching?"

"Yes. She's much worse, Aunt Robbie. I'm going back tonight. The vet thinks he may have to do it soon."

"Oh dear. Mr. Gamadge, this is my niece, Clara Dawson; and this is Sun—his grandmother is very old, and she's ill. We are all distressed about it."

"How do you do, Mr. Gamadge?" said Miss Dawson. "Are you going to save Great-uncle Imbrie for us?"

Gamadge had already taken a quick but comprehensive glance at her longish oval face, lightly tanned, with a flush on the cheekbones; at her wide forehead, short nose, and benign gray eyes. A brown riding hat came down low on her dark-brown hair, and a long, russet-brown coat hung loosely over dun-colored breeches and shining brown boots. Miss Dawson's figure was still rangy; her riding costume became it.

He thought: "I'll never get this girl," and a moment later: "Am I out of my mind?" He said: "I can try, Miss Dawson."

The cat Martin, which lived for occasions like these, put his head around Theodore's legs, crept through the doorway, and trotted down the front steps. The chow came through the car window; Martin leapt into the next area, Gamadge after him, the chow after Gamadge, and Miss Vauregard after the chow. She grasped Sun by the tail, while Martin eluded Gamadge, and dashed into the street. Miss Dawson caught him by falling on him.

"I do hope to goodness you haven't scratched your boots." Gamadge assisted her to her feet. Martin, having instantly relaxed in her arms, lay back against her shoulder with closed eyes and a pleased expression. Miss Vauregard bundled the chow into the back of the car.

"Any damage?"

"Not a bit," said Miss Dawson.

"Let me take that wretched animal."

"Oh, he's so sweet. Don't disturb him yet."

"He'll take a piece out of you, in a minute," said Miss Vauregard, getting into the sedan.

"You actually like the creatures?" asked Gamadge.

"I only wish I had one. I even have to keep Sun at a dog's boardinghouse."

"You know very well, dear," said Miss Vauregard, through the car window, "that your Aunt Angela cannot be disturbed by dogs and cats. After Ching clawed the curtain..."

Miss Dawson allowed Theodore to take Martin away from her, and into the house. She said, "He's lovely."

"He hopes to see you again." Gamadge opened the car door for her, and went around to the other side.

Miss Dawson looked at him with the detached benignity that he found so remarkable.

"I'd love to see him again."

"How about coming to tea with him?" He got in, and she started the car. "Bring anybody, or nobody. If it must be somebody, I should prefer Miss Vauregard."

"When can I come?"

"Tomorrow."

"Marvelous."

Miss Vauregard hung on to the chow's collar while he leaned out of his window, getting the breeze in his hair. Catching Gamadge's eye, she held it with a snapping black one, and shook her head.

"No good?" asked Gamadge, over the back of his seat.

"No."

"You giving me orders?"

"Information."

"What's all this?" inquired Miss Dawson, turning the corner into Park Avenue, and stopping for a light.

"We got confidential over our mint juleps," said Miss Vauregard.

"Drinking at a business conference? I never heard of such a thing."

"Your aunt and I don't have to keep our heads clear when we have a business conference. We're affinities."

"Only," said Miss Vauregard, "Mr. Gamadge doesn't seem to realize quite how we feel about getting into the papers."

"I merely think that there are worse things than getting into the papers."

"Such as losing a million dollars," said Clara demurely.

"There are worse things than losing a million dollars."

"Not many, I should think." Miss Vauregard's tone was dry.

"The Barclays say you don't like to be in the papers." Clara's glance at him was still more demure.

"They've been telling on me, have they?"

"Fred and Alma have. Fred told me how scared he was because he thought you were falling in love with Alma."

"When I fall in love with anybody, nobody will have to think about it; they'll know it, and so will the girl."

"Alma said it was silly—you'd only been acquainted for a few hours."

"I shouldn't need a few hours. A few minutes would do." Gamadge, watching the profile beside him, decided to be grateful for the mint julep; it seemed to have inspired his voice with a subtle urgency which had its effect. The flush on Miss Dawson's cheek grew deeper. She said nothing, and she did not look at him. Nobody spoke again until the car turned west from Astor Place.

"I'll let you out at the corner," said Miss Dawson, then; "Those cobbles wreck my tires." She added: "I suppose I can't go in with you, Aunt Robbie? I'm dying to see Miss Smith."

"No, dear, you cannot."

Miss Dawson drew up at the curb, and Gamadge got out. He helped Miss Vauregard to descend, and then, at Clara's request, transferred the chow to the front seat. Clara said, "I shouldn't be surprised if she turned out to be a refugee, after all."

"Very charitable of you," replied her aunt dryly. "But Miss Smith might have communicated with the family when she discovered that your great-uncle's wits were going, and that he took her for a historical character."

"If she had, she'd have lost her meal ticket. I don't believe you realize how a refugee must feel, Aunt Robbie."

"Perhaps I don't, dear."

"Shall I wait here for you?"

"Certainly not. Go home and get out of those hot things."

"I promised to pick Cameron up and take him for a turn before dinner."

"Go along then."

Clara turned the car, and Gamadge walked beside Miss Vauregard down the narrow, tree-shaded street. Grass and bushes showed at the end of it, through the iron railings of the little park. Late afternoon sunlight turned the old bricks under their feet to a deep rose color, and cast a friendly glow on the brownstone walk-ups on the left, and the high windowless walls on the right. But for a distant view of towers rising into the sky, it might have been a street in any little European town.

Gamadge paused in front of a wide gateway in a brick wall, surmounted by an arch and an old lantern.

"Gates hospitably wide," he said. "This must be a quiet, law-abiding backwater."

"It is. Uncle has never had any trouble with intruders."

"Until now." He stood surveying the brick-paved driveway, the side of the old three-storied house, the glimpse of garden beyond. A hint of white ironwork showed through vines in the distance. "The famous arbor; candid little place. I see that the windows on either side of the kitchen door are high."

"Yes; you can't see out of them without standing on something."

"And these nearer windows are well curtained."

"That's the dining room."

He followed Miss Vauregard past the high brick wall, and along the house front to the pillared portico. Miss Vauregard pulled a shining brass handle, and produced a soft, faraway jingle. A pale old man in a striped waistcoat opened the door and smiled at her.

"Well, John; how is Uncle?"

"Quite well, thank you, Madam. He is waiting for you in the library."

"Don't come up." She stepped past him into a white-paneled hall, Gamadge following.

"Thank you, Madam." He closed the front door, and stood with his hand on the knob of it, regarding her in a melancholy, questioning way.

"How is Miss Smith?" she asked brightly.

"Much better, Madam. If you have time, Eliza would like to speak to you before you go."

"I'm always delighted to see Eliza."

"We are a little worried about Mr. Vauregard, Madam."

"Oh dear. Why?"

"He seems a little restless and nervous; I don't think he is sleeping very well."

"He isn't used to guests in the house, you know, John."

"No, Madam." His look said, "Neither are we."

Gamadge followed Miss Vauregard up the shallow stairs with their delicate white rail, along a wide hallway, and into a large room which ran across the back of the house. High windows with summer curtains of glazed flowery chintz admitted light on the east, south and west. A gray marble chimneypiece stood against the west wall. The other wall spaces were filled by gray-painted bookcases, each a little temple with fluted columns and pediment. Glass wall brackets held candles. There was an old French rug on the mirrorlike floor, and a portrait over the mantel represented a self-satisfied young man in a white wig, pointing to a row of lawbooks. His coat was blue, his buttons gilt; and his little finger displayed a ring with a big red stone in it.

Old Mr. Vauregard came forward, a pleased smile on his face, and held out his hand. The original of the seal ring was on his little finger, and his long, narrow, high-nosed face looked like that of the portrait, grown old. His pale ivory skin was hardly lined, and his bright, dark eyes as clear as Gamadge's own. He stooped a little—a tall man, he now seemed to be of little more than medium height. He was perfectly turned out in gray flannel trousers and a thin, unlined, woolen house jacket, russet-brown.

"How very pleasant this is," he said. "Robina, my dear child, how did you persuade Mr. Gamadge?"

"He may not want to see the books, Uncle Imbrie," replied Miss Vauregard, embracing her uncle affectionately, "but he does want to see the house—everybody does."

"And he shall see it. Sit down, Mr. Gamadge; or would you prefer to glance at my poor little collection, and get it over with, before we have our coffee?"

"I'm afraid it can't be much more than a glance, this afternoon, sir," said Gamadge. "You'll have to turn me loose in it some time when you can spare the library, if you want an opinion that's worth anything."

"It has only one merit." His host led the way across the room to the bookcase on the right of the northeast window. "We Vauregards have never been great readers; but my great-great-grandfather brought these in this case from England with him, somewhere about the middle of the eighteenth century, and my great-grand-father bought what was known as a 'gentleman's library,' the usual classics, and installed them with the others. Here they are, in the next sections. Then my grandfather built this house—we lived first on Battery Place, and this neighborhood was quite rural. He added to the library—not very wisely, I dare say. You'll find plenty of rubbish. The point is that it's a family collection, and will remain with the house when I die and turn it over to the public."

Gamadge passed from section to section of the bookcases, hands in pockets. He paused occasionally, and once or twice he asked to see a book.

"Congratulations on your Early Americana," he said. "Very nice, very complete. Lacks one or two of the most marketable items, I'm afraid."

They had reached the shelves, glassed as were all the others, which stood between the east windows. Gamadge paused, and Mr. Vauregard, hovering, showed signs of mild excitement. "American editions of English poets," he said. "Worthless, I believe."

"Unless you have any association books among them."

"Well…I might say that I have." Mr. Vauregard's eye sought that of his niece. "Do you notice that little set—the Byron—which is so badly faded, except for one volume? Prettily gilded, isn't it? That was a presentation set, but not presented by the author, I'm afraid!"

Mr. Vauregard opened the glass door of the center compartment, and took Volume I down from the shelf. "Rather an amusing little family story connected with it—if you can bear family stories?"

"They are the breath of life to one of my profession, if they are in any way connected with books."

Miss Vauregard, looking rather bewildered, sat on the davenport beside the fireplace, nervously playing with her gloves.

"It's trifling, but so characteristic of the period." Mr. Vauregard opened the book and handed it to Gamadge, who read on the flyleaf the following inscription, in a bold and ornamental hand:

> To Fanny Vauregard
> from
> ...A Friend

"Fanny Vauregard was my grandmother," said Mr. Vauregard. "She had a very dear friend—school friend; they attended The Van Korn Female Academy, and they were very sentimental. At that time, you must know, young ladies were not permitted to read Byron's poems."

"Or much besides, I suppose," said Gamadge.

"But Byron was taboo—absolutely taboo. She and Cornelia Dykinck—by the way, Robina, do you ever see the Dykincks nowadays?"

"Well, Uncle, I'm afraid not. Old Mrs. Dykinck is an invalid, and the girl is such a bore."

"Wrong of you, very wrong; you shouldn't lose sight of the old family friends. Not," said Mr. Vauregard, archly, "that I have seen anything of them myself, for the last twenty years or so; but then, bachelors are privileged."

"They are, indeed," said his niece, tartly. "I don't remember anything about this story you're telling, Uncle Imbrie."

"You young people would never listen to any of my old stories. No wonder family traditions die out. Well, my grandmother and her friend—Cornelia Petrie, she was then—swore a mutual covenant that the moment they married, which they proposed to do the moment they left school, they would instantly purchase and read the whole of Byron."

"Leaving the spouses to their own devices for a week or so?"

"No doubt. They married, and settled down; and of course I need not tell you that they quite forgot Lord Byron."

"And all his works."

"And all his works," repeated Mr. Vauregard, laughing heartily at this mild witticism. "But my Great-uncle Charles, who was something of a wag, heard the story; and on the next Christmas—the Christmas of 1839—he picked up two little sets of Byron, exactly alike, and presented them to my grandmother and to Mrs. Dykinck."

"Delightful," said Gamadge, refraining from a glance at Miss Vauregard, who seemed suddenly to have lost much of her vivacity.

Mr. Vauregard said: "We have other odd memories connected with the set. We—ah—lost the second volume a century ago, and if you will believe me, Mr. Gamadge, it was not until last month that I was able to replace it!"

"How very odd—and how lucky," said Gamadge. "I see that it looks much fresher than the others. Might I look at it?"

Mr. Vauregard's fingers trembled as he took it from the shelf and handed it to Gamadge. The latter examined it with interest, and asked casually: "Where did you find it?"

"Well…you mayn't ask. The details of my discovery are a secret."

"The details of such discoveries so often are." Gamadge produced a little leather case containing a reading glass, and inspected Volume II without and within; he then repeated the process with Volume I.

"One would swear they came out of the same set," he declared, "if it were not for the fresher binding on your discovery."

"Wouldn't one?" Mr. Vauregard beamed.

"Only, the top edges of Volume II are a little rubbed." Gamadge peered at a double row of tiny scars, which seemed to say that Volume II had been squeezed into a space too narrow for it.

"I saw no rubbing." Mr. Vauregard peered anxiously over his shoulder.

"Microscopic. And Volume II is not foxed; Volume I is; rather badly, too, I'm afraid. And so," continued Gamadge, taking out Volumes III and IV, "are your others."

"Extraordinary," murmured Mr. Vauregard, with a dreaminess in his dark eyes which suddenly gave him the "psychic" look that Gamadge had missed before.

"You really ought to write up your story of the lost Byron. I'm sure I could get it printed for you in *End Pieces*," he said.

Mr. Vauregard looked wistful. "I wish I dared."

John the butler brought in a big silver tray and coffee service. When he had placed it beside Miss Vauregard's sofa, her uncle said: "I hope Miss Smith will come down, John?"

"Yes, Sir. I asked her, and she is coming."

Miss Vauregard indicated a chair beside the table for Gamadge, who brought the Byrons with him, and laid them on a stand at his elbow.

"The young lady who is staying with me has had a sad time of it. I should warn you," said the old gentleman. "She has been obliged for some years to support herself as a governess—in Poland, of all tragic places. She is an English girl, with all the courage of her race; but she is now what I think you call a refugee."

Gamadge murmured something, sympathetically.

"She finds herself alone in a new world," continued Mr. Vauregard, who seemed to be enjoying his own fabrications very much, "and she is dazed and still shaken by her experiences. Her escape has been in the nature of a miracle. She is shy of strangers, and she cannot yet face crowds. I hope to persuade her—gradually, of course—"

He broke off, rose, went to the door, and came back with a young woman whose hand was on his arm. She was tall, slender, and pale, with a wide, high forehead, a pointed face, and large blue eyes. She wore no vestige of make-up. Her fair hair was dressed in curls on the top of her head, a coiffure which made her long neck seem longer. The short, gentian-blue and white dress which Miss Vauregard had chosen for her became her very well, but Gamadge thought that the cornflower silk in which she had arrived from nowhere would have made her seem even more wraithlike, and far more delicately bred.

"Here is our kind Robina, my dear," said Mr. Vauregard, with touching gentleness. "And this is Mr. Gamadge. Mr. Gamadge, my ward, Miss Smith."

(HAPTER FIVE

Miss Smith

Miss SMITH BOWED FORMALLY to Gamadge, and sat down beside Miss Vauregard on the davenport. That lady had described her as very pretty; the description did not do her justice. She was almost beautiful, and she had a beautiful voice.

"I have everything I need, thanks to you, Miss Vauregard," she was saying.

"But you will want dinner gowns, Lydia." Mr. Vauregard accepted a cup of coffee from his niece. "Simple dinner gowns. We shall be going away—we must get out of the city. You will want to dress; my niece will find you something."

Miss Smith said gravely that she had not worn a dinner gown for years. "I am accustomed to nursery tea, you know. I never dined when I was in a situation."

Gamadge, feeling as if he were struggling through a Jane Austen tea party, and listening avidly to every intonation of Miss Smith's voice, told himself that so far as he was concerned, she might well be English. His ear could not catch the fault, if there were any, in her accent.

"Well, my dear child, all that is over now," protested Mr. Vauregard.

"But when I am stronger, of course I must earn my living again," said Miss Smith, looking down at her coffee cup. "That is settled."

"Time enough to talk of that when you are stronger." Mr. Vauregard, glancing at the three Byrons at Gamadge's elbow, went on: "I was telling Mr. Gamadge that little story about my grandmother and Mrs. Dykinck."

Miss Smith said that it was amusing.

"We are not a reading family; but now that I have time," said Mr. Vauregard, "and a trained taste to choose for me, and a voice like yours to listen to, my dear, I shall be asking to hear some Byron myself."

Gamadge put down his cup, and took up Volume II. "You are fond of Byron, Miss Smith?" he asked, turning the pages.

"Yes, I am very fond of Byron," said Miss Smith.

"So am I. Shockingly underrated he is, just now; one can't turn a leaf without coming on something good:

> *Cold-blooded, smooth-faced, placid miscreant!*
> *I have had many foes, but none like thee!*

Colossal—isn't he?"

Miss Smith, her head a little on one side, as if her slender neck were not quite strong enough to support it and its mass of pale-gold hair, coughed gently.

Gamadge continued: "How did the original Volume II get lost, if I may ask, Mr. Vauregard? Or is that a secret too?"

There was a pause. "We never knew what became of it," replied the old gentleman.

"No outsiders in the house at the time?"

"Nobody but Mrs. Dykinck herself, and as she had a

duplicate set, one can hardly imagine her taking Volume II, or any other volume."

"Mrs. Dykinck was here that afternoon?" Miss Vauregard, who seemed to be increasingly depressed, asked the question with a start. "If I ever knew that, I had forgotten."

"She was, but she did not know," said Mr. Vauregard, with a fond look at Miss Smith, "that anything had been lost."

"Mightn't she have lost her Volume II, and had the bright idea of replenishing it from your set?" asked Gamadge, smiling. "Stranger things have happened."

Mr. Vauregard, again laughing heartily, said that he doubted whether any female Dykinck had ever had the initiative required for such an adventure.

"Well, your lucky find is in excellent condition; one would almost say that it had been in a state of suspended animation, if books could be called animate objects. Sometimes I almost think they are." Gamadge rose, drifted back to the bookcase against the east wall, replaced the Byrons, and sauntered to the southeast window. He stood there looking out at shaven turf, narrow graveled paths, a fountain surmounted by an Italian bronze nymph, dolphin and shell—all in the worst baroque taste—and the little white arbor, now smothered in wisteria.

"I see that you are not superstitious, Mr. Vauregard," he said, without turning.

"Superstitious, my dear fellow! I think I may truthfully say that I am not."

"You have a hexagon made of iron on the premises."

"A hexagon!" Mr. Vauregard got up and joined his guest at the window.

"Your summerhouse is hexagonal."

"It is; and pray why not?"

"Doesn't Albertus Magnus, or Paracelsus, or somebody, warn us against hexagons made of metal?"

"Bless my soul, do they?" Mr. Vauregard was intensely interested. "I never heard so." He gazed at his disappearing cabinet with a kind of delighted dismay. "Do you hear that, Lydia? Hexagons!"

"All nonsense, of course," said Gamadge, "but I know I've read about it somewhere. I've read so many useless but interesting things. I think I even have a book—*Mystery and Magic of Numbers*—something of the kind."

"I should be most grateful if you would let me see it, Mr. Gamadge. Most grateful."

"I'll look it up for you."

"Would it—I know you're a busy man. Would it be too much to ask—could you look it up—ah—soon, Mr. Gamadge?"

"I'll drop in with it tomorrow; I have business downtown. May I leave it here between six and seven, say?"

"You may, indeed, and I shall take it very hard if you don't give me a minute or two of your time, when you do leave it. Robina, my child, absurd as it may seem, I don't think I ever realized until this moment that the arbor is hexagonal."

"Why should you, Uncle Imbrie?" Miss Vauregard, now definitely out of sorts, spoke crossly. "Such nonsense."

"Well, my dear, I know your healthy skepticism of old; but yours is a narrow way, after all. Straight, but narrow. Lydia's mind is more receptive to wonders. Don't you think Mr. Gamadge's information about metal hexagons very odd, Lydia?"

Miss Smith replied in a colorless tone that it was very odd. Her eyes, as they rested on Gamadge, seemed to say that he was very odd, too; but her face remained serene.

"And we must make an appointment when you come tomorrow, an appointment for you to give a day to my books. I shall be glad of your professional services," said Mr. Vauregard, delicately, as he and Gamadge shook hands. Gamadge then took Miss Smith's slender fingers in his, and their eyes met; Gamadge's as blank of expression as her own.

He followed Miss Vauregard down the wide stairs to the lower floor. They went along the hall, through an arched door, and into a narrower passage that led by way of an open doorway straight into the garden. Pausing with her hand on a knob to the left, she faced him, angrily.

"Uncle is in his dotage."

"Or very near it. He is amenable to any suggestion, if it approaches the occult, I should say."

"Hexagons! You made that up!"

"Well, I had to invent some excuse for coming back as soon as possible. Miss Smith must be scared away, somehow."

"If you didn't scare her this afternoon, she can't be scared at all. That poetry! I felt as if the ice were breaking under me."

"Wouldn't you have been thankful for a cold dip? I should. The atmosphere up there is morally stifling. Your uncle and Miss Smith are museum pieces."

"Have you really that book—about numbers?"

"I have a book about numbers. I didn't promise that it dealt with the danger inherent in hexagons."

Miss Vauregard, looking grim, opened the door on the left and they entered a pantry. Its window was set high in the east wall. They passed through it into a big kitchen, all white-painted brick and plaster. Its east windows were also high, with an open door between them which gave on the carriageway. Two south windows afforded a view of a narrow yard or drying ground, enclosed by a lattice; between them rose the ancient coal range.

A stout, rosy-faced old woman in a gray dress and a large white apron turned to greet them:

"I am glad to see you, Miss; that I am."

"Dear Eliza, we have kept you from your nap."

"I need a talk with you more than any nap." Eliza glanced at Gamadge, and Miss Vauregard introduced him:

"This is a friend of mine—Mr. Gamadge. I'm showing him the place."

Eliza bobbed at Gamadge, obviously wondering how to get rid of him. She said: "I wanted a word with you about the Master, Miss. John and me are worried about him."

"So am I, and so is Mr. Gamadge. We can talk in front of Mr. Gamadge, Eliza."

"Oh, very well, Miss, if you say so, I'm sure. Shall we go into the 'all, Miss? And Sir?"

Since Eliza crossed the passage and opened a door on the opposite side of it, and since this door led into a large comfortably furnished sitting room with a dining table in the middle of it, Gamadge realized that she had referred to the servants' hall, and that her beginnings had had a lofty and impressive background.

"Do sit down, Eliza," said Miss Vauregard. They all sat down, and Eliza plunged into her subject:

"Miss, I know you will understand. If that young lady stays, we must get in a maid. You know how kind and considerate the Master is—all laundry goes out, and all cleaning comes in. I have a kitchenmaid nine months of the year, and would have one now, but we were going on our vacations next week, and the Master was leaving town as usual. Now he says it depends on the young lady's 'ealth, and we are making out as best we can."

"I never thought, Eliza. Of course, you must have extra help. Uncle has probably been too upset by all this to think of it."

"Nor do we wish to remind him, at present. If you could—"

"Of course I will. I don't know what Uncle can have been thinking of. You don't have to maid her, I hope?"

"Not a thing has she asked me to do, Miss, not since she appeared, with no coat nor no 'at, and came to 'er senses in the drawing room. But she never steps out of the 'ouse, and it's not right that she should take care of 'erself, let alone that 'ead of 'air."

"I'll speak to Uncle. No, I'll leave him a note."

Miss Vauregard sat down at a little desk in the corner, and began to write. Gamadge said:

"The poor thing had no luggage, either, I think."

"No, Sir; she did not."

"How in the world did she lose her hat?"

"It was borrowed from a passenger on the boat, Sir."

"Dreadful thing to happen to an English lady."

"Sir, if she is an English lady she was brought up somewhere else."

"Really? Lost her native characteristics, has she?"

"I couldn't 'ardly say what she has lost, Sir, but John and I 'ave the same impression."

"Burned her clothes, Mr. Vauregard says. That shows you what she'd been through."

"Sir, when I brought up early tea, she said: 'I 'ave 'ad these things on my back for weeks and weeks, and if your 'usband will light a fire in the furnace, I will burn them.'"

"Furnace? She said furnace?"

"That," replied Eliza, with a resigned look at him, "is what she said—or so I remember it."

Miss Vauregard looked up from her writing. Gamadge continued: "I should have thought she knew nothing about furnaces."

"Don't they 'ave central 'eating on the Continent, Sir?"

"Not where Miss Smith is supposed to have been. So she burned the things in the furnace, did she?"

"Sir, she did more than burn them. She waited in the cellar until they were ashes, and then she raked out the pan."

"Raked out the pan, did she? Dear me."

"And scraped it. I think," said Eliza, in the hushed tone of shock, "she put the 'eap down the drain."

"Very thorough."

"John and I were greatly distressed, Sir; we thought 'er sufferings had sent the young lady off 'er 'ead."

"Looks like it."

"We 'ardly like the Master being alone with 'er."

"But she seems to be improving, doesn't she?"

"Quite the lady, Sir. But that beautiful thick silk the dress was made of! I 'aven't seen such silk in years. It did seem cruel to put it on the fire."

"Too good to burn, was it?"

"Fresh as when it came out of the shop, it looked."

"How was it you and your husband didn't see her arrive?"

"I was up 'aving my sleep, and John was 'aving a nap, as usual, on that sofa there. After 'e takes up the coffee at five o'clock, 'e 'as nothing to do until the sherry goes up at seven."

"Unless callers come."

"The Master only sees 'is friends very rarely, nowadays; and 'e always tells us when 'e expects them."

"These windows are screened off from the garden by bushes, aren't they?"

"What we can't make out," said Eliza uneasily, "is why that young lady should 'ave come by the garden door. The Master often takes a stroll after his coffee, and 'e says 'e saw her at the gates; why did she stand at the gates, we want to know? Miss, and Sir, I won't say it's none of our business, because we have took care of the Master for forty years; but what we want to know is—" Eliza's small round eyes stared distressfully from Miss Vauregard to Gamadge—"could the young lady be a himposter?" The fact that she had aspirated a vowel for the first time was the measure of her anxiety.

"Just between ourselves, and you, and John," said Gamadge, leaning his elbow on the table and looking at her seriously, "we are asking ourselves that question. Now, we're all in the same boat, and we must trust one another. The greatest favor you could possibly do Mr. Vauregard would be to settle the question, once and for all."

"I'm sure we—"

"Just you get John to help you, and sit down tonight and write out every word you've told us today. Every word. The new silk dress, the furnace, the scraping, and the drain. And your impression that Miss Smith is not quite so English as she ought to be. Will you do that?"

"What will 'appen to the paper?"

"Miss Vauregard will take charge of it."

Eliza turned her head and looked at Miss Vauregard, who nodded vigorously.

"He's an old gentleman, you know," said Gamadge, "eighty years old. He looks so young that one forgets it."

"I'll get John to do it, Sir. Tonight."

"Good for you."

Miss Vauregard rose, and handed an envelope to Eliza. "There you are," she said, "and I can promise you that at least you'll have another woman in the house."

Eliza bobbed them out of the garden door. They followed a very ancient brick path around the grass plot that contained the fountain, which never played any more—its shell was full of leaves, and its basin planted with a fine crop of geraniums. Gamadge had to put aside a trail of wisteria, in order to make his way into the arbor.

He sat down in a green gloom, and surveyed the back of the old house. Mr. Vauregard appeared at an open window, nodding and smiling at his niece, who stood between the arbor and the fountain; a fair, pointed face looked over his shoulder, but the rather wide lips did not smile. When the window was empty again, Gamadge came out.

"You wouldn't go into the arbor for anything, would you?" he asked. "Not even now."

Miss Vauregard said: "Of course I would."

"You didn't."

"Well..." she gave a nervous laugh. "Old habits are hard to break, at my age. How did you like it?"

"Gave me claustrophobia."

(HAPTER SIX

Inside Information

"**I** KNOW NOW WHAT YOU MEANT, Mr. Gamadge."
Miss Vauregard spoke in a hard, dry voice. They were walking
eastward through the quiet back streets of lower New York,
where even pedestrian traffic seemed almost to have ceased.
Miss Vauregard had insisted on going uptown by subway.

Gamadge looked down at her sympathetically. "You do?"

"I realized it when Uncle began talking about that other
set of books. What a fool I've been. Of course Volume II
belongs to the Dykinck set!"

"Looks that way. See here, Miss Vauregard—you'd better
fire me."

She ignored this. "Uncle wouldn't tell that old story to the
Chandors—why should he? And even if he did, how could
they, or any outsider, get hold of the Byron?"

"How, indeed?"

"You guessed it before you ever heard about the Dykincks
from Uncle. I don't see how."

"It just looked to me like an inside job. I couldn't see Miss Smith having the nerve, or the facilities, to put it over without backing from a member of the clan—someone who knew all the ropes. You thought an outsider was trying to get your uncle's money away from the family; I wondered whether one of the family wasn't trying to prevent exactly that. It would have to be somebody who had learned that Mr. Vauregard meant to give property away, and who was determined to keep the old gentleman's interests within the home. So far, I should say that it's been a huge success; he's engrossed by Miss Smith, and he already regards her as his ward."

Miss Vauregard walked along very fast beside him, her head down. "I can't believe it!" she said, in a choked voice. "I won't believe it!"

"Don't take it so hard. Look at it as a pious fraud—an attempt to prevent your uncle from doing something very foolish, something he would never have done even a few years ago, and wouldn't do now if his wits weren't befogged by fake occultism."

"I can't look at it as a pious anything; it's the meanest, ugliest thing I ever heard of. Uncle wouldn't have cut us out completely. Of course we need all the money we can get—he's sinking so much, as it is, in the endowment for the house. The poor children—Clara has nothing. Angela won't do much for us, she thinks first of Tom Duncannon. But if we can't get extra money without cheating Uncle in this shameful way, and employing a girl like that, I don't want extra money at all."

"How is he leaving it?"

"A hundred thousand to each of the children, and the residue to Angela and me. He's supposed to have a couple of millions. Oh, I can't believe any of us would stoop to such a miserable thing! You must be wrong!"

"Well—an outsider wouldn't have known how your uncle was likely to react to the arbor scene, and an outsider couldn't be sure that the family wouldn't drag the thing into the open. And—what's most important, and what bothered me from the start—nobody but a member of the family, or an affiliated member, could count on a big enough slice of Mr. Vauregard's fortune to repay them for all the trouble and risk. Not without fighting for it!" He added, with another commiserating glance: "Do try to look at it calmly. The idea was to save your uncle's money from swindlers."

"I can't look at it calmly; if we do a thing like this, we're swindlers ourselves. Would you look at it calmly?"

"No, because that kind of thing is dangerous. People who embark on a fraud—even a pious fraud—never know where they're heading for. They never know how the situation may develop, especially when they get in outside help. We don't know what the Miss Smiths are capable of, or what they'd do at a pinch. We don't know what we'd do, ourselves. I think you ought to get to the bottom of it. But you can fire me, if you like. I'll retire gracefully and ask no questions."

Miss Vauregard stopped dead. "What shall I do?"

"You'll have to decide before I see the family; because, as you no doubt realize, we shan't be able to take them fully into our confidence. Not a word about that other set of Byron!"

Miss Vauregard walked on again. "It's too horrible! As if we were a lot of gangsters! Mr. Gamadge, if we're right, I shouldn't have been allowed to engage you!"

"Well, nobody could very well protest. Besides, a private investigator can sometimes be more or less controlled by his employers, and I suppose your family knows enough about me to be pretty sure that I shouldn't blackmail them."

"When you meet them, you'll know how impossible—"

"I can't meet them, unless you decide to keep the real investigation between us two."

"But that Smith woman will tell—whoever she's in with; she'll tell all about what happened this afternoon, and everything that was said."

"I suppose she must often slip out at night and meet her friends; she wouldn't telephone. The point is, she doesn't know whether the Dykinck story impressed us, or how we mean to act on it."

"I only wish I knew how we meant to act on it! Mr. Gamadge, how can I conspire against the rest of the family? And poor Angie—she's paying you! Suppose you found out something about somebody she—Oh, dear."

"She needn't pay me if she doesn't care for my findings. You can pay me—when you get your money from the Vauregard estate," said Gamadge, smiling at her. "And don't forget that we may be wrong, after all; these people may be professional swindlers; but if they are, they're the most remarkable gang I ever heard of."

"If you could only prove that they were professional swindlers!"

"And there's another possibility, too; you won't care for it, but as an alternative it isn't too bad."

"Any alternative!..."

"How about this, then; your uncle engineered the hoax himself."

"What!" Miss Vauregard stopped dead again. Gamadge urged her on, with a hand beneath her elbow. She gazed up at him, aghast.

"Suppose he met her somewhere," continued Gamadge, "and was completely bowled over; such things do happen, you know! He wouldn't like to take the family into his confidence about a divagation of that sort! So, being unable to admit to any of you that he's about to make a perfect fool of himself, and knowing that the refugee business—his first inspiration—wouldn't hold water if you all got after it seriously, he makes up the arbor story. You can't interfere, for financial reasons; and he knows you won't put him into a madhouse. He hopes that he may gradually get up enough courage to marry her."

"Mr. Gamadge, please don't go on. It's too grotesque."

"Lots of things in life are grotesque."

"Uncle Imbrie! You don't know him. I suppose he met her at a burlesque show," said Miss Vauregard, with intense sarcasm.

"No, indeed I don't; but she's an actress, Miss Vauregard, and a trained one, that's certain."

"Uncle Imbrie! Ridiculous."

"In a way, I'm glad that it is, because if it's the truth, you're all sunk. Trying to prove undue influence is not a safe bet."

"Uncle Imbrie making up that story!" Miss Vauregard gave a short laugh.

"He made up the refugee story, and enjoyed it. Well, I've made you laugh, anyhow, and that's something."

They had reached the Fourteenth Street subway station. Neither of them spoke again until they had descended, caught an express, and reached Forty-second Street. When they were in their local, Miss Vauregard shouted in his ear:

"I must get to the bottom of it. It's all too hideous!"

The colored man sitting beside Miss Vauregard caught that, and moved slightly away from her. He was not reassured by Gamadge's answering shout: "Everything is, when you get involved in fraud and conspiracy."

They got out at Sixty-eighth Street, and took a cab. As they turned west from Lexington, Gamadge said dreamily: "I have a personal interest in all this, you know."

"Your—er—fee?" Miss Vauregard cast a quizzical glance at him.

"No, that's business. Your niece."

"Do drop that nonsense, Mr. Gamadge!"

"Miss Dawson is not for me?"

"You can't be serious."

"I don't know how I could behave more seriously than by addressing myself to the young person's guardian."

"Angela is her guardian. Clara engaged herself years ago."

"Infant betrothal? Sounds rather Hindu."

"You'll see how Hindu it is when you meet Cameron Payne."

The cab stopped in front of an ornate stone house, bay windowed, and highly decorated with flowers, fruit and foliage in gray stone. Miss Vauregard got out of the cab before Gamadge could open the door of it for her.

"Wait a minute," he said. "Do I continue my journey, or are you employing me?""

"I'm employing you. I must." She mounted a short flight of stone steps, looking pale and grim. Gamadge paid the driver, and followed her through plate-glass swing doors, impressively grilled, into a vestibule with a floor of black and red mosaic. Inner doors confronted them, with stretches of Renaissance lace behind their plate glass, which prepared Gamadge for the interior revealed when a swarthy, harassed-looking houseman answered the bell.

"Tell my sister that Mr. Gamadge is here, Luigi," said Miss Vauregard.

The houseman's white coat disappeared through an arch-way, curtained with red brocade, which divided the front from the back hall. Gamadge deposited his hat on a tremendous carved oak bench, over which hung an equally tremendous gilt-framed Florentine mirror. Miss Vauregard waited for him between the red brocade curtains at the entrance to the draw-ing room. He looked about him.

In spite of the late season, red carpet covered the floor and the staircase—a hot, bright cherry red which matched the portieres. Small pictures—oils, watercolors, etchings, even photographs—covered every inch of available wall space, and followed the staircase to the second floor. All the pictures were originals, and many of them were affectionately inscribed. A big Italian sconce, carved and gilt, and provided with a red-glass globe, hung on either side of the mirror.

"Pretty awful, isn't it?" Miss Vauregard followed his glance about the hall, and up the stairs. "My sister won't have the curtains down, or the carpets up, until she goes to the country; and she won't have anything changed. This is as it was in the nineties."

"Very handsome," said Gamadge.

She led the way into the drawing room. Here the Napoleon craze which swept the western world in the last decade of the nineteenth century was strongly in evidence. The walls were white, decorated with gold wreaths. Wreaths, crowns and bees, all in gold, sprinkled the marble mantelpiece, the Empire furniture, and the green-satin window draperies. A white marble bust on a pedestal between the windows did not, however, represent Napoleon, or even Josephine—it was Angela Morton in her prime, with wide, blank eyes, hair blown back from her forehead, and smiling lips half-parted.

"Angie bought the house furnished," said Miss Vauregard. "The furniture isn't real Empire, you know."

"A very good reproduction of it."

"She doesn't care a bit about such things; all she likes is a background."

Gamadge raised his eyes to a full-length portrait of Angela Morton in velvet and tights—no doubt the costume of Viola, one of her favorite parts. He said: "It must be fun to live surrounded by the proofs of one's glory."

"One can't blame them for hating to give it all up, can one?"

"No, indeed."

"But they lose their sense of proportion."

"Your sister supports the two young people, you say?"

"Dickie is earning something—he's a lawyer. Clara wanted to go on the stage, but Angela wouldn't hear of it. She said the child had no talent, and was only stage-struck. The truth is, poor Clara hasn't been trained to do anything—just like me—and she thought she might be able to earn her own living that way. All the young people seem to want to do something nowadays."

"Mrs. Morton doesn't sympathize with her efforts to leave home? Too bad."

"She thinks Clara hasn't the reasons for breaking away that she had. Life was a little stuffy for some of us in those days; Angela doesn't think Clara's life is stuffy."

Gamadge looked about the hot, crowded room, dominated by the effigies of its owner. He said: "Overwhelming personality, I should imagine."

"But she's so good to us all, Mr. Gamadge! We're perfectly free and happy."

"No latchkeys."

"What? Oh. No, I haven't one, and Clara hasn't. Angie hates them getting lost. Dick finally revolted; he got one when he left college and went into law school."

"No animals allowed on the premises."

"They ruined the furniture. Angie has her macaw."

"Good God."

"Now, please, Mr. Gamadge! She supports us all."

"Including Mr. Duncannon?"

"Of course not. He's been unlucky in his last plays, but he usually makes an excellent income. He adores her—it was a marriage for love."

"Everybody adored Mrs. Morton. She permitted Miss Dawson to get engaged to this Mr. Payne, and at an early age?"

"Angela doesn't care for the match—now; but that she could not interfere with."

Two men came almost simultaneously into the room: a young one, from the hall; and an older one, through the doorway that led from a room in the rear. Miss Vauregard said: "Mr. Gamadge, this is Mr. Duncannon; and this is my nephew Richard."

Duncannon came forward with the attractive, calculated awkwardness which Gamadge remembered as being an asset to him on the stage; the gait and manner of one who knows how to hold himself, but doesn't have to bother about that any more. His voice lagged, too—a cultivated drawl. He had been very handsome, but he now looked his forty-odd years; his figure was thickening, and so were the Roman features of his bronzed, discontented face.

"Awfully glad you're on the job," he said, shaking hands.

"High time, too." Richard Vauregard, a big, lumbering, worried-looking young man, nearly shook Gamadge's arm off. "Now, let's hope, we'll get some action. To the deuce with all the pussyfooting. Mr. Gamadge, have you met the zombi?"

Volume II

Warning by William Shakespeare

CHAPTER SEVEN

Head of the House

"IF YOU ARE GOING TO BE VULGAR, dear," said Miss Vauregard, who had seated herself on the settee to the right of the screened fireplace, and was glancing uneasily at Gamadge, "you may go away."

"Vulgar, Aunt Rob? Zombies aren't vulgar."

"Miss Smith didn't say she had been dead."

"Just in abeyance. Well, I don't propose to mince words about Miss Smith, I can tell you. I saw her once, and she struck me as well able to take care of herself. What do you say, Mr. Gamadge?"

"Quite well poised, in every way."

"Poised! Of all the brazen-faced assurance—but Tom's fallen for her." He grimaced rudely at his uncle-in-law. "I forgot that. He won't hear a word against her."

Duncannon walked with his long, balanced actor's step to the left-hand window. He said coldly, over his shoulder: "Go chase yourself. I don't care for your type of humor, that's all."

"'Spare her, boys; she's a woman. More to be pitied than blamed. Well, of course, she has no designs on your money; that makes a difference. We're afraid of her, and they say fear leads to brutality."

"I've noticed that it does."

"Now, please," said Miss Vauregard.

"That girl is not a common swindler," continued Duncannon, parting the lace undercurtains to look out at the wide, empty street. "There's something funny about this thing, somewhere. Don't you agree with me, Gamadge?"

"You think she may be in the house with old Mr. Vauregard's connivance?"

"That's a notion!" Duncannon stared at him, his light hazel eyes widening between their long lashes.

"A cockeyed notion." Young Vauregard also stared.

"I said it was silly." Miss Vauregard turned her eyes resolutely away from Duncannon, and fixed them on her gloves, which she had removed and was rolling into a ball.

Duncannon said, coming back towards them, "I never thought of that."

"But how else could she be there—innocently, let us say?" Gamadge asked the question mildly. "Unless, of course, she really is a refugee, and the old gentleman has concocted his romance out of too much family atmosphere."

Duncannon said firmly, "I believe she really is a refugee."

"Fine," agreed Dick Vauregard, with lowering sarcasm. "Now, if she'll just oblige with the name of the boat she came on, and hand over her papers—"

"She will, eventually. Good heavens," said Duncannon, in a drawl of disgust, "give her time. After such experiences as she may have had, it's a wonder that she remembers her own name. When I saw her, she seemed very vague, hardly normal. Trouble is, Gamadge, the whole family is so terrified of the old codger down there that they won't ask him a question about her. If they did, he might let it all out, in time. As a matter of fact, I don't think he's mentally sound—haven't thought so for some time."

"I don't think you're mentally sound," said Dick Vauregard. "Did she impress you as a suffering angel, Mr. Gamadge?"

"To be quite frank," answered Gamadge, "and without meaning to hurt anybody's sensibilities, I thought she would make an excellent understudy for your aunt, Mrs. Morton, in her new play."

Mr. Duncannon stared at him with a sort of furious disgust. Young Vauregard gently whistled.

"Not as bad as it sounds," continued Gamadge, smiling. He took a wallet out of his pocket, and removed the fragment which he had cut from the *Observer*. "Here's what Ivor Brown, the English critic, says about Vittoria Corombona—or rather, Accorambona; which he says was the lady's right name: 'She loved passionately, lived dangerously, offended the Medici and died young.' Not quite Webster's white devil, is it? Miss Smith might go back to history, and give us a new reading."

Dick Vauregard looked at him under knitted brows. "Did you like the zombi?"

"No, I did not; and she knows it."

The house man, more harassed even than before, brought in a tray of cocktails. Miss Vauregard refused one. Gamadge accepted a glass, and young Vauregard seized one, emptied it, and seized another. "I'll have yours, Aunt Robbie," he said. "I need it."

"Your manners are very bad, dear."

"Don't make a sissy of me. This highbrow theater stuff makes me feel weak."

Duncannon, sipping his cocktail, said: "Very young, still, aren't you? Don't try so hard to be a he-man."

"You don't have to try, do you?" Vauregard's irony was so bitter as to startle Gamadge; it made Duncannon flush.

"Company present," was all he said, in a tired voice.

"Sorry to offend your delicate sensibilities."

The house man had gone out of the room; he now

returned with a small silver jug, which he placed on the tray. As he did so, Angela Morton swept in from the hall.

She was a tall, large-boned woman, long-limbed and graceful, with large dark eyes, almost classical features, and a brilliant smile. Like many other actresses of her period she seemed to have no physical vanity in private life; her graying hair was carelessly arranged off her forehead, in a large untidy knot on her neck; and her green silk robe or tea gown was made for comfort; moreover, it lacked freshness. She strode up to Gamadge, her arm outstretched to its full length, her head back and her eyes fixed upon his own.

"Dear Mr. Gamadge, how very good of you, and what a comfort to have somebody we can trust, to help us! Have you had a cocktail? Luigi, where is my vegetable juice? Oh, thank you. Don't bother—I shall wait on myself."

But Mrs. Morton did not have to wait on herself. Her husband lunged forward and settled her on the little sofa opposite Miss Vauregard, with a stand at her elbow. He poured out her drink, brought it to her, and sat down at her side. Gamadge was sinking back into his chair, but she waved him nearer.

"Sit beside Robina," her mellifluous voice besought him, "and let us talk our family scandal over quietly. Where is Clara, Robina? Late, as usual; we must try to get on without her advice. Pull up your chair, Dickie. What did you think of the young woman, Mr. Gamadge? I would not see her, but my husband tells me she has looks. Do you agree with him?"

Gamadge said: "She is very good looking. About my taking the case, Mrs. Morton; it's absurd, really. I'm not a detective. I have no organization, and no facilities for this kind of work. I can't watch people, and I can't trail them. I can't even look them up, properly. Nobody but the police can really do that."

"The police are out of the question, Mr. Gamadge; didn't my sister explain that? Your observations are what we want."

"They may be worthless to you, and a waste of time."

"We'll risk it. What did you think of Miss Smith?"

"I thought her very dangerous."

"Did you really? In what way?" Mrs. Morton glanced at her husband, whose arm was lying along the back of the settee, and whose hand occasionally patted her shoulder. "Not as a siren, I gather," she went on, smiling. "Tom and Dickie complain that she looked straight through them."

"Still uninterested in gentlemen." Gamadge also smiled.

"I mean that she represents something dangerous; something crooked; something—well, let us not be melodramatic, but shall I call it something evil? I'm afraid your husband is too generous in his estimate of her. She has studied a part, and is playing it very well."

"I really think I must see her, after all. She must be very clever. Imagine going through all that, day after day, without breaking down! But then I speak as one who cannot act off the stage, Mr. Gamadge. I never could."

Gamadge, who was convinced that Mrs. Morton never stopped acting unless she was sound asleep, said "It may be possible to frighten her away."

"You won't do that," exclaimed Dick Vauregard. "She's as hard as nails."

Mrs. Morton gave her famous chromatic laugh. "You think so because she didn't respond to your blandishments, Dickie. Tom finds her more sympathetic." She patted her husband's hand, and went on, with a fond look at him: "Tom is always for the underdog, Mr. Gamadge. He thinks the girl is a sort of victim. I don't know…Uncle must be protected, whoever she is. Miss Smith might run off with the Georgian silver."

"Tom won't love you, if you talk like that, Aunt Angie," said young Vauregard.

"Just try to forget about me and my emotions," said Duncannon, in his weariest drawl. "Angela, you must see for yourself. I don't believe there's an ounce of malice in her. Gamadge is looking for a plot, so of course he finds one. The trouble is, your uncle is mildly insane."

"Nonsense, Tommy! Uncle isn't mad. What do you think, Mr. Gamadge?"

"Far from it. He thinks he has weighed the evidence and come to a logical conclusion. Unless we can show him definitely that it's false evidence, he won't be amenable to reason."

"But can we show him that?"

"I think we probably can, if we try. Tell me, Mrs. Morton; has he made a will, and do you know the terms of it?"

"He made one in 1920, just after Mother died—she was his only sister. It was a nice will, but a good deal of money went toward keeping up the old house as a museum—in perpetuity, you know." Mrs. Morton looked out of the corners of her eyes at Gamadge—the celebrated mischievous look that had once enraptured audiences. "We all believed in perpetuity then, didn't we? Of course, none of us minded his diverting half his fortune to the house, because his estate was then assessed at about two million. We aren't so largehearted, now."

"You get the rest of it?"

"Yes. Robina and I are down for about five hundred thousand apiece; my nephew and niece each get a hundred thousand."

"To show you how fair Uncle is," said Miss Vauregard, firmly, "the family gets paid first. If the estate has shrunk, so much the worse for the New York Historical Society."

"What about John and Eliza?"

"They're part of the museum endowment," said Mrs. Morton. "They stay on as caretakers until they die. It's in the bond."

Dick Vauregard said gloomily, "Perhaps he'll give the house and John and Eliza to the zombi; for old time's sake, you know."

"I do wish you wouldn't call her that, Dickie. It gives me the horrors." Mrs. Morton contracted her shoulders in a comic shudder.

"We got used to the term at college. Used it a good deal in reference to people we considered below par."

Duncannon said, looking bored, "The whole thing's at a deadlock. You can't expect Gamadge to make bricks without straw."

"Well, I have a straw or two," said Gamadge. "By the way, Mr. Vauregard informed us that on the day Miss Wagoneur disappeared, there was a Mrs. Dykinck in the house. Friend of his grandmother's."

"Now I think of it," said Mrs. Morton, after a pause for reflection, "I believe she was there."

"I gather that there are still Dykincks living in New York."

"Yes—old Mrs. Kilaean Dykinck and her daughter. They are still in East Thirty-fourth Street, where they've been for ages."

"Are they the only Dykincks left?"

"So far as I know, they are—thank goodness. They're rather stuffy. The Dykincks intermarried too much; they thought nobody but a Dykinck was good enough for a Dykinck. I always said poor Rose wasn't allowed to marry because there was no Dykinck left for her."

Dick Vauregard remarked that not even a Dykinck would probably have been willing to marry Posy.

"She's just a pathetic, silly creature, and she's always been suppressed by that mother of hers," said Miss Vauregard, who had been watching Gamadge in some bewilderment.

"Did you see her at the Billings wedding?" asked Dick. "You weren't there, Aunt Angela, were you?"

"No, dear, I have given up weddings, and all formal functions. After all, one needn't persist in boring oneself all one's life."

"You were there, Tom. I saw the old girl tackling you, too."

Duncannon said that he vaguely remembered her.

"Nothing vague about my memory of Posy!" declared young Vauregard. "She came up and asked me if I wasn't a Vauregard, and said the families used to be so intimate in the old days, and wasn't it a shame to lose sight of old friends. Then she went off and cornered Cam Payne. I think I saw her interviewing Clara, too. The old freak must be well over forty."

"She can't help that, Dickie," protested Miss Vauregard.

"I mean, she was got up like one of the Floradora sextet. Ostrich feathers, all kinds of trimmings."

Gamadge said: "I should rather like to meet the Dykyncks. They might have family legends, too—connected with the arbor mystery."

"Well, perhaps I might give you a letter. I don't know what excuse there could be—and old Mrs. Dykinck is an invalid. She doesn't leave her room, I believe." Mrs. Morton gave him a puzzled look.

"Say I'm thinking of writing a book on the unwritten history of New York. Something of that kind. And if you'd be so good, you might also give me a letter to the Chandors. Tell 'em I'm putting cults and occultism into the book."

"Well, that I'm afraid I can hardly do," said Mrs. Morton. "The Chandors wouldn't take kindly to it at all. I went into New Soul just for fun, and the Chandors weren't any too pleased when I got out of it, about six months ago. They were afraid I should drag Uncle off with me. As a matter of fact, he wouldn't be dragged. He loved it. But he's been too busy with Miss Smith to go on with it since May—or with any other outside interest."

"Aunt Angie's a caution when she gets going on a new fad," said Dick Vauregard. "Remember how you used to try to convert us to New Soul, Aunt Angie? 'All is illusion, and the veil is lifted.' I don't think you got a customer, though, not even Tom."

"Unfortunately," said Duncannon, with a teasing but affectionate look at his wife, "she got old Mr. Vauregard into it."

Mrs. Morton clasped her bosom. "I have repented in sackcloth and ashes, you know I have, dearest! These Chandors went all out for poor Uncle, Mr. Gamadge; they're very clever, very sympathetic, and lots of important people consult them."

"May I use the Vauregard name?"

"Of course, but it may not get you an audience! They live at the Palazzo, Central Park West."

"Does the Chandor system include ancient sorceries? Table tipping, materializations, and so forth?"

"Oh, no, nothing so primitive. They're not even astrologers. It's all on a very high plane: mystical reunion with nature. You regain physical and spiritual youth. I never got very far with it, because I couldn't make out what any of it was all about. It was rather fun, for a while—one felt uplifted."

"I wondered whether Miss Smith might have been an answer to prayer—conducted by the Chandors."

"I wondered, myself. But they're intensely respectable, and I understand that they're prosperous. I hardly think they'd mix themselves up in a thing like this. I'll go and write you the Dykinck letter, but it may not get you into the presence. The Dykincks are almost too good for daily use, you know."

"Miss Dykinck seems to have been chatty at the wedding your nephew talked of. Perhaps a telephone call would do, Mrs. Morton. I hate to put you to the trouble—"

"They have no telephone," said Miss Vauregard. "I discovered that when I tried to get in touch with them about war work."

"Not even a private wire?"

"No, I'm afraid the poor things are dreadfully hard up nowadays."

Mrs. Morton went into the room behind the green parlor, which seemed to be a small, dark library. There was a desk in front of its one window, at which she sat down with her back to the drawn portieres. The doorbell rang. Dick Vauregard, who had been frowning at his feet, now addressed Gamadge curiously:

"You said Miss Smith was dangerous. How do you mean, dangerous—apart from the danger to our money?"

"When a thing of this sort is being carried on, regardless of risk and trouble, one never knows what it may lead to."

Duncannon said sharply, "I don't know what that implies."

"Well, technically at least, a crime is in process of construction; and there's always the chance that one crime will lead to another."

"I don't see why."

"A second one may be necessary to back up or conceal the first. Classical example, much used in secondary education: *Macbeth*."

"Nonsense. If Miss Smith were cornered, she would simply pack up and disappear, I suppose," said young Vauregard.

"Let us hope so."

Miss Clara Dawson came in, her cheeks glowing. She was followed by a tall young man of Saxon fairness, who walked with the aid of a stick. Miss Dawson seemed to be in the highest spirits.

"Hello, gang," she said. "Hello, Mr. Gamadge. Great-uncle Imbrie thinks you're a wonderful man. He adores you. Let me introduce Cameron Payne."

Mr. Payne, who also seemed to be in high spirits, and who had a radiant smile, shook hands.

"You certainly made a hit down there," he said.

Miss Vauregard exclaimed: "Clara, what have you and Cameron been doing?"

"Don't be like that, Aunt Robbie; we couldn't resist. We've seen the zombi."

CHAPTER EIGHT

Outside Information

Mrs. MORTON CAME BACK into the drawing room, an envelope in her hand. She looked ill-pleased.

"Clara," she said, "you were to tell nobody."

"It never entered my head that you could mean Cam, Aunt Angela. You told Tom."

"Tom is my husband. You are not married to Cameron Payne yet, so far as I am aware."

Payne said, in a light but masculine singsong that consorted admirably with his angelic coloring: "Easy does it, Mrs. Morton. I shan't spread it." There was nothing angelic about the way his eyes crinkled at the corners when he smiled, or about the teasing humor with which he looked at her. He stood carelessly leaning on his stick, poised on one foot, the other knee bent slightly. He wore a thin gray suit, the loose, fashionable cut of which seemed to minimize his lameness.

"Of course Cameron won't tell." Clara pushed a chair up behind him, and he sat down in it without looking at her;

his act, as well as hers, seemed automatic. She remained standing beside him, a hand on the chair back, while with the other she pulled off her felt riding hat. She cast it on a table some distance away, and smoothed back her thick, soft brown hair with the gesture of one who knows that it is, and will remain, neatly in place. "Uncle gave us sherry," she said. "Why didn't somebody tell us that the zombi—excuse me, Tom—why didn't some of you say how good-looking she is?"

Mrs. Morton handed the envelope to Gamadge. Her brilliant smile had returned, and did not alter as she said: "I hope that joke about Tom and the—and Miss Smith will wear thin after a week or so. We can't hope to hear the last of it sooner, I suppose. Infants!"

"Why shouldn't Tom admire her? She's perfectly lovely, and Cam thinks so, too."

"Beautiful," agreed that young man, turning his impish smile on Gamadge. "But a trifle dumb, perhaps?"

"Dumb? She's putting on a wonderful show—you'll have to give her that," said Dick Vauregard. "She's anything but dumb."

"She's a little spooky," said Clara, "but I might not have thought so if I didn't know the arbor story."

Duncannon said: "You're a fair-minded girl, Clara; didn't she look to you as if she might have been through so much that it had knocked her out, for the time being?"

"Yes, she did; but I thought that was part of the show, Tom."

The doorbell rang again.

"Why don't you get a picture of her, Mr. Gamadge?" asked Clara. "Somebody would be sure to recognize it, she's so wonderful-looking. Uncle said you were going back there tomorrow, before dinner. You could take along one of those little tiny cameras, and snap her through a hole in your coat, or something. Isn't that what detectives do?"

Gamadge began: "That had occurred to me; but—"

Dick Vauregard interrupted, with some irritation "Give the man credit, Clara! And do sit down, can't you? You're keeping him on his feet."

"No, no; I must be going. There are slight difficulties in the way of my snapping Miss Smith through a hole in my coat, Miss Dawson."

"But there are little cameras no bigger than a cigarette lighter; Cameron has one."

Payne said, with his humorous smile: "It's a nice little gadget, but not constructed for snooping."

Gamadge's quick look found no malice in the young man's face, nor had there been any in his tone; but he replied with an amiability which certain persons had in the past found reason to distrust: "My snooping is done in the grand manner. I don't know my job well enough to hold a card up my sleeve, much less palm it. No deception, ladies and gentlemen."

The house man came in, looking wild, and announced: "Mr. Bridge is calling."

A short, stocky man with a pale, flat face and round eyes entered slowly. His expression of acid resignation did not change when Mrs. Morton, from her sofa, extended her long arm in the loose green-silk sleeve.

"Darling Weddie! I had given you up. Was that your ring, ages ago? Luigi is so slow."

"You run the poor devil off his legs. I was looking at the little Drouet again."

"What fascinates you so about that landscape?"

"Make a nice set for a Tchekhov play."

"Mr. Gamadge, Mr. Bridge. He directs the Mermaid Group. He's persuading me to have a last fling in such a wonderful play. Can you keep a secret?"

"Try me."

"Would you come to see me as Vittoria Corombona?"

Bridge said: "People will come to see anybody as Vittoria Corombona."

"Now, Weddie, is that nice of you?"

"It's a glorious idea," said Gamadge. "I'll come, don't worry."

"Have you brought the costume sketches for me?" asked Mrs. Morton eagerly.

Bridge took a folder from under his arm. "Yes, all except Brachiano. Duncannon will have to go to the Morgan library, with a card, if he wants to see that."

"And now we have practically everything!"

"Except money," said Bridge. "If we don't do it right, the police will close us up; there's only one way to get by with Webster—put on so many frills that nobody will know what it's all about."

"Where is Luigi? Oh, there you are; a cocktail for Mr. Bridge, and won't you stay for dinner, Weddie? Can't you? Too bad. Let's see…this is Wednesday. How about Friday? Without fail? Good. Must you really be going, Mr. Gamadge? You'll let me know all about everything? Thank you so much."

Gamadge made his adieux. When he came to Clara Dawson, she said: "Tomorrow, don't forget."

"I won't forget."

"When Great-uncle Imbrie said you were going down there, I was afraid you had forgotten our tea party."

"No, indeed. I was careful to arrange for that."

"Love to Martin."

"Thank you, he'll be touched."

Miss Vauregard said nothing when he took leave of her; but her eyes were anxious and questioning. He gave her a friendly smile, and was off.

He took the first taxi he saw, and was at home in five minutes. As he dashed up the steps Harold came out of the front door. Not the least of that youth's peculiarities was his dislike of sit-down meals, and his preference for strange foods, eaten in solitude and at counters.

"You just caught me," he said.

"That's what I hoped to do. Can you deliver a note for me?"

"Right now?"

"In a cab."

"O.K."

Gamadge turned into the office and wrote the note, which he enclosed in an envelope with Mrs. Morton's.

"Here you are," he said. "I'm going out to dinner, and I may not see you later. First thing tomorrow I want you to get me the best and smallest miniature camera to be had for money. How much do they cost?"

"Don't know. I'll get it at Forbes', where we have an account."

"I want to photograph marks on a book, and if possible I want to photograph a woman. Indoor work. The camera will have to be very candid."

"O.K."

"I want to use it tomorrow."

Harold placed his snap-brim felt on his black hair, and went out. Gamadge took a shower, dressed, and went to his club. There he dined with a friend, and played bridge afterwards. During the course of the evening he acquired certain information.

From an old gentleman:

The Dykincks were church set, and were supposed to have about enough money left from their invested fortune to pay their taxes. They had sold all the New York property they had inherited except the Thirty-fourth Street house, rented their Newport cottage, and were no longer bothered by requests for subscriptions. The mother (who had been a Dykinck, too) was an invalid. The girl was tied to her—one of those deplorable things—and didn't go out much, either.

From a somewhat horsy young man:

The Vauregards used to be horse fanciers, but none of them rode now except the girl, and Mrs. Morton only drove when she was in the country, old hacks she had had for years. They never showed horses. The girl and Dick still belonged to the Riding Club, but Dick had no time now for riding.

Cameron Payne had been a polo player, and had had a bad accident—not at polo. Some kind of spill. Duncannon wasn't a riding man—went in for fast motoring. Quite a decent sort, but he and Dick Vauregard were not supposed to get on.

From a young actor:

Duncannon had never been star material, used to get by on his looks, and was now definitely on the skids. Had had some bad luck, besides; two of his recent plays had been flops. He had been in Angela Morton's company six years before, and had been shoved by her into the part of Christian, when she undertook an ill-fated revival of *Cyrano*. Mrs. Morton had fallen in love with him during the short run, and had married him in a month.

"They say he really did fall in love with her, too," said Gamadge's informant. "She had a lot of appeal, they tell me. She won't let him go into pictures."

"Did he get a chance at pictures?"

"He did about five years ago. She wouldn't hear of his going to Hollywood." The young actor laughed, in a cynical manner. "She says the pictures are not art."

"Has plenty of money, hasn't she?"

"I don't know why she should have. She's spent a lot on Duncannon, and I hear she supports a whole raft of poor relations."

From an athletic member:

Cameron Payne was an orphan, twenty-eight years old, an ex-polo player of some reputation. He had had a riding accident four years previously and would be knocked up for life. Popular guy, even now, but of course he had more or less dropped out of things. Had a little money, enough to get on with, belonged to a good club, played cards a good deal. Lived in a flat by himself, somewhere. "Was going to be a metallurgical chemist, but had to give it up. Fooled around in somebody's lab, now and then. Hard luck—time must hang heavy on his hands. He never cared for anything but sports."

Gamadge went home at midnight, and found two notes on his bedside table. The first was from Harold, and was short:

They had me wait on the stoop while they
wrangled the answer.

The second was written in a tremulous, flowing hand, on thick, black-bordered paper; it said:

The state of Mrs. Kilacan Dykinck's health may or may not permit her to receive Mr. Henry Gamadge tomorrow morning. However, if he will call at eleven, as he suggests, he will be informed whether Mrs. Dykinck can have the pleasure of seeing him. Wednesday, June the Fifth.

Gamadge reverently studied the Dykinck crest, which seemed to consist of a gloved hand brandishing a carving knife, and then retired to bed.

At nine o'clock on the following morning he asked Harold to call the Chandor apartment. "Tell them I wish to consult them about a literary matter," he said, "and that I was referred to them by the Vauregards."

Harold went into the office, and came back presently to say that the Chandor secretary sounded like a tough proposition, and requested a letter. Gamadge, annoyed, penned the following:

CHANDORS:

Mr. Henry Gamadge, author of *The Technique of a Book Forger, Super-Charlatans, The Race of Chatterton*, etc., etc., contemplates writing a semihistorical book on the city of New York, one section of which will be entitled "Cults and Illusions".

He feels that he ought to devote space in this portion of the work to Chandors, and is prepared to give them full credit (in footnotes) for their cooperation.

They were recommended to his attention by Miss Vauregard, and also by Mrs. Thomas Duncannon (Mrs. Morton). Mr. Gamadge would like to call upon Chandors at their earliest convenience—if possible this afternoon.

Thursday, June Sixth, 1940.

Harold was asked to deliver this epistle by hand. He withdrew, and Gamadge took down several reference books, in which he immersed himself until his assistant's return. By that time he was convinced that of all early Dutch settlers and merchants, the Dykincks had probably been the dullest and most blameless. They had built nothing, founded nothing, and created nothing except Dykincks. They had apparently done nothing but make and save money, and how they had managed to lose it all, Gamadge could not imagine.

Harold came back very morose.

"The secretary is a big fat man with a bald head. He took the letter, and I waited in a little room with stars on the ceiling. There was a blue book on a table called *New Soul*. The feller came back and gave me this." He handed Gamadge a blue envelope, with a star on one corner of it. "Gave me a nasty ugly look, too. They must've not liked what you wrote them."

Gamadge opened the letter, unfolded a sheet of paper sprinkled with stars, and read in typescript:

MR. HENRY GAMADGE:
SIR:
There is no mystery about New Soul, except insofar

as all is mystery. Miss Vauregard, with whom we have communicated by telephone, informs us that you are a well-known and accomplished writer, and an expert on documents. We fail to see how we can assist you in your work; we do not advertise and we abhor publicity.

However, we are willing to discuss the matter with you this afternoon at two o'clock.

Yours,

ASTRA CHANDOR.

Gamadge said: "Telephone that I'll be there."

"You better take me along."

"Nonsense. The best people go there."

"They wouldn't if they got the look that secretary handed me."

"I just made them a little nervous. Did you get me that camera? Good. Let's see it."

Harold produced a little object, so enchanting in its compact perfection that it engrossed both of them for some time. Gamadge then went to his room and put on his best town clothes. He gazed earnestly at his shoes to assure himself that they were in no need of a polish, took up a soft hat and a pair of gloves, and left the house. A bus at the corner deposited him at eleven sharp within a block of the Dykinck residence, which stood on the south side of the street, in a depressing row of brownstone houses, all alike, and all losing flakes and chips from their gritty surfaces. The street had deteriorated; children shouted across the asphalt, and one of the houses had a card in its front window, announcing: "Vacancy."

CHAPTER NINE

Peacock Blue

GAMADGE MOUNTED the high stoop and pulled a bronze knob. He then entered the vestibule, and stood, already a trifle depressed, in contemplation of walnut double doors; their upper halves were of glass, ornamented with a ground-glass pattern—birds and flowers.

After a considerable wait he was admitted by an elderly parlormaid in a long black alpaca dress, a long white apron, and a fluted cap. She took his card, left him standing in the front hall, and went upstairs.

Gamadge laid his hat on a marble-topped console, and looked about him. Walnut folding doors shut him off from the drawing room; the huge mirror above the console sprouted hooks on either side of it, and umbrella stands below; beside the stairs a narrow hallway ended in another glassed door, through which filtered a pale, uncertain light. The Dykinck house was dark, stuffy, and as quiet as the grave. Gamadge leaned against the newel post, and faced the closed doors of the drawing room; thereby enabling whoever it was that peered at him through the crack to get a good look at him.

The maid came downstairs, and pushed the folding doors wide. The observer had withdrawn. Gamadge, feeling a little eerie, stepped past the maid into the dusk of a long room, with brown shades pulled down over the tall windows, and shrouded furniture standing about like boulders. Another huge mirror confronted him, high enough to reflect the immense bronze chandelier. His feet slid on Holland drugget.

A female form, tall and apparently much bedraped, stood with its back to the windows. As the maid departed, it said in a high voice: "I am Miss Dykinck."

"So good of you to let me come," replied Gamadge.

"It is a great pleasure; and Mamma loves company. She is not always up to it."

"Very kind of her to put herself out."

Gamadge began to discern a shadowy face under a large hat with a pink rose on it, a figured silk dress which reached the lady's ankles, and, finally, an out-stretched hand with a frill about the wrist. He shook the hand, and Miss Dykinck sat down. Gamadge groped for a chair in front of her.

She had a sharp, pale face, surrounded by tendrils of brown hair; bright brown eyes, flecked with yellow; a high nose, and a mouth which looked as if it had just been tasting something sour. The corners of it drooped, and the upper lip was drawn a little away from the prominent front teeth.

"I must apologize for keeping you in the hall," she said, "but the maid lets no one in until she is sure of them. And I must apologize for the drawing room; we are not supposed to be in town, of course."

"Very pleasant and cool in here."

"Mamma is not well enough yet to move to the country. Did you know that I had a peep at you, while you were in the hall?"

"Had you, though? I'm glad I passed muster."

"As we have no man on the premises, Mamma is a little nervous."

"You are quite right to be careful."

"Besides," and Miss Dykinck laughed with abandon, "I have made a vow that no man over thirty shall ever again cross this threshold. Old men are so dreary."

"I shall have to be going, then, I'm afraid, Miss Dykinck; I'm thirty-four."

"You don't look it, Mr. Gamadge; I shall amend my vow; no man who looks more than thirty shall come into the house, except on business. It's not always so easy," said Miss Dykinck, laughing again, "to get up a bridge game in the circumstances; but I don't care."

Gamadge thought that Miss Dykinck's defense tactics were rather interesting, and quite excusable. "Hard on us," he said. "We can't help our ages."

"Or our preferences—can we?"

"As a matter of fact, I notice ages very little; it's personality that counts with me," continued Gamadge, keeping up his spirits with some difficulty.

"I'm afraid I am not so philosophical. Mamma must be ready to see you; shall we go up?"

Gamadge felt that he had passed muster a second time. He preceded Miss Dykinck (by request—didn't the old books of etiquette insist upon this?) up the stairs to the second floor. They went along a narrow hallway to the front of the house, and entered a large sitting room; its ebonized and gilded furniture was upholstered in peacock-blue plush, and the black-marble mantel-piece upheld an ormolu clock and vases, all under glass domes.

A very old lady with an egg-shaped head sat beside the farther window. She wore purple foulard, white-spotted, and was swathed in a white shawl. A clover-shaped table, covered with blue plush and fringed, stood beside her; there was a large rosewood box on it.

"Well, young man," said Mrs. Dykinck in a deep, hoarse

voice, "here I am, all ready for you; but I don't see how I can help you about your book. Posy, give Mr. Gamadge a chair."

Gamadge took a bamboo rocker from Miss Dykinck, saw her disposed on an ottoman, and sat down. Mrs. Dykinck observed him through steel-rimmed spectacles.

"I was quite touched to get a note from Angela Morton," she said, with considerable dryness. "They have quite dropped us."

"Now, Mamma!" Miss Dykinck's upper lip drew away from her teeth in her characteristic smile. "You dropped Mrs. Morton for ages—after she first went on the stage."

"It wasn't done at that time. Nowadays, we make compromises. How does she wear, Mr. Gamadge? Those big women usually age so fast, I always think."

"She is still vital and impressive, Mrs. Dykinck."

Mrs. Dykinck laughed hoarsely. "She was always a wild, bold girl. From the nursery. They say she has gone in for spiritualism."

"Not spiritualism, Mamma; the Chandors are not spiritualists."

"Some trickery of the kind, at all events."

"Oh, no, Mamma; the Chandors are not like that t'all. I met Chandor at a tea, once; he was really very charming. We had quite a discussion on—what is it?—New Soul."

"He should never have been introduced to you; and if he had been, by some oversight, you should not have talked to him. You are not only a lady—you are a Churchwoman."

"Oh, he was quite harmless; and New Soul is not so very heretical."

"I wonder if Angela Morton still dabbles in that kind of thing. She used to go in for astrology."

"I believe she has dropped it all, for the time being," said Gamadge.

"And how are the boy and girl turning out? Posy met them at a wedding, not so long ago, and she was not very well impressed."

"I thought their manners poor, that's all," said Miss Dykinck. "Clara Dawson was too much occupied to waste time on anyone not in her set, and the boy was offhand. The husband," continued Miss Dykinck, smirking humorously, "struck me as an agreeable sort of person."

"But rather old" ventured Gamadge. They exchanged a mirthful glance. Mrs. Dykinck again protested:

"My daughter Rose is far too democratic socially, Mr. Gamadge. She will talk to every Tom, Dick, and Harry at these functions."

"You know very well that you wouldn't like it if I came back from them without any gossip for you," retorted Miss Dykinck gamely. "Dick Vauregard is getting to look quite like his father, only much bigger and nicer."

"I hope he has not too much of his father in him!" rumbled the old lady. "Cyril Vauregard spent all his share of the money before he died; threw it out of the window. What we used to call a man about town, Mr. Gamadge."

"They call them playboys now."

"Horrid expression."

"Cameron Payne was at the wedding," said Miss Dykinck. "Did I mention him, Mamma?"

"You did, Posy, several times."

"I sat beside him for half an hour. The poor boy was quite by himself on his sofa. I could have cried."

"He is able to walk about, I believe," said Mrs. Dykinck peevishly.

"But not for long, they say. He has become very spiritual since his accident. Witty, though; we had great fun over some of the types at that wedding. Do you know him, Mr. Gamadge?"

"Hardly at all."

"He was a lovely child, and now he is really beautiful. I hope Clara Dawson is not going to neglect him. I hope she appreciates him properly."

"Angela Morton won't like supporting them both," said

her mother. "I had an idea she wanted Clara for Dick. In that case, they could very well have lived on their Vauregard legacies, put together. I wonder how poor old Imbrie Vauregard is getting on, by the way—he must be ninety. We haven't seen anything of him for ages. How long ago was it, Posy, that he gave that tea party, or coffee party, and left you out?"

"Perfect ages. He only likes very young girls, you know."

Considering Miss Dykinck's own expressed preferences, Gamadge thought that this remark might have been made with less acerbity. He said: "I give parties myself, once in a while. I hope I shall be able to persuade you into coming, some afternoon."

"Who chaperones for you?" inquired Mrs. Dykinck.

"I wish you would, Mrs. Dykinck!"

"Nonsense. I am thankful to say that my chaperoning days are over."

"Miss Vauregard might take on this party."

"She would do quite well. Robina Vauregard has a good deal of sense, I always thought."

"Old Mr. Vauregard told me, in connection with this book I think of writing, that an ancestor of yours was a great friend of his grandparents. I hoped you might have letters."

"So that's what you came to find! Cornelia Dykinck was my great-aunt." Mrs. Dykinck's white, ringed hand stretched out towards the rosewood box. "We are not a letter-saving family, I am sorry to say, especially of recent years; but there are some—"

A bell jangled in the depths of the house. Mrs. and Miss Dykinck became alert, and waited in silence until the ancient parlormaid appeared panting in the doorway.

"Miss Rose's hair tonic." She advanced, a white package in her hand, and placed it within the outstretched fingers of the old lady. Mrs. Dykinck examined it from all angles, and then gave it to her daughter.

"Put it in my room, Anna," said Miss Dykinck. Anna retired, and Mrs. Dykinck opened the rosewood box.

"These are the only old letters we have," she said. "I went over the bundles this morning, and my daughter says that there is nothing you ought not to see."

"In your part of the book," said Gamadge, "I shan't be dealing with any period after 1840."

"Then you may borrow these two packets. We expect you to be most discreet, Mr. Gamadge; nothing must be published, or even alluded to, without our express permission."

"I shouldn't think of it," said Gamadge, taking the letters, and wondering whether he wouldn't have to write the confounded thing, after all.

"I thought you might care to use some of these." Mrs. Dykinck, evidently rather eager and fluttered, produced a small heap of daguerreotypes from the box, their cases in the usual state of disrepair. Gamadge opened one, and gazed mournfully at the vanishing and ghostly countenance of the Dykinck within. He said they might prove valuable.

"You may not be aware that my daughter Rose is the last of the Dykincks; she is not sure whether she would care to have her picture in your book; historically, it might be of interest."

"I hope I may have a photograph?"

"There's rather a good one," said Miss Dykinck, "but it's rather old."

"Send it to me, if you will." Gamadge, who had been feeling more and more of a brute, comforted himself by reflecting that the Dykincks seemed inclined to purchase immortality rather cheap. "By the way," he continued, "old Mr. Vauregard spoke of two little presentation sets of Byron—one in his possession, one perhaps in yours."

Mrs. Dykinck looked blank. "Do we own a set of Byron, Posy? We have some old books, but I don't know what's there."

Miss Dykinck said, "I don't know, myself."

"If a Vauregard presented them, there might be a little story in it," said Gamadge.

"Take him down, Posy, and show him the library," said the old lady.

Gamadge rose. "I do hope you understand, Mrs. Dykinck, that this kind of research takes a long time?"

Mrs. Dykinck said she understood; but Gamadge, as he wrapped the letters and the daguerreotypes in a piece of paper retrieved for him from the wastebasket by the last of the Dykincks, could not help wondering how long it would be before her mother joined their ancestors. Posy, he was certain, could be more easily dealt with.

He made his farewells, and followed Miss Dykinck out of the room. Mrs. Dykinck suddenly called after him in her resounding bass: "Why don't you get married?"

"I will if I can."

Again by request, he preceded Miss Dykinck down the stairs. She took him along the hall, and into a small, squeezed apartment behind the drawing room, with a ponderous mahogany bookcase in the darkest corner of it. The doors fitted so tightly that when she opened the middle section it left its frame as if reluctantly, with the ghost of a sigh.

Gamadge felt a slight but unmistakable thrill when he saw the row of little brown and gilt books, with the gap between Volume I and Volume III. He removed Volume I with some difficulty—the old shelves had warped, and left a faint double scar on its top edges. An inscription on the flyleaf read:

To Cornelia Dykinck
from
A Friend.

"Interesting," said Gamadge. "I should like to borrow Volumes I and III, if I may. Too bad Volume II is missing; or have you lent it?"

Miss Dykinck peered at the shelf in a manner which showed that she was puzzled, as well as nearsighted. "Missing?"

"Yes. I hope it's not lost?"

"I'm sure I don't—nobody ever looks at these books."

"Or stolen?"

Miss Dykinck turned her head to stare. "Who would steal a book out of a set?"

"Who, indeed?"

"They were all here when Anna and I dusted them, before Easter."

"Very odd; spoils the set."

Miss Dykinck looked angry, and very much puzzled. "Mamma would be—I can't imagine what's become of it!"

"So few people would have an opportunity to smuggle a book out of this room, too; or at least I suppose so. Your maids wouldn't?..."

Miss Dykinck dismissed this suggestion with no more than a satirical smile.

"Who does come into this room," persisted Gamadge, "besides yourself?"

"Nobody except my Lenten sewing circle. They overflowed, last time, from the drawing room. In Holy Week. Perhaps," and Miss Dykinck's nervous giggle sounded as if, in spite of her obvious and growing uneasiness, she rather enjoyed the idea, "perhaps one of the girls is a kleptomaniac."

"I suppose your mother's friends aren't kleptomaniacs, either?"

"They never come in here. They go up to her."

"In fact, nobody but the sewing circle ever does overflow into your library, nowadays. Well, it's a fascinating little minor mystery." Gamadge glanced at her face, which looked like a mask of perplexity under the shadow of her hat brim. The doorbell jangled downstairs, and caused a diversion; Miss Dykinck listened with interest while heavy steps came up from the Cimmerian darkness of the basement.

The maid Anna passed the library door, with a side glance at the couple within, and presently a masculine voice could be heard inquiring for Miss Dykinck. Its owner was apparently left to wait in the hall while Anna mounted to the second story.

"What's the matter with her?" inquired Gamadge.

"That was for you."

"She always speaks to Mamma first."

"What in the world for?"

"Poor Mamma hates to feel out of things," said Miss Dykinck brightly.

Gamadge, again impressed by her gameness, surveyed her in silence. The maid came slowly down again, and entered the library.

"Your books, Miss Rose. Your mamma hasn't finished one of the last lot; she says she'll pay the extra charge for keeping it over."

"All right. Had he the new ones I asked for?"

"Your mamma is only keeping one of them. She says you won't care for the other."

Miss Dykinck, somewhat annoyed, peered at a book in a library jacket, which the stolid Anna gripped firmly in both hands.

"Oh dear," she murmured. "I'll go up and speak to Mamma. No, never mind. Let it go."

Anna went off, and a moment or two later they heard the front door slam, shaking the house.

Gamadge said: "As the gentleman said to the lady in the old play, 'This I have heard of before, but never believed.'"

"What old play?"

"*Love for Love.*"

A ladylike squeal made Gamadge realize that he had twice used a word which could never pass unremarked in the presence of Miss Dykinck. He went on: "You know, I was just thinking: Suppose, for the sake of argument, that you had acquired some friend—we will say X—whom your mother might be expected to disapprove of. No, wait—it's only a hypothesis. Hang it all, most of us require a little privacy, now and again; are we guppies?"

"Men look at these things so differently," protested Miss Dykinck.

"Do they? Well, anyhow—I believe you have no telephone."

"The ringing bothered—"

"Just so. Suppose you wanted to get into communication with this X; you could go out half a dozen times in a day and call up from a drugstore, until you found your party at home. But what I should like to know is, how in the name of Childe Roland and the Dark Tower could X get into communication with you? Not by telegraph or by letter; the message might be opened by mistake. Am I wrong? I see that I am not. X couldn't because the faithful Anna would announce the caller to your mother before you knew there was such a person as X in the house. So if you wished to entertain X at home, you would have to make the appointment; and you would have to let X in, yourself—rather late, say, when the good Anna had retired to bed. X wouldn't ring, of course, but would knock gently on the door. And X couldn't leave by the front door, because it slams loud enough to wake not only Anna, but your mother, too."

"This is all very silly, Mr. Gamadge," said Miss Dykinck; and Gamadge, for the first time in his life, saw what is meant by "bridling."

"No, it's an interesting piece of induction. You would have to let X out by the area gate."

"Are you planning to call, one night?" inquired Miss Dykinck archly.

"By Jove, I'd like to! As a matter of fact, I flatter myself that Mrs. Dykinck approves of me thoroughly as a good young man; rather dull, but quite presentable. Look here, Miss Dykinck; I believe I can locate your missing Byron for you."

Miss Dykinck became rigid. Finally she said: "I won't trouble you, thanks."

"No trouble at all. I ought to be able to get it back for you quite soon."

"Mr. Gamadge, I…"

"Don't be distressed, Miss Dykinck; please don't. I'm the soul of discretion. Nobody will ever know where your Byron was—except those who know it already. And not even X will know that I got it back for you. You really ought to have it."

Miss Dykinck looked at him, and saw that his smile could be a very friendly one. She said, in a trembling voice: "You're absolutely wrong. I don't know where the book can have got to."

"And you needn't know it. I shan't communicate with X in any way—I shall simply get it and bring it back. I don't at all like it's being where it is. It might get you into a spot of publicity."

Miss Dykinck, very much frightened, searched Gamadge's face. "I cannot think what you mean."

"I'll do the thinking, if you'll trust me. But in order to identify your Byron, I must have Volume I and Volume III."

"Take them. I don't know what you're talking about. It would kill Mamma, if—"

"Mrs. Dykinck will never know a thing about it."

Gamadge added the Byrons to his now considerable bundle, and asked for more paper. Miss Dykinck opened an oak desk, and hunted about in it until she found a creased square of Christmas paper with holly on it, and a length of gold twine.

"Splendid," said Gamadge. He turned the paper inside out, wrapped up the books, the letters and the daguerreotypes, and tied them securely. "Thanks very much, Miss Dykinck; I'll have a try for your Byron this very afternoon. Don't forget that you're coming to my next doings."

He hurried out and along the hall. The lugubrious Anna surged up from the basement stairs before he had reached his hat, but it gave him some pleasure to slam the front door in her face.

He strolled westward, and had not reached the corner before Miss Dykinck came down her steps and flitted in the opposite direction. He watched her turn into a corner drug-store.

"X is going to get an earful," he murmured, and looked at his watch. It was twenty minutes to one.

He got on a bus, which was already crowded by a herd of other people who were going home to lunch. As he swung on his handle, he cogitated. As soon as X heard from Miss Dykinck, and realized that Volumes I and III were going to be compared with Volume II, and no later than that very afternoon, X would feel strongly impelled to get hold of Volume II before Gamadge did. But was that possible? Until after five, nobody could get past John and Eliza unseen; after five, Mr. Vauregard would be in the library, guarding his own treasure. It could probably be stolen under the old gentleman's nose, but in that case Mr. Vauregard would know who the thief had been. No, Volume II would remain where it was until it had had its picture taken.

Gamadge frowned, and then shrugged. Nonsense, he thought; no cause for worry. He was not, after all, dealing with the Medici.

CHAPTER TEN

All Is Illusion

W HEN HE REACHED HOME, Gamadge sought
Harold in the office, and handed over Volumes I and III of the
Dykinck Byron.

"There are minute rubbings and scars along the top
edges of these," he said. "I want photographs, much enlarged.
You'll find a break in the sequence—unfortunately. I have to
take a photograph of Volume II myself. I only hope Mr.
Vauregard will let me; but I don't think he'll be able to resist
the baby camera. My picture will have to be fitted in between
your two, somehow. Can you manage with the laboratory
camera?"

"Sure, I can."

"Have your lunch, will you? I want some help after I swallow mine."

He swallowed his, and then spread the Dykinck letters
out on a table beside the library window. "Start on these," he
said. "Begin with the year 1840, and sort out anything that

refers to the Vauregards, with special attention to the dates immediately following May third."

A cab got him to Central Park West shortly before two o'clock, and stopped in front of the old Palazzo apartments. Huge potted palms still bloomed among columns of variegated marble, and turbaned Moors (bronze gilt) upheld clusters of multicolored light globes. Gamadge went up to the top floor in a cage elevator, open on all sides.

He got out of it into a high, bare hall, and rang at a door with CHANDOR on it in blue lettering. It was immediately opened by the individual whom Harold had not cared for—a bald, peering man of immense size, whose manner to clients might be good, but who surveyed Gamadge without affection.

He looked at Gamadge's card, and then led him down a long passage with two bends in it, and into a big, surprising room. It was a kind of sun parlor, with starred, dark-blue awnings adjusted against the glare of the sun. A range of windows on three sides let in air, more sun, and the troubled roar of the streets below. Anything less soothing than this room, decorated as it was in light-blue and silver, with stars everywhere, Gamadge could not imagine.

Two persons rose from large blue-and-silver chairs as he came in; a handsome, big woman, faultlessly garbed in dark blue, with a diamond star on her left shoulder which Gamadge imagined to represent many fees, and large ones. She had a jolly smile, which beamed upon Gamadge while her small bright eyes appraised him.

The tall, thin, gray-headed man beside her looked like an actor. His regular features and waxy complexion needed a touch or so of grease paint to make them impressively handsome, but even now he was very good-looking. He did not smile at all—in fact, his expression was ominous. He said: "Stay and take notes, Rubens."

Gamadge remarked, amiably: "My assistant wanted to come with me; perhaps I ought to have let him."

"Now, now; you two!" protested Mrs. Chandor, showing brilliant teeth. "Sit down, Mr. Gamadge. I'm delighted to meet you." She sat down herself, and Rubens accommodated himself at a table, upon which he laid a notebook.

"Just for the record," said Mr. Chandor. He lifted his hand, a slim and pale one, and waved it horizontally in front of him, level with his midriff. "You don't object?"

"Not a bit."

"Sit down, Mr. Gamadge."

"When you do."

Chandor lowered himself into a chair, his eyes on the visitor. Gamadge pulled up a hard, spindly affair with a star surmounting the back of it, and sat down also.

"Our business name is Chandor, but in private life we are Mr. and Mrs. Zanch," said Mr. Zanch. Gamadge bowed.

Mrs. Zanch said: "Such interesting books you must write. We couldn't read them, of course, because we don't accept crime."

"Nice, not to have to," said Gamadge.

"We don't quite understand how we can help you. There is no mystery, as I said in my letter, about New Soul. It is merely a system of thought. What can you do with it, Mr. Gamadge ? It would take you years merely to learn to put it into words."

"Didn't you put it into words in your book, Mrs. Zanch? You have written one, I understand."

"That is for initiates, who have taken the preliminary steps towards the light. I really cannot see—"

"My wife means," said Mr. Zanch, also smiling, but without mirth, "that she'd like to know what the racket is. Don't be annoyed."

Gamadge, looking anything but annoyed, said that he wouldn't.

"We are business people; New Soul is not only a practical system of life, it's a business—and a very good business, too. We have a special commodity that people need, want, and pay for. Anything that menaces that business," said Mr. Zanch, "is a racket, to us."

"Naturally. And if the business menaces somebody, then the business is a racket to him—or her," said Gamadge, cheerfully.

Mrs. Zanch said: "Now, now. This isn't the way to go about it at all. Mr. Gamadge isn't a blackmailer—ridiculous; and he can see just by looking at us that we are not fortune tellers, palmists, or mediums. We don't care about going into your book in the section that deals with them, Mr. Gamadge."

"Oh, you wouldn't."

"We don't care about going into it at all," said Zanch, his tone suddenly violent. "We have a lawyer, and we shall take good care not to go into your book, in any section whatsoever."

"I'm sorry. New Soul sounded interesting, to me, and I could treat it seriously. Since Mrs. Zanch—or both of you— have written a book yourselves, I supposed that you were not averse to print."

"You can't deal with it intelligently."

"I could refer to it intelligently, perhaps," suggested Gamadge, looking surprised. "What's the difficulty? There must be something. You're not by any chance worrying because I heard of you through the Vauregards and Mrs. Morton?"

The Zanches were silent. Then Mrs. Zanch said: "Mrs. Morton left us rather abruptly. She is a woman of whims—very flighty, I am sorry to say."

"Artistic temperament."

"Far, far too much of it! We could have given her balance and repose; but she was a difficult case. Charming woman, of course," said Mrs. Zanch.

"We have the best and most delicate-minded people in our seminars," said Mr. Zanch. "Any breath of dissension frightens them."

Gamadge looked sympathetic. "As a matter of fact," he said, "I don't know why old Mr. Vauregard shouldn't endow New Soul; he would be allowed to endow a hospital for the body, why not one for the mind? Or soul, of course. He would be allowed to build one. The family couldn't do a thing about it. I really do not see the difference. Except, of course, that there's a touch of popular prejudice against cults."

"We are not a cult, Mr. Gamadge." Mrs. Zanch's smile was almost a grimace, so forced had it become. "We are, as I keep telling you, a system. Look out of that window."

Gamadge did so, and then gave her a politely questioning glance.

"What do you see?" asked Mrs. Zanch. "Sky."

"Of course. But the stars are there, Mr. Gamadge; the stars are there! Why can't you see them at this moment?"

"Too much light?" asked Gamadge, with the nervous uncertainty of a candidate taking an I.Q. test.

"Too much light; the light that shows us things which are of no importance to the spirit—things which distract the soul. We teach these light-blinded people to look beyond that empty sky, to pierce illusion; to lose one star, and find the countless stars that it conceals."

"I see," said Gamadge. "You pierce the illusion of light, and find the twilight of the soul. What a title! 'The Twilight of the Soul.' Couldn't you use it, Mrs. Zanch?"

Mr. Zanch said roughly: "Don't bother with him, Astra; you can see to look at him that he's light-bound."

"A materialist, I'm afraid," agreed Mrs. Zanch.

"And we don't want you interpreting us in your book."

"I shouldn't dream of doing so, if you object; in fact, I am willing to give you a promise in writing that I won't even mention you, or New Soul either. I'll give it to you now," said Gamadge; "then, when I make my request, you won't call me a blackmailer again; and before witnesses, too," he added, reproachfully.

"Request? What request?" Zanch fixed suspicious black eyes on him.

"I only want to know just what old Mr. Vauregard was going to do for New Soul, before his family got after him."

The Zanches gazed at him, and Mrs. Zanch suddenly laughed. "Of all the impudence!" she said.

"Not at all. Why should you object to satisfying my curiosity? I have no witness here; and if I mentioned such a thing in my book, you could get terrific damages out of me for libel."

"Nothing of the sort was ever discussed. Really, Mr. Gamadge! If Mrs. Morton wishes to ruin us by spreading tales among our clients, she will have to go about it another way. You talk of libel; there is such a thing as slander." Mrs. Zanch laughed again, highly amused. "To send you here with your story about a book!"

Gamadge said: "Mrs. Morton was rather averse to my coming, but I persisted. Of course, I can ask the old gentleman himself, and he may tell me—who knows?"

He got out of his chair. Zanch said: "Wait a minute. I don't get this at all. What use are you going to make of the information, if you get it?"

"I'll be perfectly frank with you. I have reason to think that Mr. Vauregard has fallen into less scrupulous hands than yours."

Mrs. Zanch drew in her breath. "Ah! I knew he would. Poor old gentleman. If you knew what we saved him from, Mr. Gamadge! Crystal gazing and clairvoyance, I give you my word!"

"He wasn't above table tipping, I swear he wasn't," said Zanch.

"Well, somebody's after him; and I just wanted to get an idea what they may think they can get out of it. If it's anything considerable, the family will do something drastic—" He stopped himself from adding: "again."

The Zanches looked at each other. A hoarse voice from the corner where Mr. Rubens scribbled in shorthand said gloomily: "I bet you it's the Knights of the Temple crowd. He kept asking about them."

After a long pause, Mr. Zanch spoke between his teeth: "It's a crime. He'll sink into Black Magic, that's where he'll end up. Very susceptible subject. Hankered after phenomena. My wife hasn't been in a trance since since we discovered New Soul, but she would have done anything, rather than throw him to the wolves."

"What are the Knights of the Temple likely to get out of it, do you think?" asked Gamadge. "Much?"

"Anything," said Mrs. Zanch. "Almost anything, that is. The first thing they would get would be the old house, and the upkeep; but not any such upkeep as he planned for it when it was going to be a museum. Oh, no."

"Dear me," said Gamadge. "And I suppose that bequest would take precedence; get paid before the family legacies were settled."

"All things considered," said Zanch dryly, "I suppose so, too."

"Well, I must be going. Thank you both for being so helpful, and I only wish you'd reconsider about my book. Look here; won't you let me send you the chapter, if it ever gets written? You might actually like it, you know."

Mrs. Zanch said, with graciousness, that she thought that might be a good idea. Her husband remarked jocosely "Too bad to disappoint you. Old what's-her-name—Cybele—the outfit on the second floor; they want a ghost writer, I understand."

Gamadge laughed, and said that he would remember that fact. He shook hands with the Chandors, and went out, escorted by the bald man, who was in a thawing mood.

"The boss was peeved at first," he said, "because he got busy and found out you did detective work."

"I've done it twice, and I hardly ever remember that I have done it. Sorry to upset him."

"For Gawd's sake don't let anybody try anything raw with the old gentleman—Mr. Vauregard. It would kill him."

"I'll do my best."

Gamadge walked home through the park, feeling his usual pleasant nostalgia at sight of the fountain below the Mall, the old green balustrades, the boats on the lake. He sat down under a big tree, in a byway well screened from motor traffic, and reviewed the situation.

There had been a good deal at stake, apparently, when somebody decided to play the arbor game; quite enough to justify a certain amount of risk. Well, Gamadge did not doubt that Miss Wagoneur-Smith could be scared away, but what then? The old gentleman seemed determined to make a fool of himself in one way or another; how could X hope to restrain him from further excursions into the inane? Once again Gamadge's thoughts made him uneasy. He told himself that he was getting too hardboiled for polite society, represented by the Vauregard family and its connections; threw away his cigarette, and pursued his way along avenues of dusty trees.

He found Harold sorting Dykinck letters.

"How'd you like the Chandors?" he asked, looking up as Gamadge came in.

"Not much. They're disappointed. Old Mr. Vauregard certainly intended to do something big for them. They were teaching him to see the stars at midday. Zanch—that's Chandor—was certainly a medicine man of some kind, once; Mrs. Zanch comes from the West, and has been brought up among the spirits, I should say; it's her life. She made me think of a magnificent and glorified trained nurse. I shouldn't be surprised if she did some people as much good as their pills and electric sun lamps do."

"Ten letters for you to look at," said Harold. "Vauregard references, five."

Gamadge looked through the five. "All from Cornelia Dykinck to her husband Deken. Very interesting."

He selected one, and read:

Sixth May, 1840
MY DEAREST DYKINCK:
I am glad you had a good voyage, and that you have engaged passage on the same ship. Do not forget to

buy the furred greatcoat in Hamburg; it can be bit-
terly cold, there, as you know, and the travelling is
so bad.

You remember the cold I caught in the Swiss
diligence, though it was August.

I had coffee with the Vauregards on the third,
and the oddest thing happened. The governess disappeared! That charming girl they had from
England. They are greatly put out, fear a scandal of
some sort, and are making a mystery of it. I did not
think it very odd at the time, she might very well
have run out on an errand without her hat, but she
has not returned! I sent to enquire next morning,
and when Sue came back with the news that she was
still away, I confess I thought instantly of the dashing Charles. Fanny says there is nothing in that,
Miss Wagoneur never looked at him, and he is still
in Albany.

I shall keep you informed in my weekly letter of
this upset in the Vauregard circle, but have promised not to mention it, so you must be very careful.

The dear children miss you...

Gamadge cast the letter aside, and seized upon the next
one, which was dated "Twentieth May." He read eagerly:

...The great Wagoneur mystery is a mystery yet, or
so Fanny pretends to everyone but myself. They are
giving out that she returned to England suddenly.
As you know, that is all nonsense; what I told you in
mine of last week is a fact, but we must be careful
not to repeat it, as Fanny is distressed, and no doubt
wishes she had never breathed a word to me about
it.

Did I tell you that the girl took a book with her
when she decamped? As a blind, of course, so that

they should think she was going into the arbor to read for half an hour. It is one of that set of Byron that Charles gave to Fanny, when he gave me mine. Fancy!...

"Where's the other letter? Where's the other letter?" Gamadge hunted about on the table.

"What other letter?"

"The letter of May thirteenth. Where is it?"

"There isn't any letter of May thirteenth."

"There must be...Good heavens—X!"

"What do you mean, 'X'?"

"X got the letter, too, hang it all!"

"I don't know anything about the case," said Harold, putting the letters together, "so I don't know what you're talking about."

"Cornelia wrote to her absent spouse weekly, and there's a letter missing—the one that explodes the Great Wagoneur Mystery. X got Miss Dykinck to show him the letters, as well as the Byrons; perhaps he's writing a book, too! Poor Miss Dykinck must think we mean to flood the market. He stole the letter of May thirteenth, and he stole Volume II of the Byron set. Of course he had to have that letter—it blows Miss Smith higher than a kite, or would if old Mr. Vauregard saw it. Well, I bet on the dashing Charles—I always suspected him."

Harold gathered up the papers, and rose. "You want these in the safe?"

"Stick 'em in, but they're no use to me. Well, I only hope X hasn't dared telephone Miss Smith; if he has, and repeated Miss Dykinck's story of this morning, I doubt if I get to see the zombi again at all."

"I don't care who the zombi is," said Harold coldly, "but who is this X?"

"Don't I wish I knew ! Never mind; I shall do a lot of guessing, I can tell you. It's somebody Miss Dykinck has taken a fancy to, and whom she has been entertaining once or twice of an evening, unbeknown to her domestic Gestapo. It's a young or youngish man, and a not unattractive one. I say young or youngish, but I think Miss Dykinck would stretch a point, if she liked the fellow."

"This is your guess?"

"It's my guess. What sort of visitor would be banned by Mrs. Dykinck, I wonder? A young man—she wouldn't like Posy to make a fool of herself; a married man; a divorced man; a man of evil repute; a man not socially acceptable to a Dykinck."

"Still guessing?"

"No, I think that part of it's certain. This person (ridiculous to suppose that Miss Dykinck would go to any trouble to see a woman), this person is trying to keep the Vauregard money in the family."

"Do they need money?"

"They do. Even Mrs. Morton does—to finance a probably unremunerative theatrical production. She's set her heart on it."

Theodore came into the room, and announced (with a broad smile): "Miss Dawson and Mr. Payne."

CHAPTER ELEVEN

Volume II

"I'M AFRAID WE'RE awfully early, it's only a little after four," said Clara. "Cameron has an engagement later. I brought him with me—do you mind?"

In her dark-blue dress sprinkled with bright flowers, and her neat, uptilted hat, she looked older than she did in riding clothes; Gamadge thought she also looked tired.

"Delighted," he said, shaking hands with her. Payne stood in the doorway, leaning on his stick; Harold, sliding past him on his way out, certainly appeared to be of a lesser breed, and decidedly without the law. "She always lugs me around everywhere with her," said Payne gaily.

"Of course I do. Isn't this a nice room!" She glanced about her. Her eyes came gently to rest on Theodore, who was busily arranging chairs and a low table in front of the davenport.

"Young gentleman find this sofa comfortable," said that functionary, and departed for the tea tray. Payne limped over to it, and Clara settled him on it with a cushion behind him. She then sat down beside him.

Gamadge brought cigarettes and matches, passed them, and seated himself on the other side of the tea table.

"You bet it's a nice room. Nice house." Payne's eyes crinkled as he also looked about him. "Improvement on the kind of hole I live in. I hate a hotel."

"Convenient, though," said Gamadge. "You're independent. Whenever I go anywhere, or come back, there's the deuce and all to pay. It seems to me they're always wanting to houseclean, or something. God knows how often they wash the windows."

"Pathetic," smiled Payne. "I could easily burst out crying."

"I feel like it, sometimes. By the way, Mr. Payne, you don't have to drink tea, you know."

"I've always wanted to try it."

"Sure you wouldn't prefer something more stimulating?"

"Sure."

"Are you comfortable, Cam?" asked Miss Dawson.

"Quite."

"Let me just—"

"Quit fussing, my angel."

"When we are married, I shall have a sofa just like this one."

"If we are married, you mean. I'm not sure yet that I'll have you, you know." Payne turned and smiled at her.

"Don't be so rude; what will Mr. Gamadge think?"

"We know what he thinks, now; that I have a nerve, letting you marry a crock. Hello, isn't that the back of my club I see out of the window?" He pulled himself to his feet, and steered himself, rather crookedly, across the room. As he stood looking out of the big window at the awninged terrace opposite, Clara said: "Poor Cammy."

"Yes. Too bad."

"He can never get better."

"Pretty grim for him—and for you."

"He's awfully plucky." She added, after a pause, "It was all my fault."

"Yours?"

"We were riding, and we took a jump, and I let my horse crowd him. We came down on top of him."

Theodore came in with the tea tray, and Cameron Payne came back to the sofa. He said, "We're neighbors. The Humbert—that's where I live, if you call it living—it isn't so far off, either. West Fifty-eighth Street. We might have a game, of an evening. Do you like cards?"

"Very much."

"Piquet? Bezique? Cribbage?"

"All the two-handed games."

"We must play. It's so damned hard to get up a bridge four."

"Come in whenever you like."

Theodore left them, and Miss Dawson poured tea. Payne, tasting his, said: "Delightful new beverage; I'm glad I stuck to it. Do you disapprove of Clara telling me about her Great-uncle Imbrie and the femme fatale, Mr. Gamadge?"

"Not in the least. That makes only eight in the know, excluding Miss Smith herself, and her friends."

"We ought to start an Arbor Cult, or something. Hello."

Martin the cat had come in quietly, looked the party over, and decided to leap upon the knees of Mr. Payne. He lifted his teacup out of the way, and Clara said: "Oh dear. Cats always go for the people that don't like them."

"I'll remove the brute," said Gamadge.

"Not at all. He doesn't bother me," declared Payne.

"He does like dogs, though, thank goodness," said Clara.

"That reminds me. How's the sick chow, Miss Dawson?" asked Gamadge.

Her face clouded. "She died last night. The vet had to…"

"Oh, I am sorry."

"Doctor Wadley said it was better. She was so old, and she's been ailing a long time. We all went over to see her, before he..."

"I'm glad you have the other one. Wadley's my vet, too. Good man."

Payne said, between bites of his muffin: "I didn't realize cats needed vets."

"Oh, Lord, they're perfect hypochondriacs. Always something wrong with them."

"Never tasted better muffins," said Payne, accepting another. "About Miss Smith; what I say is, live and let live. What if she does get a slice of the money? He's happy, and nobody's much the worse for it, so far as I can see. The family wouldn't dream of interfering if he bought himself a yacht or an airplane."

"But he's such a darling, and he's being taken in by this female," protested Clara. "I hate to think of it."

"He's having the time of his life. Getting a great kick out of it; she just suits him. Anybody can see that."

Clara seemed more troubled by this lighthearted view of the situation than Gamadge thought necessary.

"Cam, please," she said. "It's so ugly."

"Oh, twaddle."

"I don't think you ought to—"

"Just let me mind my own business, for once, like a good girl."

There was something behind this exchange, Gamadge decided. He said: "I agree with Miss Dawson. It's ugly, and it's dangerous."

Payne replied, very urbane: "Well, of course you have to say so. You're thinking of your job."

Clara said: "Don't be that way, Cam."

"What way?"

"If you are rude to Mr. Gamadge, he won't play cards with you."

"For the love of heaven, can't you let me alone?"

Gamadge said: "Of course it's my job to extricate Mr.

Vauregard; Mr. Payne is quite right. Strangely enough, I think I'm making progress."

"No!" Clara was excited. "Can you tell us about it?"

"Not quite yet."

"The thing is," she said earnestly, "you ought to get a picture of her."

"I'm afraid I may not be able to manage that."

Payne's interest had apparently waned. He was glancing about the room again. "You have plenty of books," he said. "Nice habit, reading; too bad I can't."

"Didn't they teach you, darling?" asked Clara; her serenity had returned, and she was polishing off a little cake with great appetite.

"They couldn't teach me to like it. Well, Clara, we won't have a place like this, unless Uncle Imbrie leaves you a damn sight more than he's likely to; anyway, no matter how low we sink, we can't settle in The Humbert."

"It's a bachelor apartment," she told Gamadge, "and I'm the only woman that ever went up in the elevator. The boy told me so."

"A cripple has special privileges," smiled Payne.

"The more the better," said Gamadge.

Payne again got to his feet and limped around the room, examining the pictures, the ancient maps, the celestial and terrestrial globes that stood waist-high on either side of the fireplace. He ended at the farther window, where he stood with his lame foot propped against the low sill, the sun glinting on his hair. Martin had slid to the floor, and was rubbing himself now against the stick in Payne's hand.

"Don't let him knock your cane out from under," said Gamadge.

"You bet I won't."

Clara was leaning back, her head against a cushion; Gamadge contemplated her gravely, and when she caught him at it, did not look away. They exchanged a long, friendly gaze. She said "It's restful here."

"You look as if you could do with a rest. I suppose it's your dog, and all."

"Yes, and that business at Uncle Imbrie's."

"Upsets the whole family, I suppose."

"It makes everything seem queer and unnatural. Nobody agrees with anybody else what to do. They are so nervous. Poor Aunt Robina feels it a lot."

"Intolerable situation."

"We all want the money, so I suppose it's hypocritical for me to mind talking about it all the time."

"Not at all."

"I wish sometimes I could get away from every single thing."

She caught Gamadge's eye again, and something she read there held her own. He said: "Wish I could do something about it."

"You can't."

"I know that."

"It's so restful here."

Payne came back to them. "All right, Clara. It's getting on to five; if you're ready."

She got up. "We loved it, Mr. Gamadge."

"Come again. This bachelor establishment does let women up; welcomes them, in fact."

"I'll bet." Payne shook hands. "We'll have those card parties. I don't play for anything much, but I keep my end up."

"You'll probably clean me out," said Gamadge. "I play nothing regularly except bridge."

He went down to the door with them, and saw them into Clara's sedan. Theodore, clearing away in the library, remarked that that was a fine couple, and a mighty fine young gentleman, "Be about perfect, when he gets over that bust-up he had."

"That's the trouble." Gamadge stood aimlessly in the window where Payne had stood, and gazed out at nothing. "He won't get over it."

"Too bad; but he's good enough the way he is. Looks like one of the archangels, he only needs big wings."

"All is illusion."

"That young lady, she'll stick to him."

"Play piquet with him all her life—unless when she gets old he ends by not liking her any more."

Theodore straightened himself to stare. "Never heard you say nothin' like that, Mr. Gamadge; not in your born days."

"Live and learn."

Gamadge went into the hall and dialed the number of the Morton house. When he got Miss Vauregard, he said: "I'm going down there in half an hour. I think I have something. I'll begin to break it to him—very gently."

"Oh, do be careful. He'll be so shocked."

"I'll be very careful. It will take some doing, though."

"Do you think I ought to be there with you?"

"No, much better to keep the family right out of it. Let him suppose it's the idea of a distinterested outsider."

"I'm so nervous, I think I'll go out for a walk. Be sure to telephone me later."

"I will." He added: "Your niece brought her intended to tea."

"Don't say I didn't warn you. It's a fixed idea."

"Oh, I understand perfectly what you meant. As from one human being to another: Is your niece in love with this young man, or is it romantic self-sacrifice in the classic tradition?"

"Hundreds of girls have been in love with him."

"I don't doubt it. Is she?"

"They've known each other always—too long to be romantic."

"Did she really crowd him at the jump?"

"She will always think so. She was only sixteen, and he was an experienced rider, but you can't do anything with Clara, if she gets an idea like that into her head."

"How about him? I thought him a little offhand."

"Just his manner. Clara is all he has."

"Rather casual with his treasure."

"That's his manner, Mr. Gamadge. He's been wonderful about his injury."

"Still, from one human being to another: Do you like this match? Tell me honestly."

"Well...who knows how poor Cameron may turn out? Of course I wish things were different. One can't urge her to desert him."

"At any rate, there'll be three of us from now on; she will stick to him, and I shall stick to her."

"You can't mean it."

"Can't I?"

"That kind of thing leads to all sorts of trouble."

"Not at all; I shall make myself inconspicuous."

Miss Vauregard made a sound expressive of incredulity, and hung up. Gamadge chose a book from his shelves, and wrapped it up with Volumes I and III of the Dykinck Byron. He then descended to the laboratory, where Harold was enlarging photographs, and took more expert instruction in the management of his new camera. He finally put it in his pocket, and left the house. It was five forty-five o'clock.

He took the Fifty-ninth Street subway, got out at Astor Place, and walked to Traders Row, arriving there at six fifteen. A yellow, cloudy light fell on the little street, where no passerby ever seemed to walk, and where the houses were as blank and apparently untenanted as if they had been house fronts on a stage. The Vauregard gates stood wide. Gamadge paused for a moment, noted the closed kitchen door and the green solitude beyond, and passed on to the white steps and portico.

Old John received him as if he had been a guest of years' standing: "Will you go up, Sir? Mr. Vauregard allows me to spare myself the stairs."

"How is Eliza?"

"Very well, Sir; having her afternoon rest in her room. We are working on that paper, Sir."

"Fine. How are you getting on with it?"

"Very well, Sir. I—I hope we are not doing an injustice to the young person."

"You won't do that."

"Shall you be wanting coffee, Sir? I can make you fresh."

"No, indeed."

"I hope you can wait for sherry, Sir. I take it up at seven, when I fetch down the coffee tray."

"I'm afraid I can't. Is Miss Smith in the library, do you know?"

"She was not there at five. She may be in the garden, Sir. They are often there after coffee. Mr. Vauregard likes a stroll before dinner. He is expecting you, Sir, and you will find him upstairs."

Gamadge mounted to the second story. Pausing in the library doorway, he saw the old gentleman's head above the back of the davenport. It was drooping, as if Mr. Vauregard was in a doze.

Gamadge said: "Good evening, Sir." And then, receiving no answer, he repeated: "Good evening, Mr. Vauregard." He rounded the end of the davenport, stopped abruptly, and said: "My God!" His eyes went from the dusky and contorted face to the hand bent strangely inward on the chintz cushion; he saw the broken Spode cup on the parquet floor, and the river of spilled coffee. He stared for another moment, turned, and dashed from the room.

CHAPTER TWELVE

The Macbeth Formula

GAMADGE TOOK THE STAIRS three at a time. He glanced into the drawing room, the dining room, the pantry and the kitchen, and then went through the back doorway that led into the garden. It was empty, and so was the arbor.

He came back and opened the door of the servants' sitting room. John lay on the couch, snoring lightly. At Gamadge's voice he sat up with a start.

"John," said Gamadge, "when were you last in the library?"

"When was I..." The old man was only half awake. "At five, Sir, when I took up the coffee."

"Where have you been since?"

"Here, Sir, except when you—"

"Eliza upstairs all that time?"

"Yes, Sir. She goes as soon after five as she...Is anything wrong, Sir?"

"Just tell me this: So far as you know, nobody came to have coffee with Mr. Vauregard?"

"No, Sir."

"Miss Smith with him when you took the tray up?"

"No, Sir. What—"

"Do you keep everything wide open down here, even when you take your nap?"

"Mr. Vauregard is in and out...The kitchen door—Eliza locks it. Mr. Gamadge, Sir, what has happened?" The butler got to his feet.

"Mr. Vauregard is dead. Hold on there—sit down. Any brandy anywhere? Dining room? I'll get you some. Don't you stir, now; you can't do a thing."

Gamadge ran to the dining room, found cognac in the buffet, and came back with it. He poured some into a water glass on the dresser, and stood over the butler until he had drunk it. Then he said: "I know how you feel—it's pretty bad."

"What—what was it, Sir?" gasped John.

"That's the trouble; he's taken poison somehow. Steady, there—you're not to go near the library. Understand? I'm calling the police."

"Police!"

"I've got to. I want you to go up and see if you can find Miss Smith. She isn't down here, or in the garden. Will you do that for me? Then you're to go up to Eliza, and keep her right in her room. I'm doing the best I can for everybody—take my word for it."

"Yes, Sir." John got up. He looked vague. Gamadge said in a sharper tone: "Just go up and find Miss Smith. If you can't find her, call down; I'll be in the pantry."

The old man went along the hall and up the stairs. Gamadge, listening, heard him mount the second flight without turning down the hall. He then dashed out again, and into the arbor. He had not been mistaken on his first hurried trip; there was a smudge of cigarette ash on the white iron bench—

somebody had flicked most of it off. He studied the grass, and found no match or stub; there was, however, a neat hole punched in the soft ground at the left of the entrance—a corner where the sun never shone. He stared at it angrily, left the arbor, looked about on the grass between it and the paved walk that circled the fountain, and went back to the house.

As he entered, he heard old John's voice from the floor above: "Miss Smith is not here, Sir."

"Sure?"

"Yes, Sir." His voice was shaking.

"Then go up and break the news to Eliza, and for your life, don't either of you leave your room. And don't be frightened—I'm standing by."

Gamadge still hugged his parcel under his arm. He mounted the stairs again, and made for the library. Casting no glance at the bent figure on the davenport, he crossed to the bookcase between the east windows. The Byron set confronted him, but it was again incomplete—Volume II had once more been withdrawn from circulation; this time, thought Gamadge with considerable relief, for good and all.

He unwrapped his parcel, laid its contents on a table, and carefully removed the inscribed flyleaf from Volume I of the Dykinck Byron. He then opened the bookcase, shoved the set along, and squeezed the Dykinck Byrons, Volumes I and III, in at the end of the shelf. He rewrapped his own book, *Mystery and Magic in Numbers*, making as bulky a parcel as he could of it, and took it with him down to the pantry, where he had seen a telephone. He dialed the Morton number.

"Is Miss Vauregard in?" he asked.

The houseman's indistinguishable mumble faded, and presently Miss Vauregard spoke.

He said: "This is Gamadge, Miss Vauregard. I am speaking from Traders Row. I have bad news for you. Can you take it?...Yes, it's Mr. Vauregard...Yes, he is. I found him so. He had been dead some time, I should think more than half an hour....Are you all right? I'm awfully sorry to keep you talking,

but if you can manage it, I want you to listen; it's most important...Take a minute...Good, I knew you'd stand by.

"This is our one and only chance, because I have to call
the police...It was poison, I think he had it in his coffee...Miss
Smith isn't in the house or on the place—can you understand
me? Good for you. Volume II is missing again...Yes, it's gone.

"Try to listen carefully, now: Get hold of the rest of the
family, and see whether they can account for themselves from
five o'clock on, until about six. I was expected any time after
six, you know, and John saw your uncle at five. If any of you
can't produce witnesses to provide a complete alibi, you must
tell the police the arbor story.

"Why? Surely you see it. You must tell the whole thing,
with just one reservation, what only you and I know—the tie-
up with our friends in Thirty-fourth Street. Don't drag them
in. The police will never get that line at all, because Volume II
is gone. Don't you see? Without it there's absolutely no connection—I've seen to that.

"What? Oh, I'll tell the police the refugee story—that's all
I'm supposed to know. I'll wait for you to divulge the other...
Miss Vauregard, you must divulge it! They're going to look for
motive, and we must give them Miss Smith...No, they won't
come to our conclusions; they can't. Volume II is gone. Don't
you see? There is nothing to connect any of you with it. Let
them get after Miss Smith, and keep after her; if they know
she's a swindler, they'll follow that line indefinitely...We can't
help where it leads; don't think of that! Think of all the inno-
cent parties.

"And don't communicate with me from now on—much
better not. I just came in about the books. When you tell them
the arbor story, and they question me about it, I can look out
for myself. Remember, don't hold out on them! Only, those
people called D, it would be tough to drag them in. They're
not going to be useful. I must hang up, can't wait another
moment. Till later. Good-bye."

Gamadge hung up and dialed another number.

"Police? Henry Gamadge speaking, from the old Vauregard house, Traders Row. I called at six fifteen, or near it, and found old Mr. Vauregard dead…Poison, I think…No, I didn't…No, I won't…Yes, I will."

When the police arrived, they found in Mr. Henry Gamadge a model witness. He allowed himself to be marooned in the drawing room, a charming apartment wherein he sat as in a stupor, nursing his parcel and asking no questions. He told his story patiently to three different sets of officials, he offered his fingers for printing with an air of candid interest, and he did not mention the fact that he was getting hungry.

At last a thin-faced, dark man with a narrow blue eye came in, introduced himself as Detective Lieutenant Durfee, and asked to see the contents of Gamadge's parcel. "The old fellow—Daggett, the butler—said you brought one. Any objection?…"

"None at all." Gamadge handed it over.

Durfee untied it, and gazed inquiringly at *Mystery and Magic in Numbers*. He said, "I understand you're an authority on books and documents."

"Kind of whoever said so."

"I had Miss Vauregard on the telephone; she says she introduced you."

"Yes."

"Mr. Vauregard wanted to see this?"

"Yes. It's nonsense, but he liked to fool with such things."

Durfee looked at a picture of a pentacle within three concentric circles, and returned the book to Gamadge.

"This young lady that was staying in the house—this refugee. English girl, I understand."

"So Mr. Vauregard told me."

"She hasn't come back yet. Didn't take her hat with her."

"No?"

"Could you describe her?"

"I could, but I only met her once, yesterday. Tall, slim, very fair, rather long blue eyes, pointed face. Fine, thin, rather

long nose. Long neck, lots of thick, fine hair. Very good-looking."

"Lady, I suppose?"

"Ladylike. Quiet, good manners, rather formal and old-
fashioned."

"Family tells me she was a governess."

Gamadge gently sighed.

"Seems the deceased didn't say much about her."

"He didn't to me."

"You hear that refugee story from the family?"

"Yes."

"What did you think of it?"

"I thought that whatever the details of it might be, they
would turn out to be entirely creditable to him."

"Felt that way, did you?"

"Oh, yes; most high-minded old gentleman."

"We haven't been able to get hold of the family lawyer
yet—Bedlowe. He's in the country. The family doesn't know a
thing about Mr. Vauregard's affairs, except that he made a will
years ago. We hate to lose any time over routine, when it's a
case of homicide."

"Is it a case of homicide?"

"No poison container present; unless," said Durfee,
jocosely, "you removed it."

"People have been known to take a capsule or a tablet out
of a pocket, and swallow it, I suppose."

"We'll know more about that later. What did you think
about the servants? The family says they're out of the question."

"Oh, absolutely, I should think."

"The poor old cook—Mrs. Daggett—she's so laid out we
got a woman up from the department to look out for her. Nice
woman, Mrs. Daggett likes her."

"I should say Miss Vauregard was the person for that
job."

"We don't want the family down here, yet; I'm going up to

see them this evening. Funny, the way that yard door was left open when the servants weren't on the spot."

"I understood from John the butler that Mr. Vauregard was going out."

"Even so. Still, Daggett says they never have been burgled. How about getting the time straight? You were to drop in between six and seven, and you got here and up to the library at about six fifteen?"

"Six eighteen, I should think."

"You looked at the body, didn't touch it, and came right out again. Didn't touch it." Durfee questioned Gamadge with a sharp, inquiring glance.

"No. He was dead, I could see that. I supposed you didn't want me to examine him or offer my opinions. I know nothing about such matters."

"So you came right out again. Nothing unusual about the place, except the dead body, and the broken coffee cup?"

"I saw nothing unusual; I was there about a quarter of a minute, and I had only been in that room once before—yesterday."

"Why did you decide he was dead?"

"Because he'd taken cyanide."

"You're up on poisons?"

"One reads so much about that one. Cyanide gives people that blue look, doesn't it? And of course the broken cup, and that pond of coffee on the parquet, showed he'd only had a sip of it."

"A sip was plenty. It was his second cup, unless somebody else had one, and washed up afterwards. Well, you went down and broke the news to Daggett. Five minutes?"

"About that, and five more to hunt for Miss Smith, and a short five to telephone Miss Vauregard and the police."

"Which brings us to six thirty-eight, when you called us. We were here at six forty-four."

"Er—Miss Smith didn't have coffee with Mr. Vauregard?"

"Not unless she washed her cup afterwards. Mr. Daggett says there are exactly two cupfuls gone out of the pot. The deceased took two cups of an afternoon, and was always finished with his second by five-thirty. There's an alcohol lamp under the urn, and he kept it going in case a friend dropped in. Old Daggett didn't clear away until he brought up sherry at seven—he's got rheumatism, and the old gentleman spared him."

"No cyanide in the coffee pot, I gather."

"Probably not, but we'll have it analyzed. It doesn't smell of any. The point of all this is that whoever put cyanide in that second cup of coffee knew all about the house, and the habits of the deceased, and knew that he wasn't likely to have unexpected callers any time. There was just one time of day when a thing like that could be pulled off in this house."

"By an outsider."

"Yes. The Daggetts seem to have been making out some kind of a statement about this refugee, Miss Smith. Queer things they noticed. They say the list was for the family."

"They're devoted old servants. They'd worry about a stranger coming in from nowhere."

"And the old gentleman didn't give out much information about her, I understand."

"Very little."

"Would it inconvenience you if we looked you over—just to keep the records straight?"

"Go ahead," said Gamadge, laughing. "Only of course I should have shot the poison container down the drain."

Durfee smiled grimly, and looked Gamadge over himself. He showed interest in the little camera, and borrowed it "for a day or so." He looked into Gamadge's wallet, but did not notice or remove the flyleaf inscribed "Cornelia, from a Friend," which nestled among clean banknotes. He investigated Gamadge's fountain pen, which was full of ink, apologized civilly, and let him go home.

Harold met him in the front hall, eyes bulging. "You've been getting us into trouble," he said.

"Called up for my dossier, did they?"

"Twice. How do you like being on the wrong side of a murder case?"

"Quite restful; I left them to it, poor devils." Gamadge cast his hat on the hall table, and went upstairs to the library. The dinner table was set, as usual, beside a window; but Athalie the cook had taken the unusual step of coming up and waiting for him at the door.

"Nine o'clock, Mr. Gamadge," she said, "and what about your squab?"

"What about it?"

"You want a chaud-froid, or will I put it back in the oven and dry it up some more?"

"Give it to me the way it is, I want it now. Sorry, Athalie, the police got me."

While he ate Harold hovered near him; which was also unprecedented. Gamadge said at last: "Sit down, won't you? What are you worrying about?"

"You cut loose from those Vauregards." He produced an envelope. "This came by Postal messenger boy, but I didn't exactly like to interrupt your dinner."

"You will all end by driving me crazy. Can't I even have my mail any more?" Gamadge seized the letter, opened it, and read as follows

DEAR MR. GAMADGE,

You cannot desert us. The police are here, and they have seen me, and I am sending this off while I can.

None of us except Angela has an alibi for this afternoon! Imagine our hurting poor, poor darling Uncle! I was out for my walk, Dick walked home from his office, Clara was driving with Sun, and Cameron Payne was somewhere on a bus, and never got back to the Humbert until six, or later. Tom Duncannon was driving, too, and has only just come home. Angela was here, and is prostrated.

She won't allow us to tell the police one word about the arbor. I can't act alone. Won't you please come up, about half past ten tomorrow morning, before Mr. Bedlowe gets here, and reason with her? He's coming at eleven—we finally found him at his Westchester club.

Please help us.

Yours,

ROBINA VAUREGARD

Gamadge pocketed the letter, and went on with his dinner. When he had reached the coffee, he said: "All right, Harold. It seems I'm still on the case. I think I'm going to need you, from now on. Listen, while I tell you a fairy tale."

Harold listened in silence. There was a pause while Theodore cleared away, and then, while Gamadge smoked, his assistant pondered. When he spoke he surprised his employer:

"This Dykinck bird."

"What about her?"

"She probably told him this noon that you took those letters and those books. He knows that you know he took the missing letter, and that second volume."

"What of it?"

"What of it? She'll connect him with this murder, unless she's loony; even if she is loony, she'll connect him with it when and if those people tell the police the arbor story."

"She'd connive at ten murders before she told her story. Do you think she'd allow those girls in her sewing circle to know that she let X in by the area gate? I honestly believe she'd die first."

"He can't bank on that. He won't take a chance on it. He'll go there, and he'll—X is no sissy."

"He can't get into the place without making an appointment with her—he can't even get into communication with her."

"She may have made the appointment with him when she telephoned him today."

"He won't go near her now; not on your life! He can't risk it, with me in the know. It would sink him to be seen there."

"He'll risk it, all right. You got her into this—"

"I like that. She got herself into it. Here I am, in the worst jam I ever was in since I was born, and you talk to me about Miss Dykinck. I kept poor Miss Vauregard at the telephone when she was hardly able to talk or listen, telling her to keep the Dykincks out of it. If she remembers to, she's an even better sport than I thought she was. Miss Dykinck!"

"She's the one that's in the jam. He may go around there this evening—"

"Talk sense. Time enough to worry about her when and if the Wagoneur story gets into the news. It never may."

"Who is this X, anyhow? Duncannon, or young Vauregard, or Payne?" He paused, and added: "Or Bridge, or Chandor, or somebody else?"

"Payne? Payne?"

"Miss Dykinck likes him, and he's engaged to one of the Vauregard heirs."

"And he's a lame man who walks with a stick."

"Seems to get around, though. They left before five. She could have driven him down there in twenty minutes. She could have waited around, and driven him back."

"Have you ever seen Miss Dawson?"

"Yes, but you always told me never to go by what people look like."

"If I did, it's the only time I ever generalized in my life, and I take it back. Would you mind telephoning the Morton house for me? If a cop answers, say you want Butterfield, not Rhinelander. If somebody else does, say Mr. Gamadge will call on Miss Vauregard at half past ten o'clock tomorrow morning."

CHAPTER THIRTEEN

Mrs. Morton Cannot See It

WHEN GAMADGE PRESENTED himself at the Morton house next morning, Luigi the houseman received him tragically, and took him directly up to the second floor front. This seemed to be Miss Vauregard's workroom. A small, curly desk which Gamadge thought must be the first and only one she had ever had was littered with bills, address books, laundry lists and canceled checks. There was a little ancient typewriter on a table in front of a window, with telephone directories piled on the floor beside it. Miss Vauregard came in through a communicating door, which led to her bedroom.

She looked haggard, and her eyes were raised to Gamadge's with so much distress in them that he spoke even more gently than he had intended.

"You are making a great mistake, Miss Vauregard."

"I had to talk to you!"

"Let's sit down and talk, then; but you shouldn't have written to me, and I shouldn't be here."

He saw her installed on a lumpy sofa, and sat down in front of her, leaning forward. He continued with extreme gravity. "Our attempt—my attempt—to scare Miss Smith away has been only too successful—it has ended in this tragedy. Now the whole thing is out of our hands, and in those of the proper authorities. Unless you can be frank with them, you don't want me near you."

"But the police don't know anything about the arbor story—they won't ask you any questions."

"Durfee asked me questions yesterday, and I sailed a little too close to the wind in my answers. I can't stay on the job and conceal evidence, Miss Vauregard."

"But if I do persuade Angela to tell the whole story about Miss Smith, the police will know that we employed you. You'll get into trouble with them."

"No, not serious trouble; I was employed by you, and I was trying to get you to give them the story. All I had done was to work on Volume II, hoping to prove that it didn't belong to the Vauregard set. Well, Volume II has disappeared, and how I was working on it even you don't know. The police won't be interested in my twaddle about states of binding, now that the book's gone."

"But you don't want me to tell about the Dykincks."

"Their evidence won't help the police."

Miss Vauregard said, looking at him doubtfully "Mightn't they know who took the second volume?"

"If they do, they won't tell, and nobody will get it out of them."

"Some outsider could have got hold of it."

"True. It's not a physical impossibility."

"I'm convinced that we were absolutely mistaken about everything. I can't forgive myself. One of the family might have put that woman in the house, though my instincts were always against it; but none of us is capable of this frightful thing."

"If you have come to that conclusion, you want me less than ever."

"But they say the police are so stupid. You could persuade them to drop all this nonsense about our alibis. Why do they bother about it, when they haven't even found Miss Smith?"

"Perhaps they think Miss Smith is another victim."

Miss Vauregard stared at him. "She can't be!"

"They don't know that she isn't a refugee. They don't know that she didn't witness the murder. You must tell them that arbor story."

"Oh, why didn't we all meet people we knew, yesterday afternoon! You know yourself, Mr. Gamadge, that one doesn't, especially at this time of year."

"Of course I know it; I walked through the park yesterday and didn't meet a soul. At least, I met about a thousand souls, but nobody I knew, or—so far as I can tell—that knew me."

"Why can't the police understand that?"

"They have to follow a logical course of conduct. Look here, Miss Vauregard; you've been through a lot, and you're not by any means up to par, and I don't intend to take a high moral attitude; but you're not after the truth, any more."

"Yes, I am. I just don't want the police to make any mistakes."

"You don't care whether they make mistakes or not, so long as they make them about somebody outside the family. Who shall blame you?"

"But Miss Smith is the logical person to suspect! She must have had something to do with it!"

"If she's found, she may have a story to tell that will blow the case sky-high, and then where will you be? You say she's the logical suspect; but why should she kill Mr. Vauregard, unless she was acting for someone who had an interest in his estate?"

"He may have given her—"

"Then why not merely vanish? Miss Vauregard, I'm awfully sorry to bully you like this; but do look at it sensibly. If anything leaks out—and I may tell you that the police have seen that report John and Eliza were drawing up, and they're all ready to ask themselves whether there wasn't an imposture going on—they'll want to know why you didn't any of you dare to tell them that Miss Smith was a swindler. Tell them now and they'll go after her and her friends. I know you're frightened; but you can't help what's happened, and you can't fight this kind of situation. It's madness to try."

"Angela won't do it."

"I'll talk to Mrs. Morton. If she won't agree, I'm out of the case. So I'd better say good-bye now." Gamadge took her hand and smiled at her. "Until all this is a thing of the past, you know."

Miss Vauregard said, chokingly: "You warned us all."

"I blame myself for underrating the risk. What I or anyone could have done, in the peculiar circumstances, I hardly know."

He shook hands with her, patted her drooping shoulder, and went down to the drawing room.

There were four people in it, but Gamadge's eyes went first to Clara Dawson, who stood in a window, looking out. When she turned there was horror in her face, and a certain bewilderment, but her eyes did not cloud at the sight of him. "She isn't afraid of me," thought Gamadge, "and perhaps that's no compliment to either of us."

Mrs. Morton was pacing the long room. A thin, flowing black dress trailed behind her, and its wide sleeves fell back from her arms as she clasped her head in her hands. She would always dramatize a tragedy, that was her nature; but she was obviously distracted.

When Gamadge came in, she stopped and faced him. "Mr. Gamadge," she wailed, "why didn't we take your advice in the first place? Why didn't we call in the police?"

"Please relax, dearest." Duncannon, who stood with an elbow on the mantelpiece, watched her rather anxiously. "You'll be ill." "Yes, for heaven's sake, Aunt Angie!" Dick Vauregard, astride a chair, spoke with impatience. "Take it easy. Now that Gamadge is here, we must discuss the thing quietly, you know. He can put you in the soup."

"He can put us all—he can ruin us all!"

"Not me, because I don't care."

"Mr. Gamadge!" Mrs. Morton addressed him wildly. "That girl was a tool of the Chandors. They put her in the house, and she told them all his ways, and when they faced exposure she helped them to come in and kill him."

"Is that what you're going to tell the police, Mrs. Morton?" asked Gamadge quietly.

"I have told them. This morning, as soon as I had heard from Mr. Bedlowe, I called Mr. Durfee up and told him again. Mr. Bedlowe now says that Uncle was going to create a new trust, and that it would have meant making a new will. He spoke to Mr. Bedlowe about it in January. Mr. Bedlowe warned him that as things are now, it would mean cutting down the endowment on the house, and perhaps altering our legacies; but Uncle only laughed, and said that that would all be taken care of. It's quite evident that the Chandors had got hold of him, and that when I interfered they simply pretended to drop Uncle, and put this girl in the house. Mr. Bedlowe is perfectly horrified at this police talk about our alibis."

"You have one, I believe, Mrs. Morton."

"But the others have not, so far. Of course they must have been seen by somebody, between five and five thirty."

"Do the police put your uncle's death as early as five thirty?"

"Not much later. Oh, I cannot bear to think of it!"

Duncannon said: "We have to go over the situation, I quite realize that; but would you mind, Gamadge, steering away from details as much as possible?"

Dick Vauregard gave a short laugh. "Let's pretend," he said.

Mrs. Morton drew herself up. "No, I must face it. I will not have such stuff in the papers," she said. "One never lives it down. My husband was trying his new sports car, and he paid two tolls on the parkway; is it his fault if the man didn't remember him?"

"If you want to protect yourself and your family, Mrs. Morton, tell the police the arbor story, and tell them now."

"That I shall not do. It is unnecessary. The mere fact that the girl has disappeared is enough to implicate her."

"If you want to implicate her, and keep her implicated, you must save the police from wasting time on that refugee angle."

"Must?" Duncannon looked up, and gave him a haughty stare.

"Must. Remember that Miss Smith may turn up with some story of her own. Get in first with your own version, the true one, and it will be believed and attended to."

Mrs. Morton sank down on the settee. "They will get all sorts of grotesque notions into their heads, and the newspapers will be awful. They will say there is insanity in the family. They will make fun of us. We shall all be ruined."

"Those considerations won't weigh with the police if they find out that you have been withholding evidence against Miss Smith. Tell them that at first you couldn't take Mr. Vauregard's delusions seriously, but that now you feel you ought to hand over everything, fantastic though it may sound to them."

Mrs. Morton gazed at him, and her lustrous eyes fell. She said: "If I feel that I cannot follow your suggestion, can I count upon you to be discreet?"

"Oh, yes. I shall be completely out of the case, from now on."

Duncannon said: "Mr. Gamadge will know better than to spread stories about Angela Morton."

Dick Vauregard suddenly exploded into violence:

"You conceited, gibbering fool! I can't help it, Aunt Angie! What kind of nitwit is he, to threaten a man like Gamadge, and now, of all times! As a lawyer, let me tell you that you people don't know your own luck."

"Should we have been just a little luckier, though," queried Duncannon, in a soft voice, "if our dear Robina hadn't persisted in getting an expert in?"

"Don't worry about the expert," said Gamadge. "The only evidence that I had went when Volume II of the Byron set did. But if I'm to keep quiet about it, I must withdraw from the affair entirely. I accept no responsibility for what happened, but perhaps I ought to have looked at the thing with more detachment, and faced the possibility that we were dealing with people who stick at nothing. Don't play their game, Mrs. Morton—you are warned."

Mrs. Morton again took her head in her hands. Gamadge, with a nod to the assembled company, left the room.

He was joined on the front steps by Dick Vauregard, who asked, rather eagerly: "That your car?"

"Such as it is, yes. Want a lift somewhere?"

"Breath of air. Those people are driving me crazy. Bunch of ostriches. Where are you going?"

"I was bound for home, but—"

"Just drop me there, wherever it is. I'll walk back." They got into the car, and the young man continued:

"Some house of mourning! Poor old Great-uncle, I swear I think Clara and I are the only ones of the lot who cared a hang about him. Even Aunt Rob is dithering about the police, and what's going to happen to the estate if we're all locked up for life as conspirators to murder. I swear they all act as if they'd done it."

"Well, your great-uncle was behaving very sillily; I suppose some of them couldn't help wishing he'd depart this life before he behaved even worse; and when such wishes are staggeringly fulfilled, nice-minded persons feel guilty."

"Then I'm not a nice-minded person. Guilty! With crooks like the Chandors and the Smith woman in the offing!"

Gamadge did not reply until he had negotiated a green light, just in time. Then he said: "I was right about the danger, wasn't I?"

"Yes, confound you, you were. Who'd have thought it?"

"Shakespeare thought of it, and he thought Macbeth should have waded back to shore before he slaughtered all the innocents."

Dick Vauregard gave him a quick, almost frightened look. "What do you mean?"

"Only that."

"But in this case there are no more—those people won't kill anybody else. They don't have to."

"Relax not thy vigilance. The murderer always thinks he has to, when he does it."

"But how am I to watch, when I don't know…"

"Just keep an eye on them, and on yourself."

"I can certainly look after myself."

"Do it, then, but don't take your personal safety for granted. Nobody is big, strong and clever enough to do that with impunity."

Young Vauregard, after another frowning look at him, fell silent. When they reached Gamadge's three-story brick house in the East Sixties, they found a car at the curb. A friend had stopped by to inveigle Gamadge up the Hudson. He proposed a short day of golf at their Westchester club, dinner, and a little bridge afterwards, if they could keep awake. He was a person of large philanthropies, and when he saw Vauregard's wistful face, he included him in the invitation.

"I don't think I'd better," began the young man, awkwardly. "There's been a—I don't know whether you know—"

Gamadge's friend, who had given Dick Vauregard a sharp look when introduced to him, said cheerfully: "Nonsense. I suppose you don't feel up to much; come along anyway. Do you good. Probably won't see a soul you know, we're all fogies up there. Come as my guest, we'll get you home early."

Vauregard said he would love some golf, but he wouldn't stay for dinner. He supposed he could get a taxi back to town?

"Sure you can."

"Come along," advised Gamadge.

"It's awfully good of you." Vauregard sprinted for a cab, and returned within twenty minutes, his golf tweeds on and his clubs over his shoulder. They were nearing Riverdale when he asked, with a doubtful, rather shy look at Gamadge "Want to see something?"

"I always want to see something."

"I may be wrong, but I think you will, if we stop at the Brightstone Inn. It's just along this back road on the right."

"I wouldn't mind seeing a cocktail."

"From what I gathered earlier today—and I wasn't eavesdropping, either; he was talking on the library telephone—you'll get a glimpse of something besides a cocktail."

Gamadge's friend drew up at the Brightstone Inn, but elected to remain in the car. Gamadge and Dick Vauregard entered the cocktail lounge, and were rewarded by the sight of Mr. Duncannon, or as much as could be perceived of him behind discreet palms, in close conversation with a blond young lady, cheerfully dressed in Morocco pink. He caught their eyes, arose, and strolled forward, while his companion hastily downed a cocktail, and ordered another.

"Hello," he said, with extreme nonchalance. "Want you to meet Miss Garfield. She's going to be in our show, and we've been talking over our scenes." He gave Dick a casual, slightly amused glance. "Perhaps you've met the young lady?"

"No, I don't meet young ladies, much," said Dick.

"Theatrical phrase. We're an old-fashioned profession." He led the way back to his table.

Dick muttered in Gamadge's ear: "Runs to blondes, doesn't he? Miss What's-Her-Name is the spitting image of the zombi."

"No, she isn't," said Gamadge, who did not seem particularly amused, and who bowed to Miss Garfield gravely. While they waited for cocktails, he inquired, politely surveying her plump person:

"You're going to be in the Webster play, I believe? Very interesting."

Miss Garfield's blue eyes twinkled. "Yes, and I'm going to be just as rotten as Tom is. Mr. Bridge is wild. He says I'm not the type at all, and he says Mrs. Morton is only having me in it because I won't get any sympathy from the audience."

"Quiet down," said Duncannon, removing the new coktail from in front of her. "Don't talk such rot."

"But I ask you, Mr. Gimmidge, Gummidge, I'm sorry. I ask you, can I do that part? I ask you. But of course, you don't know the play, nobody does, why should they?"

"If you mean *The White Devil*—" protested Gamadge.

Miss Garfield laughed loudly, and Duncannon scowled at her. "I can't help it," she said. "I can't get over that title."

"But it's such a good one! Think of it in red lights! I know the play very well, Miss Garfield. Are you by any chance playing the countess—Isabella?"

"Chance is good! No chance to it, but I'm playing it." Miss Garfield's round face beamed at him. "Can you imagine me? I'm Tom's wife, and he has me poisoned so he can marry Mrs. Morton. I tell him it ought to be the other way around, but did you ever notice, these handsome men never have any sense of humor."

Mr. Duncannon's sense of humor, if he had one, did at the moment seem to have failed him. So had Dick Vauregard's. The latter swallowed his cocktail, got up, and said roughly: "Ought we to keep your friend waiting, Gamadge?"

"Perhaps not." Gamadge also rose. "Good luck, Miss Garfield—you never know. Perhaps you'll walk away with the show."

"I only have a couple of scenes."

"Yes, but my goodness, think of the speech where you get finally mad and say what you'd like to do to Vittoria Corombona!"

Miss Garfield shrieked again, and Duncannon said: "If you start reciting that speech, I'll carry you out, Gloria!"

Gamadge, laughing, said that he should love to hear Miss Garfield recite, but that he must go. He shook hands with her, nodded to Duncannon, and followed Dick Vauregard from the room.

"They always come here," growled that young man.

"To discuss the play?"

"Aunt Angie doesn't know a thing about it. I wouldn't tell her for anything. She thinks she got that little devil into the show herself; you ought to have heard Tom wangle it!"

Gamadge asked: "Did you bring me here to acquaint me with your step-uncle's more obvious failings, or to convey something more subtle?"

"I want you to see the whole situation. Perhaps you'll feel more like telling me exactly what you were warning me about, now that you've met Miss Garfield."

"I am delighted to have met Miss Garfield, and I only hope that Providence will spare me to see her play the Countess Isabella, 'sister of Francisco de Medicis, wife of Brachiano.'"

He added, after a pause, "Is Mrs. Morton quite, quite mad?"

Vauregard replied in a low voice: "She'll come to her senses sooner or later."

The golf game was a success; it seemed to cheer the young man. Somebody gave him a lift back to town before seven, and the other two had their dinner early, and a rubber of bridge afterwards. Gamadge was deposited at his door promptly at eleven o'clock.

He was sleepily removing his tie when the telephone beside his bed rang softly.

"Hello," he said. "Gamadge speaking."

A husky voice answered, very low: "This is Angela Morton."

Volume III

*Obsequies by
John Webster*

CHAPTER FOURTEEN

Too Many Murderers

GAMADGE COLLECTED HIS faculties. "Yes, Mrs. Morton?"

"Mr. Gamadge—can we be overheard?"

"No, quite safe."

"I have been thinking about what you said this morning; thinking and thinking all day long. I must have your advice."

"You have had it."

"Oh, that; I shall talk to the police—tell them about everything; everything you want them to know."

"You're very wise—but there's no question of my wanting anything, Mrs. Morton."

"I understand that." The hurried, husky voice was impatient. "I must have your advice before I talk to them. As—as a friend. Could you advise me as—as a friend, Mr. Gamadge? I feel that you understand these things. Your opinion is valuable, and you have a broad, civilized point of view."

Gamadge frowned a little, but he said: "Thank you."

"It's an imposition—I do so hate to ask it of you; but could you—could you possibly come up to the house now?"

"Well, I—"

"It's the only opportunity I have to see you alone. I don't want anyone to know."

Gamadge paused. Then he asked: "Where are they all?"

"They're all upstairs. They've gone up for the night. I saw the servants up, too, and Luigi has gone home."

"Where's Mr. Duncannon?"

"In his room; we said good night."

"Anybody able to listen in at your end?"

"I turned the switch off. Mr. Gamadge, I wouldn't ask you if I didn't absolutely have to see you. Those police will be back again tomorrow. I must have your advice. I don't know where to turn."

"You had it this morning. Better consult Bedlowe."

"I want to talk to you first. You will tell me what I ought to do. You don't know the whole—you may be able to think of something."

"Oh. How will you manage about letting me in?"

"Don't ring; I've put the door on the latch. Come in when you get here; I'll wait in the library. I'm there now. How soon can you get here?"

"A very few minutes."

"I am nearly mad. Cameron and Bridge were here for dinner, and I could hardly—thank you so very much."

Gamadge replaced the receiver, retied his tie, and wearily reassumed his tweed coat. He picked up a soft hat, and went quietly out of his sleeping house.

Regretting, not for the first time, that he lived in an east-bound street, he caught a taxi at the corner and got out at the corner of the Morton block. It was almost dark, and as silent as a street in a dead city. He walked to the Morton house, where no light showed, climbed the steps, and entered the vestibule. He turned the heavy bronze door handle, and pushed.

He found himself in complete darkness, except for the

feeble glimmer of light that came from the drawing room. This proceeded from a red-shaded lamp in the library, whither he walked silently over the thick carpet.

Mrs. Morton sat at her desk with her back to him. She still wore the flowing black dress, but she now seemed to have brightened it by fastening a scarlet ribbon around her neck; the ends hung down her back almost to her waist, and one of them had a tassel on it.

"Mrs. Morton," whispered Gamadge. She did not move; her hand, beside the telephone on which she seemed just to have replaced the receiver, did not move. Gamadge reached her side in a second, lifted the hand, let it drop, looked at the face—one that he would not have recognized—seized the telephone by the tips of his fingers, and dialed.

"Police. This is Henry Gamadge. Can I get hold of Detective Lieutenant Durfee? The Vauregard case."

After a pause he spoke again.

"Lieutenant Durfee? I'm Gamadge. Mrs. Morton telephoned me to come up, fifteen minutes ago—less. I found her dead, in her library…Strangled with one of her curtain cords… They're all upstairs, gone to bed…Of course. Certainly I'll wait."

He replaced the receiver, and leaned for a moment against the edge of the desk. Presently he got out his handkerchief, dried his forehead and the palms of his hands, and slowly replaced it in his pocket. He then crossed to the curtained doorway on his left, stood for a moment looking up at a raw and dangling end of silk cord, and went through into the back hall. He followed it, passed between other portieres, and found himself at the foot of the front stairs; these he negotiated two at a time.

The upper hall was dimly lighted. He turned to the right, reached the open door of Miss Vauregard's sitting room in half a dozen strides, and entered. It was dark, and the communicating door was closed. He knocked on it, gently.

Miss Vauregard spoke immediately: "Who is it?"

"Gamadge."

"Mr. Gamadge!"

"Your sister sent for me. Where is your nephew's room, please?"

"Upstairs, in the front. Why did Angela—where is she?"

"She isn't here. I'll come right back and explain. Will you wait for me?"

"Yes, but…"

Gamadge fled up the stairs to the third floor, and banged on the door of the front room. A drowsy voice said something. He banged again, and Clara Dawson came out of the door at the other end of the hall. At the same moment Dick Vauregard opened his; he was in his pajamas, and looked half awake.

"Gamadge? What is this?"

"Your aunt—Mrs. Morton. She's dead…in the library."

"What? What's that?"

"Try to get it. She's dead—been killed. The police will be here any minute. Get hold of Duncannon, break it to him, and if possible keep him upstairs. I haven't a second—I must get back to Miss Vauregard."

After a wild, blank look at him, Dick Vauregard leaped down the stairs. Gamadge went along the hall, and stood looking at Clara; her neat, soft hair was unruffled, and she wore a white-dotted, dark-blue foulard dressing gown over pajamas that matched it. She stared at him, frozen.

"Clara," he said, "it's up to you. Go down there and tell Miss Vauregard, and get her in shape to talk to the police, if you can. Where's some whisky?"

"In the dining room."

"I'll get it. Can you put this through?"

"Yes."

He ran down ahead of her, gained the first floor, and dashed to the big dining room at the back of the house. He rummaged in the sideboard, and came upstairs breathing hard, a bottle in his hand. Miss Vauregard sat on the couch in her sitting room, a Japanese kimono over her nightgown. Clara, beside her, was saying: "I don't know, Aunt Rob; I don't know."

"Glasses," said Gamadge. "Three of 'em. We all need some of this."

Clara went into the bathroom and returned with a tumbler, a medicine glass, and an eyecup. Gamadge filled them all. He put a hand behind Miss Vauregard's head, and held the little beaker to her lips.

"That's right," he said. "You'll be better in a minute."

He watched her for a moment, frowning anxiously at the sight of her pinched face and circled eyes, and let her head drop back against a cushion. "Had yours, Clara? No? Down with it; and here's to better days."

Clara, agate-gray eyes on him, drained her thimbleful.

"There's the bell. Just tell the police everything, Miss Vauregard, every single thing—except Dykincks. No Dykincks."

Gamadge ran down, opened the front door, and allowed a blue wave more or less to meet over his head.

At one thirty A.M., he found himself, not quite asleep and by no means awake, in the hot little back room which was called by courtesy the library. Mrs. Morton's body had been removed, but drawn curtains shut off the drawing room and the back hall. The family were upstairs, a policeman dozed in the vestibule, and most of the press had departed. Gamadge felt like a stranded jellyfish, floating gently about on an ebb tide.

Durfee came in and sat down opposite him on a hard, high-backed Florentine chair. "Do you ever call at a house," he asked, "without finding a corpse in it?"

There was an expression on his face which Gamadge had seen before on the faces of policemen. He said: "Only happened twice."

"I should have decided that twice was too much; only, from what Miss Vauregard and the rest of them tell me, I understand I'm dealing with a pro."

"Nonsense. I'm not a detective at all. I only took this case because there was a book in it." He closed his eyes wearily, and added: "Poems of Lord Byron, Volume II."

"I know; and now that it's gone, you have no evidence. If you were a detective, I could have your license for holding out on me last night."

"Consider that I have one, and take it, with my love," replied Gamadge. "I hate these cases."

"So they tell me. Miss Vauregard tells me you wanted the police called in, right from the start. She says you've been at them since the other murder, trying to get them to call us."

"I like working with the police. Much easier."

"If you had been, we might have saved these people's lives."

"I doubt it."

"This party knew that you were nosing around, and got scared, and cleaned up just ahead of you, both times. First, you thought you had something on that Smith woman, connected with that book; and I may as well say that I never heard such a story in my life before."

"Very odd story indeed."

"Then Mrs. Morton made up her mind to tell us all about Smith, called you up to confer with you, and was overheard and strangled with a piece of curtain cord."

"Mrs. Morton didn't call me up to say that she was going to tell you about Miss Smith."

"No?"

"Certainly not. Why should she get me up here to go over that, again? I'll tell you why she called me, and you can go on from there, with my best wishes."

"Thanks."

"Mrs. Morton got me up here to tell me that she knew who her uncle's murderer was, and how she knew it."

Durfee looked at him in silence.

"She knew who he was," continued Gamadge, "because she was a member of the conspiracy. This case reeked of theater from beginning to end. Miss Smith was certainly an actress; Mrs. Morton got hold of her somehow—she would have been likely to know plenty of young actresses, out of a job and perhaps desperate—and put her there in Traders Row to keep Mr. Vauregard's money in the family; she had a big stake—something like five hundred thousand dollars, perhaps more.

"I realized quite early in the game that a member of the family was in the plot; no outsider could have known enough inside detail to put the thing through, and no outsider could have been sure of big enough money to risk such a thing."

"They talk about these Chandors," said Durfee. "I've heard of them."

"Mrs. Morton learned—probably from her uncle, while they were both interested in New Soul—that he was thinking of doing something for them. From what they said to me, I think he was going to transfer the old house and its endowment to them."

"You saw these Chandors?"

"Yesterday. It was my duty, and I did. Mrs. Morton couldn't stand it, broke with New Soul, and worked up another interest for the old gentleman. She probably meant to send Miss Smith out of the picture, as soon as she thought he was sunk in the arbor thing for keeps."

"How about her keeping the Chandors in on it?"

"Possible."

"Who was it got nervous, and killed Mr. Vauregard?"

"It wasn't just a case of nervousness, Durfee; he was killed to preserve the family fortune no matter what happened."

"Mrs. Morton would stand for a thing like that?"

"Certainly not; she was almost knocked out by it. Could hardly believe her senses. If ever I saw a frightened woman, I saw one this morning. Tonight, she wanted my advice on how to wriggle out of the mess without giving away her own part in the conspiracy. I could only have advised her to throw herself on the mercy of the court. She wouldn't have done it."

"But this accomplice didn't know she wouldn't."

"Just so."

"He heard her telephoning, and killed her as soon as she hung up."

"That's it."

"We think he hid out there in the hall; that's where he cut off the piece of curtain cord."

"I saw it."

"Three steps across this carpet—she wouldn't hear a thing, and probably didn't even turn her head." Durfee looked at Gamadge, hesitated, and continued: "Nobody could hide there until the servants went up to bed by the back stairs. The three women went up about ten thirty. The house-man left earlier—he lives out. There were two guests for dinner—Bridge, the theater manager, and young Payne, the Dawson girl's fiance. She's a nice girl, Miss Dawson; sat beside her aunt, tears rolling down her face, answered all my questions without any fuss, didn't ask any of her own. But she sticks to it that she left young Payne at his apartment Thursday afternoon around five. Drove herself here and there and around and about until six twenty, when she garaged her car. The dog was with her."

"You sound as if you didn't put much faith in her statement."

"The boy at The Humbert, Payne's apartment house, says Payne didn't come in till six fifteen. He doesn't use the stairs; takes the elevator."

"What does Payne say?"

"Says he meant to do some photograph developing, but it was such a nice day he got on a bus."

"People do."

"I can't see Payne on a bus. Miss Dawson garaged her car at six twenty, all right, and took her dog over to that place she keeps him at, and got home at six forty-five, or thereabouts. Last night Payne and Bridge let themselves out of this house, the man having gone home. Bridge went first, about ten to eleven; Payne a trifle later. One of them could have pretended to go, of course, and hidden behind those curtains that shut off the back hall."

"Payne's a cripple."

"And rides on a bus. You can stand on one foot and operate that curtain cord—or anyway, I can."

"As for Mr. Bridge, I am not in love with his personality, but Mrs. Morton was not only going to star in his new piece, she was going to help finance it. And if he stood on one foot, I bet he'd fall over."

"Miss Vauregard, Miss Dawson, Mr. Duncannon, and young Vauregard—all right on the spot," said Durfee.

"And me," said Gamadge, with a glance of mild surprise.

"Talk sense. The old gentleman was dead, according to the M.E., before you ever left your own house, much less reached Traders Row. We don't want too many murderers in this—got enough as it is. These murders are connected."

"But if the Vauregard mob pulled these killings off," said Gamadge, in a reasonable tone of voice, "they probably employed a paid assassin or two. Me, for instance: Gamadge the Strangler."

"You think it's funny to suspect any of 'em, do you?"

"Certainly not. There's always Miss Smith, though, isn't there? Or some other outsider. Let's see: Mrs. Morton, as you know, put the door on the latch for me. She then retired to the library, where we now are. Well, you know what happens when you put a door on the latch. You open the door part way, and you feel around the edge of it and press the button. Anybody who was standing in the vestibule, or on the steps, or at the foot of them, would see your hand, and what it was doing; but you wouldn't see them."

"If somebody just happened to be standing there, they could see it," said Durfee, looking at him with some amusement.

"No 'happen' about it. Suppose Mrs. Morton intended to

tell me the whole thing, including the name of the murderer. She might have telephoned to that person beforehand, and advised departure for climes unknown."

"So the party comes around, just in time—"

"Comes around the minute she telephones, and waits around for me to go in."

"Intending to finish you off, as well as her?" Durfee's smile broadened.

"Why not? The party doesn't wish to disappear, and evidently has no objection to taking human life."

"It's the darndest complicated rigmarole I ever listened to."

"Rather involved, I admit."

"But of course," said Durfee, with a sharp look at him, "it takes the thing out of the family."

"I only met them day before yesterday," said Gamadge. "And they stand to gain not only what they get from old Mr. Vauregard's estate, but what Mrs. Morton got from it, and her own property besides."

"Had she much?"

"Young Vauregard drew up her will for her. He says this house goes to Miss Vauregard; it has two mortgages on it. Five thousand apiece to the nephew and niece, and the rest to Duncannon."

"When did she perpetrate this atrocity?"

"When she married. Of course Duncannon now gets her share of old Mr. Vauregard's property." Durfee coughed. "Never saw any man so upset as he was over his wife's death. He's dazed. We had to get the M.E. to give him a sedative, and then call his own doctor. We put a man up with him for the night—feller's half out of his head."

"He seemed much attached to his wife."

"Of course, he's an actor," said Durfee reflectively. "Young Vauregard—well, I suppose you can't expect him to jump out of a window because he's lost his aunt and his great-uncle. He seems more mad than anything. Boiling about this Smith woman. Now, Duncannon thinks she was a refugee, and a mighty nice one."

"Yes. That's what he has said right along."

Durfee contemplated Gamadge for a few moments, seemed to reflect, and then asked: "Are you still employed by these people?"

"Oh, no. I think Mrs. Morton fired me this morning, or rather yesterday morning, when I bullied her about telling you the arbor story. Poor woman, what a spot she was in!"

"Of course none of this stuff you told me is evidence."

"No, just conjecture."

"It may cut a few corners for us."

"I hope it will."

"If anything more turns up, you'll hand it over?"

"Naturally; but I'm out of the case. I hope."

"It's too bad you didn't get a line on the Smith woman, through that book."

"I wasn't so much trying to get a line on her, as trying to get rid of her."

"You see what that got you."

"Yes. Got the family the Vauregard money."

Durfee gazed at him, somewhat baffled. "You're a queer guy. Don't get anybody else killed, will you?"

"I'll be careful. Are you giving the whole Smith-Wagoneur story to the press, Lieutenant?"

"Certainly are. They'll have all details by tomorrow noon. The more publicity on Smith now, the better."

"Was that poison Mr. Vauregard had in tablet form, do you mind telling me?"

"Potassium cyanide solution. He got it in his second cup of coffee."

"Oh. If Miss Smith didn't put it there, perhaps the fellow took away the container to saddle the job on her. I mean, people usually do try to make it look like suicide, don't they?"

"Now what are you getting at?"

"Just talking in my sleep." Gamadge rose, wobbling slightly, and steadied himself against the back of his chair. "As you see. Anything more, or can I go home to bed?"

"Nothing at present. If you get any ideas, just cooperate, will you? Don't forget how this thing got away from you. You might find yourself in a tight place, sometime."

"Oh, I hope not. Good night."

Gamadge made his way past the uniformed man and out of the house. He had his picture taken as he descended the steps. Before he walked away he glanced up at the front of the Morton residence, which was now blazing with lights from roof to basement, and which his exhausted fancy pictured as almost literally bulging in the grip of its two mortgages. Another flash in his eyes made him blink and start. He grinned at the grinning cameraman, and went off down the dark street.

CHAPTER FIFTEEN

Martin Becomes a Guinea Pig

NEXT MORNING A SIGN on Gamadge's door said "Keep Out," and his bedside telephone was switched off; so that he did not waken until ten, or appear at his breakfast table until ten thirty. He seemed, however, to be in a brisk and purposeful mood, which ill accorded with the careworn look of Theodore as he handed the bacon.

After a glance at the papers, in which the second Vauregard murder had found its way to a place where war news had had pre-eminence for weeks, he threw them aside and looked about him.

"Where's Martin?" he asked.

"In the lab'atory, Mr. Gamadge, keepin' Harold company. Harold, he don't feel so good this mornin'."

"Too bad."

"He see us in the paper, and he go down and shut the lab'atory door."

"He's too sensitive. Go down to the laboratory and get

Martin out of there, will you, and into his basket. This is the day he has that wart taken out of his ear."

"That cat's as well as ever he was in his life. You goin' to upset him for nothin'?"

"Doctor Wadley said it might be a focus of infection."

"Doctor Wadley's too fussy. That cat ain't been sick since Christmas, when he stole those shrimps mayonnaise."

"You get him into his basket."

Gamadge finished his breakfast, called Wadley and made an appointment, had a cigarette, and went downstairs. Theodore stood in the front hall, a large coffer-shaped basket on the floor beside him. There was a cab at the door.

"Doctor Wadley won't be workin' today, it's Saturday," protested Theodore.

"He's there, I called him."

Gamadge picked the basket up by its handle; it was not only lopsided, but it became lopsided at a different angle with every step he took. He got it to the curb, and the driver of the cab, viewing it ungraciously, said that Gamadge would have to hold it on his lap.

"I know that; I held it on my lap from New York to Boston once; my friend doesn't care for baggage cars." Gamadge got in, and adjusted the basket on his knees. He then took the orange paw which presented itself to him through a little window practiced in the wickerwork, and held it faithfully until the cab arrived at Wadley's address.

The veterinary had his quarters on the top floor of a tall building, and they had been described by Theodore as "good enough for folks." There was a front office, a waiting room furnished with comfortable chairs and a sofa for collapsed pet owners to lie down on, a big, modern surgery, and a laboratory in the rear. Gamadge sat admiringly beside the glass-topped operating table while Doctor Wadley wrapped Martin in a bath towel, told him he was a good boy, and applied a local anesthetic to his ear. Martin shrieked, Gamadge winced, and Wadley conjured him to hold on to the bath towel.

"Sorry my assistant isn't here today," he said. "I gave him the Saturday off. Owners are never any good at this sort of thing."

The wart was off in a moment. Martin stepped out of the towel, stretched and shook each leg as if to convince himself that no bones were broken, and then seemed to dismiss the whole thing from his mind. He jumped down and was making for the waiting room door, when Gamadge caught him up and cradled him in his arms.

"You're a martyr, old boy," he crooned; "that's what you are."

Wadley raised his eyebrows in amused tolerance of this spinsterish exhibition, said that there would be no trouble with the ear, and added: "Just give me a call, if he shows a tendency to scratch it."

Gamadge placed Martin in his basket, and fastened the lid.

"By the way," he said. "Miss Dawson tells me that you take care of her dogs."

"Miss Clara Dawson?" Wadley paused, in the act of gathering up his instruments.

"Yes."

"I've taken care of all their animals for years. I never was more shocked in my life! First the old gentleman, on Thursday, and now this ghastly thing about Mrs. Morton. I only knew Mr. Vauregard through that French poodle he had, but—why, it's incredible! The papers seem to think it must have been that refugee he had staying with him. Unbalanced by her troubles, went out of her mind, got some kind of persecution complex involving the whole family. They say the police can't find her."

"No. You had to put Miss Dawson's old dog out of the way, the other night, she says."

"Yes. Fine animal—that kennel has the best chows in the country, I always say. I wanted to do it before; when a dog gets blind and deaf, can't enjoy its food, has rheumatic pains, it's time for the poor old thing to go. Nice family, I don't like to think of them in all this trouble. Every one of them, except Mrs. Morton, came over here on Wednesday evening to say good-bye to the old dog. Even Duncannon came. He used to breed Afghans, but he sold 'em."

"Pretty touching, that. All here, were they?"

"Miss Dawson came with young Payne—sad case, that, isn't it? Duncannon drove Miss Vauregard over. Dick—I took care of his Scotties when he was a little fellow, before his father died—he turned up later. They all waited until I'd given the hypodermic. I wouldn't let Miss Dawson wait in here, though; never do. She was upset enough as it was."

"Milling around for some time, were they?"

"Quite a while. I called up earlier, before six, and told Miss Dawson it ought to be done, but she asked me to wait until later, so they could all come. Mrs. Morton—poor woman—she never cared for animals."

"She had a macaw."

"If you call that an animal; I'm no bird man."

"Decent of you to stay late, and humor the family. Did you keep your assistant on, too?"

Doctor Wadley, slightly surprised at the question, said no, he had let Thompson go home. "Didn't need him. The dog was lying quietly, half conscious…"

"What do you use in the hypodermic?"

"Potassium cyanide solution."

Gamadge lighted a cigarette, and Wadley gathered up his instruments and took them over to the white-enameled sink. Suddenly he turned, stared at Gamadge, and said: "My God."

Gamadge returned his gaze, but said nothing.

"That's what the papers said. In the coffee. But…"

"Was the stuff lying around handy, Wednesday night?"

"It was, but—Gamadge, you don't mean—"

"It isn't easy to come by."

"No, that's what I thought when I read about the old gentleman and this refugee. Good Lord, I—"

"Where was it, while the family milled around, and you were working over the dog?"

"In the laboratory, on that shelf just inside the door there. I got the jar out of the locked cupboard before I went out for my dinner. Place was all locked up, of course, while I was away." Wadley's red, good-natured face had taken on a purplish hue.

"Let's see it, will you?"

The veterinary, after another stare at him, went into the laboratory and came back with a small, squat jar, plainly labeled; there was a bit of adhesive plaster sealing the glass stopper. He put it down on the operating table, and they both looked at it.

"My God," said Wadley, "we're both crazy."

"Is there a sink near that shelf it was standing on?"

"Right beside it. Why?"

"Can you tell whether any of it's missing, Wadley?"

"Of course I can. I put four ounces into this jar out of the supply, did it myself; I don't allow anybody else to handle such stuff. I filled my hypodermic, and that's all that I used of it."

He took the jar into the laboratory. Gamadge waited, finally taking Martin out of the basket, for company.

When the veterinary returned, his purple hue had faded to mauve.

"Gamadge, my God, there's nine minims gone."

"Nine drops exactly?"

"Yes."

"It couldn't have evaporated?"

"Nonsense. But it's all nonsense! Those people—they didn't know they were going to have access to the stuff!"

"Couldn't have got spilled somehow?"

"Look at the jar; that's why I use it—so it won't tip over; but if it had, we'd have known it."

"Yes; '...how faint the peaches smelt.'"

"What say?"

"You would have smelled the stuff. Well, old man, I have no right to ask you to keep quiet about this for the moment—"

"I only wish I could keep quiet about it forever! I can see all the headlines, if it ever gets into the papers: 'Vet careless with deadly poisons.'"

"Not at all; 'Distinguished veterinary surgeon aids police.' You leave it to me. I've seen Durfee—"

"That's so, you found the body!"

"Both bodies."

Wadley stared.

"So I'm more or less in touch with the police. I'll be discreet; just let me handle it."

"Glad if you will. There must be some mistake, Gamadge! Nice people like that coming over to see the old dog."

"Let's hope there is."

Gamadge once more bundled Martin into his basket, bade farewell to the distressed Wadley, and drove home. He released Martin in the hall, and telephoned from his office:

"Henry Gamadge speaking. Is this the Morton house?"

"It is."

"Lieutenant Durfee there, by any chance?"

"He's busy."

"Ask him if it will be all right for me to come up and call on Miss Vauregard or Miss Dawson."

"Miss Vauregard is in bed; she can't see anyone."

"Miss Dawson, then."

After a wait, Durfee said: "Hello."

"Any objection to my coming up and seeing Miss Dawson, Lieutenant?"

"Any objection to telling me what you want to see her about?"

"Well, of course I'm out of the case, professionally; but I have an idea you might be interested in, only I have to do some checking up first. I thought Miss Dawson might help."

There was a long pause. Then Durfee said: "I had a call

this morning from a man named Schenck—insurance investigator."

"Oh, yes; I know him. Delightful, isn't he?"

"I don't know how delightful he is, but he's as sharp a customer as I ever met. He and I have come together now and then on business."

"I hope he cooperated. Schenck always wants everybody to cooperate."

"Yes, he did; he says you cooperate."

"Very nice of him."

"Quite excited he was, when he saw the papers. Wanted to know," said Durfee, with a kind of wonder, "if you were on the case!"

"I hope you snubbed him."

"He told me a lot of funny stuff. See here; if you talk to the girl—any of these people…"

"Well?"

"Schenck says you don't hold out on the police."

"Oh, never. What I was going to say was, that if I get this information from Miss Dawson, I shall turn it over to you and ask you to help check up on it. I have no facilities for digging up information, and I can't make people give me any."

There was another pause. Then Durfee said: "Just want us to do a little work for you?"

"I'm doing a little work for you."

"What's your interest in doing it?"

"Entirely noble. I have an idea that some of these people might get framed, if we're not careful."

"Nice of you to help. See here; Schenck said you didn't snoop off by yourself and look for information."

"Certainly not; I was asked to assist the state police."

"Well, I ask you to assist. If I let you see Miss Dawson, you tell her to be frank with us. You gave 'em some good advice before—give her some now."

"They don't take my advice."

"Have a try at it."

Gamadge hurried out, and was glad to find his own small car at the curb, with the garage man in it. They exchanged a few words, the garage man walked away, and Gamadge got under the wheel and drove up to Seventy-fourth Street. That thoroughfare presented a busy and crowded aspect; several cars were parked near the Morton house, and sightseers gaped at it.

A policeman let him into the hall, giving him at the same time what Eliza Daggett might have described as an old-fashioned look.

"Protecting the family, are you?" asked Gamadge cheerfully. "That's good. Anybody else on the job?"

"There's a man inside the basement door, and one in the backyard. Nobody could get across those fences without a ladder but the officer is there."

"Splendid."

"You're to go up to the second floor front."

"Thanks." Gamadge was about to do so, when a procession issued from a backroom on the next story, and began slowly to descend the stairs. It consisted of Duncannon, elegantly tailored, with a black Homburg hat on the side of his head; a plain-clothes man, who had him by the arm; Luigi, completely demoralized, carrying three pieces of handsome luggage; and a terrified maid, laden with a bundle of coats, three walking sticks, and an umbrella.

"What's all this?" Gamadge turned in astonishment to the officer beside him. "Are they arresting Duncannon?"

"I wouldn't know."

CHAPTER SIXTEEN

"Various Forms of Distraction"

THE PLAIN-CLOTHES MAN, a thin, carroty individual who looked as if he had not had much sleep for some time, was not, Gamadge saw, so much escorting Duncannon as propping him up. He addressed Gamadge in some bewilderment, under which lurked a faint amusement:

"That sleeping stuff he had last night didn't work good; we neither of us had more than a couple of naps. But now it seems to have come back on him."

Duncannon's face was greenish, and his eyes were nearly closed. He lurched against the banisters, and said thickly: "All I want is to get out of this house. Just get me out of this house."

"O.K., O.K., we're going."

They reached the bottom of the stairs in safety. The maid flung her burden of coats over the rail, propped the sticks and the umbrella against them, and scuttled off through the curtains into the back hall. Luigi put the bags down, hovered distractedly for a moment, and followed her. The detective steered his patient to the oak bench, where he sank down, his head lolling. The Homburg hat fell off, and was picked up by the uniformed man. If Duncannon had only been wearing a ruff and trunk hose, Gamadge thought, he would have been exactly right for a Medici after a banquet—or after a dose of his own aqua tofana.

"What'll I do with him?" asked the detective, annoyed.

"Get me out of here," muttered Duncannon.

"All right. I'll send for a cab."

"Cab? No cab. My wife's closed car."

The plain-clothes man caught sight of Luigi, who had been peeping behind the hall curtains. "Here, you, call up the garage and get him his car," he said.

Luigi vanished. Duncannon's escort looked down at his charge irresolutely. "Perhaps I ought to have the doctor for him, again."

"Where's he going?" asked Gamadge.

"Wish I knew. He wants to go to the Waldorf. Durfee hasn't talked it out with the rest of 'em, yet; they're all in the dining room—the whole works. The D.A., the Commissioner, Bedlowe the lawyer, and young Vauregard."

Duncannon half opened his eyes, of which the pupils were almost invisible. "Waldorf," he said, "or jail. Anywhere, out of this place. It's unsafe for human habitation, and there probably won't be a living soul left in it by the beginning of next week."

"Don't talk that way." The plain-clothes man prodded him gently in the ribs. "Wake up."

"I am awake. I said to Angela: 'Let's pack up and get out of here, take a flat. Let the house go for taxes—that'll freeze out the whole bunch of 'em.' That sister of hers—always interfering, always talking about keeping down expenses. I said: 'We won't keep down expenses while the family's so big.' Thick as thieves, she and Clara. Payne laughing at 'em all. Dick couldn't stand the house—never stayed in it, if he could go somewhere else. Carrying on about the zombi. That poor little zombi!" exclaimed Duncannon, suddenly violent. "Poor little thing, perhaps she's dead, too. Everybody dead, like those plays Angie was so crazy about." He rose, lifted an arm, and maintained a strange, stiff pose, his eyes on some imagined gallery, his left foot well behind him. He declaimed, hollowly:

'Remove the bodies.—See, my honoured lords
What use you ought make of their punishment:
Let guilty men remember, their black deeds
Do lean on crutches made of slender reeds.'

And that's the play Angie wants me to play in. She can't do that stuff. I can't do that stuff." And indeed, Mr. Duncannon's recitation left much to be desired.

The uniformed policeman stood rooted in his tracks; another official was peering over Durfee's shoulder between the hall curtains; and no less a personage than Bridge, the producer, gazed at Duncannon from the entrance to the drawing room.

"All we need is a stenographer," said the plain-clothes man.

"He must be shamming," murmured the policeman.

"You want a statement?" Duncannon looked about him, and seized a protruding knob on the gilt mirror frame to steady himself. "I'll make another. Give me police protection, and I'll do anything."

"Protection from whom, Mr. Duncannon?" asked Gamadge, in a calm, carrying voice.

Duncannon eyed him. "You're the fellow Robina brought in."

"That's who I am."

"You know something, Gamadge? My wife was ashamed of her profession. Wouldn't let that girl Clara Dawson go on the stage—Oh, no. Knew too much about it, she said. Couldn't keep off it herself, though. Thought I was so lucky to marry into such a family. What do I get for it?"

"Lots of money," said Gamadge gently.

"I won't live to get it. Not on your life," said Duncannon.

"Here, now," protested the plain-clothes man.

"It's all a plot. They've framed me. Don't you know the name of our new play?" He squinted in Bridge's direction. Bridge, who looked as if he were attending a rehearsal, and disliking it very much, said nothing. *"The White Devil* is the name of it," continued Duncannon, "but it's got another. Don't make out you don't know it, Bridge!"

"I know it, all right."

"Tell 'em, then; tell 'em!"

"The History of the Duke di Brachiano and His Two Wives; of Which He Killed the First." Bridge recited it in a monotone.

"Yes, and that's what they'll all say. It's a plot."

"We've had enough of it." Durfee surged into the hall. "No more acting here, if you don't mind, Mr. Duncannon. McGann, hasn't that car come?"

The policeman opened the door, looked out, and said that it was there—"with a chauffeur."

"Then put him into it and take him down to the Waldorf, Simmons, for the love of Pete. Stick to him like grim death. If he won't have you, he can't stay."

Duncannon was assisted out of the house and down the steps. Three photographers snapped him as he stumbled into the big car; he insisted on pausing, doubled up and with a foot inside the door, to turn his head and solemnly remove his hat. The effect was one of extreme drunkenness, and the delighted cameramen were evidently accepting it as such.

Dick Vauregard joined Gamadge in the vestibule, and watched the shining Rolls move away.

"Listen," he said. "Forget that business at the Brightstone, will you?"

"Forget it? You went a mile out of your way to impress it on me," objected Gamadge, with a look of surprise.

"That was yesterday." The young man, white-faced after a heavy night, and coatless, seemed more disheveled than he actually was. He was a type whose lumbering bigness requires continual valeting. He went on, choosing his words: "Truth is, I'd been getting sore at him for a long time. He's perfectly right—none of us liked him, and he knew it. If Aunt Rob had known about his girlfriends I bet she'd have taken Clara and left the house. But just the same, he was fond of Aunt Angie, in his own way, and I'm not skunk enough to try to put a thing like this on him."

"You never felt it your duty to let Mrs. Morton know that he was—er—broadening his interests?"

"Aunt Angie never believed anything she didn't want to. She would have had a headache, got Tom on the carpet, believed every word he said to her, and thrown me out as a troublemaker."

"Mr. Duncannon realized all that, I suppose? I thought he was rather cool when we walked in on him yesterday."

"He wasn't as cool as all that, but he knew I wouldn't talk."

"Did you see his performance, just now?"

"Some of it. I'm sorry for the guy. When he comes to, and lets himself face all this, it'll knock him silly."

"I suppose he isn't used to drugs of any kind?"

"Drugs! He and Aunt Angie coddled themselves like two old invalids. He's always going to Lestrange about something, usually his precious throat. The house reeks with his sprays and gargles half the time. He's cut down on liquor, and he's stopped eating too much. Weighs himself six times a day. Makes me sick, to think of his getting all that money—our money." And Dick Vauregard looked decidedly sick, as he said the words.

"How does he think he came to get it?" asked Gamadge. "Do his maunderings mean anything in particular?"

"He's just letting off a lot of stuff he's been keeping bottled up for years."

"He doesn't really accuse anybody of these murders?"

"He can't imagine who's responsible, any more than the rest of us can. Last night, when he first saw her in the back room there, he went right to pieces; if he'd had any suspicions, he'd have come out with them. All this talk of his is the result of that stuff they gave him."

"None of you has any ideas on the subject? Not that I expect you to confide in me, of course."

"I wish I had anything to confide. We've given up. Aunt Rob has gone to bed and pulled the blanket up over her ears; can't face it, much less discuss it. Clara and I stick to it that it was the Smith gang—we can't see any other explanation at all. We say Aunt Angie recognized the girl from our descriptions, and that the gang killed her to prevent her giving them away."

"How do you figure that the gang got in?"

"None of us can figure it, unless she let somebody in herself, not knowing he was in with them."

"But she must have made an appointment, to do that. Was I to meet this somebody?"

Dick Vauregard, looking uncomfortable, said he didn't know.

"And I don't see,'" continued Gamadge, "why they're turning Duncannon loose, and keeping the rest of you cooped up. The police usually make a beeline for the biggest financial motive."

"They're not turning him loose."

"I bet he could evade that weary cop, if he wanted to."

Young Vauregard looked at him. "It's crazy to think that he would hurt Aunt Angie. Crazy."

"Your tone lacks conviction."

"I can't help my tone. And I can tell you, I'm not sorry to be cooped up for a day or two. It's better than having to rush down to headquarters every time they want to ask us a question, and it's better than being trailed by newsmen and cameras, or having a character like that fellow of Duncannon's trailing around after us. Being a lawyer myself, though I'm not much of one yet, I can see the point in their methods; but it's hard on the girls."

"The police can't coop you all up forever."

"They don't know what to do about us. Old Bedlowe is hovering around reminding them of points of law they probably never heard of—I hadn't, myself—and they can't very well throw us all into jail as material witnesses. They'd like to. The trouble is, there's such a dickens of a lot of money involved—for Aunt Rob and Duncannon, anyhow—that they hate to take their eyes off us and look elsewhere."

"I dare say they are looking elsewhere, though."

"Well, they're all out after Smith, and they've had these Chandors up here, and they've actually got poor Bridge on their list, as you know."

"But they haven't heard about Miss Garfield."

"Hope they won't. We don't want that kind of thing brought into it to amuse the tabloids."

"The police would like additional motive on somebody's part. They'd embrace Miss Garfield with open arms."

"See here—you won't put them on?"

Gamadge said: "If they ask me whether Duncannon had women friends in the profession, I shan't lie about it; but they won't ask me. They won't have to. Miss Garfield and anybody else of the kind will emerge; don't fool yourself."

Dick Vauregard said, after a pause: "Cameron Payne—he always was a clever brute—he says that Uncle probably found out for himself about the Smith swindle—the book gave it away to him, somehow. I suppose it ought to have dawned on the poor old thing that there might have been a duplicate set somewhere in the world."

"It didn't seem to be dawning on him when I left him on Thursday afternoon."

"Well, Payne says Uncle Imbrie couldn't face the blow to his pride, or his feelings, or something, and killed himself. He says John probably found him, and saw the bottle, and got rid of it—so the Vauregards wouldn't have a suicide in the family."

"Very clever indeed. Has he obliged the police with the theory?"

"No, but he's dying to. He says Miss Smith found Uncle dead, and rushed off in a panic. I should think she might—shouldn't you?"

"All things considered, yes."

"What I can't make out is, where she's got to."

"That doesn't bother me at all."

"Doesn't?" Young Vauregard glanced at him, puzzled.

"Not at all. To the police she is a phantom; one pale girl among millions. To those of us who saw her she is almost as spectral; a colorless picture, which would be changed practically out of recognition by any applied color at all. If you saw her in the street with darkened hair, eyebrows, and eyelashes; with her eyes made up—or unmade; they looked extra-long to me—and a good deal of make-up; with smart clothes, and a hat, are you sure you would know her?"

Dick Vauregard stared at him. "I'm sure I shouldn't!"

"Remember, there's no picture for the papers to display. Unless she makes a rather spectacular appearance somewhere, she probably won't be found. Of course, if Duncannon should by any chance know her, he may lead us to her."

Vauregard said, uneasily: "Payne thinks she had nothing to do with these—murders."

"Did Mrs. Norton strangle herself, according to him?"

"Oh, he says a sneak thief wandered in here last night while the front door was unlatched, and killed Aunt Angela in a panic, when he found her in the library."

"Well—er—not quite so clever, that one."

"Cam says it's perfectly reasonable. There are hordes of professionals just waiting for a chance like that; they snap up your umbrella or your parcel if you leave it on a counter for a second. They're always looking for a way to get into houses."

"Have the police sewed him up, too?"

"Cam?" Young Vauregard looked surprised, and then rather horrified. "He's right out of it. He wasn't here, and he's lame, and he only has a contingent interest in Clara's hundred thousand. For heaven's sake don't let Clara hear you say a thing like that!"

"I should have thought that the police would consider him an interested party."

"If they do, they haven't said so."

"You're not going to be a trial lawyer, are you, Mr. Vauregard?" asked Gamadge, smiling.

"I certainly am not. Arguing is the worst thing I do. Just nice quiet patents, under Bedlowe's wing." The young man stood frowning out at the parked cars, the staring people, and the sunny avenue off to the right. "We couldn't do anything much today, anyhow, on account of Uncle and Aunt Angie; but it's decent weather, for a change, and I certainly wouldn't mind being out in it. Do you know what? I bet they'll try to keep us caged up here until after the inquests."

Durfee, behind them, said: "You're an ungrateful sort of a character; here the city's paying three men to look out for you, day and night. Will you give me a minute before you go upstairs, Mr. Gamadge?"

Gamadge followed him into the drawing room, where Mr. Bridge sat alone, contemplating the portrait of Angela Morton as Viola. He wore a pale silk suit, belted at the waist, and his Panama hat lay on the sofa beside him. His hands, in creamy doeskin gloves, clasped the knob of his cane, and his chin rested on his hands. He looked disgusted.

He said, turning his eyes on Gamadge: "Lots of managers wanted to kill her at one time or another, they say; but I hadn't got as far as that, yet."

"Don't talk foolishness, Mr. Bridge," said Durfee.

"You ask me what our financial relations are. We hadn't any. I had no money, she had no money—or said she hadn't; the moving picture people wouldn't look at us, and old Mr. Vauregard never put cash into her plays. He didn't like her being in the theater, and I don't know what kind of fit he would have thrown when he found out she was thinking of going back to it. I thought the Webster play would run because of the production; she thought it would run because the critics would say she was greater than Rachel in it; nobody else thought it would run at all."

This speech, made in a colorless voice, seemed to exhaust Bridge. He closed his eyes.

"No harm trying to find out if you were in her confidence," said Durfee irritably.

"Oh, I was." Bridge opened his eyes halfway. "Don't worry. She confided in me, all right—all her hopes, fears and ambitions about Duncannon," he said, in a sour voice. "Did you hear him tearing off the last lines out of the Webster play, just now?"

"Man was doped up with his sleeping powder."

"He does it much better when he's doped up. I was quite surprised. All he did at rehearsals was grab his stomach with both hands. Angela thought he was a great romantic actor. Well, I've paid the artists something on the stage sets and the costumes—perhaps Duncannon will reimburse me, now that he's come into all this money; and perhaps not. They say you met that Smith woman—Lydia Smith, whatever she called herself." His eyes turned to Gamadge again. "Somebody said something about your saying she could play Vittoria Corombona."

"I thought she might very well play the character that Webster based his Vittoria on."

"You know anything about the theater?"

"Only what I see when I pay for a seat."

"If they catch her, and let her go again, I might have a look at her. From the way Duncannon talks, I bet he'd back her in *The White Devil* himself."

This was too much for Durfee. "I wouldn't exactly put my money on it, if I was you," he said. "Thanks, Mr. Bridge—I guess that will be all, for now."

Bridge rose, placed his rather wide-brimmed Panama on his head, drew up the spotless gloves on his hands, and rolled out on his short, thick legs without another word or any glance of farewell. Durfee, sardonic, watched him go.

"That character never thought up any such scheme as the Smith scheme," he said.

"That character has thought up many interesting, involved and lucrative schemes connected with the theater," said Gamadge, "but far be it from me to suggest that he could or would stage a *Tragedy of Blood* in real life."

Mr. Zanch, correctly and quietly dressed, came between the curtains from the library. Upon seeing Gamadge he stopped, and his narrow, handsome face was alert and watchful.

"The clairvoyant," he said.

"The who?" inquired Durfee, lowering at him.

"The gentleman who looks for trouble, and finds it. Mr. Gamadge paid us a call, on Thursday afternoon; recommended by Miss Vauregard."

"That so?"

"That is so. Quite interested, he was, in poor old Mr. Vauregard's money. If ever I saw a barefaced shakedown pulled off, it was the one he pulled off on us. You ought to ask him about it, Lieutenant."

"Pulled some information out of you, did he? Wish he'd tell me how he managed it."

"He managed it by threatening to show us up in a book. My wife rather took to him; wouldn't let me have him thrown out, or arrested. She's psychic. Know what she said after you left, Mr. Gamadge? She said you had a very dark aura, very dark indeed. Dark and opaque. Bad combination."

"I must do something about it."

"Drop that line, Zanch," said Durfee. "We are not interested. You've made your statement, for what it's worth, and you can go. We haven't got done with you yet, though."

"If there is any law against telling people how to think sanely, my wife and I have not heard of it."

"You've got more than one hardheaded businessman to put money into your thinking plant."

"We need a plant, yes. An academy."

"Never heard of anybody like Miss Lydia Smith, never heard that *Sleeping Beauty* story until you saw it in the papers, and didn't even know Byron wrote poetry. Thought he was an explorer, I guess," said Durfee.

"Quite ironical, are you not?"

"You and your wife look out for yourselves. Every time we get a good hook into you, some rich, brainy guy tears it out again. It can't go on forever."

"Can it not? You must study Confucius."

He went out, and Durfee sat down and pointed with some abruptness to a chair near him. Gamadge drew it up, and sat politely on the edge of it.

"Now! We've got rid of the nuts at last; or most of 'em." A flicker in his eye brought an answering spark from Gamadge's.

"I'll have to be going myself, pretty soon," he replied.

"Just hand over that evidence you think you have, first, if you don't mind."

"It isn't ready for you yet. I have to see Miss Dawson first."

The look that Gamadge was used to evoking on the faces of policemen again appeared on the countenance of Lieutenant Durfee. He said, after a moment: "Quite outspoken and candid, you are."

"Always. Didn't Schenck say so?"

"See here. That girl has something on her mind."

"No!"

"She's a type that can't lie and not show that she's lying. She could give a better account of herself on Thursday afternoon, all right, and she could account for Payne. She won't do it. You try to make her see where that gets her."

"Try to make me see what on earth you can do about it."

"Not much, unless the office decides these people are as unimportant as I'm beginning to think they are."

"Have you really got three men on this job, here?"

"Yes, and three men are going to stay on it, night and day, till we get a line on the Smith woman."

"Old school friend of Miss Dawson's, perhaps?"

"Or of Vauregard's."

"Or of Duncannon's."

"That character wasn't putting on an act. He's scared out of a year's growth. Scared silly."

"This house would scare me—scare anybody. I'm glad you have three men in it. Hard to get out of it, but just as hard to get in."

"You go up and talk to that Dawson girl. Old Vauregard died over an hour before our man saw him. We want some of these people to think up somebody that got a glimpse of them between five and five thirty-five, or five forty. The rest of 'em tell a straight enough story, not that it's good for anything; but Miss Dawson doesn't. Oh, by the way—here's your camera, and you'll find a nice new film in it; just the way it was. A nicer little box I never saw."

"Who handed the papers that line about Miss Smith getting persecution mania and wiping out the Vauregards?"

"Bedlowe. It's just," said Durfee, without resentment, "one of the stalls we've been getting. Have to expect 'em, from friends of the family."

CHAPTER SEVENTEEN

Sickness in the Family

As GAMADGE ENTERED Miss Vauregard's sitting room he was met at the door of it by Sun, the big chow. Sun looked at him inquiringly, reflected, and then waved his tail.

"Oh, good," said Gamadge. "I'm glad you have this fellow."

Clara got up from Miss Vauregard's desk. "I had to have him. Poor Aunt Rob didn't think it was so very nice of me, getting him here the day after…But I had to have him."

"She's hit by this as nobody else can be. How is she?"

"I'm worried about her, she seems so dazed. The doctor wants her to get away, but she wouldn't, even if they'd let her."

"They'll let her; I'm going to get you both out of here in no time."

She looked up at him wonderingly. There was a great change, this morning, in Clara Dawson. It was not surprising, it was decent and natural that she should have lost her headlong high spirits, but her spontaneity had gone too. Her eyes still had the shallow, agate-like quality that Gamadge had seen in them the night before; not hardness so much as withdrawal. She did not look frightened, she looked intensely and strangely preoccupied.

"How could you get us out?" she asked.

"Not unaided; you must help a little."

"I can't help at all."

"Yes, you can." He pushed up a chair for her, with its back to the light; and when she had sat down, he pulled another squarely in front of her. "Now," he said, in a businesslike tone. "Has there been any sickness in the family, lately?"

The unexpectedness of this opening confused her so much that for a moment she was unable to speak. At last, tearing herself out of that quiet, guarded concentration, she said : "I don't think so...no."

"Nobody been ailing in any way at all during, say, the last week or so? Megrims, aches and pains, hangovers?"

She considered. "Aunt Rob had one of her attacks of rheumatism."

"Take anything for it?"

"Only what Doctor Lestrange always gives her—aspirin."

"Does she keep a supply in the house, or did she have to send out and get some?"

"She got a new bottle of fifty tablets from our druggist."

"Who's he?"

"Thorwald, on Madison Avenue." Gamadge's sharp questions were drawing her out of her abstraction. She was interested, curious, entirely bewildered by them.

"Durfee thinks it's fine, the way you answer questions without asking any of your own." As she stared, suddenly on guard, he went on: "Anybody else need medicine?"

"I had a sty in my eye last week. The oculist took it out and gave me a prescription for something in a little tube—you squeeze it under your eyelid, and rub it around."

"What oculist?"

"Doctor Owen, West Fifty-ninth Street."

"Any more casualties?"

"We all had something the matter! Dick and Tom Duncannon caught cold last Saturday at the ball game. Tom had a sore throat—he got something to inhale. Dick has nose drops."

"All from Thorwald?"

"Yes."

"Your aunt, Mrs. Morton?"

"I don't think—yes; she did. She had a headache the other day. She says—said—nothing did them any good except Pyramidon."

"How about Payne?"

"He's never sick." The veiled look was in her eyes again. "He just has some stuff to take when he—when he can't sleep."

"Thorwald, again?"

"No, he gets it through his own specialist, Doctor Schildmann."

"Morphia, or something milder?"

"Something much milder. He never has morphia."

"Well, I want you to go and get me all these drugs and medicaments, every one of them. If Payne won't let me have a look at his, I'll burgle his flat."

Clara looked badly frightened. "Is it important?"

"Very."

"The police have been all over our things. They took Dick's pistol and his guns. They took Tom Duncannon's collection of daggers. Do they think we're going to go around the house, shooting and stabbing one another?" He looked at her, and she said, her face white, "I forgot. I keep forgetting about Aunt Angie—I can't make it seem real."

"Go on forgetting about it. I don't suppose Durfee pinched your drugs and medicines? Then get them for me. Just what you mentioned."

She went out, returning presently with a pasteboard box

cover, on which was displayed a collection of tubes and bottles. Gamadge fingered them, and also smelt them.

"Aspirin, little screw-top bottle, piece of cotton on top of the tablets; each tablet marked 'Bayer.' Ephedrine, plain; brown bottle, rubber-capped nose dropper; colorless liquid, doesn't smell of anything. Chloretone Inhalant—recalls unhappy memories of steam sprays. Pyramidon; each tablet has a rosette on it; small tin tube. Another small tin tube, that you squeeze; cunning little nozzle. This the sty-soother?"

"Yes."

"You put all these things back where they came from, Clara."

"Mr. Gamadge—Cam's sleeping stuff?"

"I'll talk about it when you come back."

She went off, and returned after two or three minutes empty-handed.

"Now," said Gamadge. "Would you help me to get a look at Payne's sleeping medicine without his knowing about it?"

She studied his face for so long that at last he said, impatiently: "Whatever else you know or don't know, you're pretty certain of one thing—or you ought to be, by this time; I'm not out to make trouble for you, or for anyone you—er—hold dear."

"You don't like him, Mr. Gamadge."

"Compared with his feeling towards me, mine towards him verges on idolatry; but as we both like you, you can't expect too much of us when it comes to admiring each other. I fully respect the priority of his claim, however, although he doesn't think I do."

"You don't know him, Mr. Gamadge. He never complains; he—"

"Just laughs it off. I know. The trouble is, that system can be carried too far. One mustn't laugh everything off, you know—it's not polite, and it's not safe."

"He's been so wonderful, and it was all my fault."

"Don't you cry, now!"

"I'm not going to."

"How can I get a look at his medicine?"

"Do you really think there may be something wrong with it? You must see it, then, of course. But—"

"But he won't show it to me—he'll tell me to go climb a tree. I should, in his place."

"He's coming up here after dinner, about eight thirty."

"Can I get into his flat?"

"I think so. Everybody's always dropping in and waiting for him. It's on the third floor, rear....I don't like doing this behind his back. Can't I tell him to take the tablets to Schumacher, and have them analyzed?"

"Schumacher is Schildmann's druggist?"

"Yes."

"The point is to keep this line of inquiry entirely between you and me, for the present. And there's no time to be lost."

"It's just that I do so hate to take advantage of him."

"Better than letting somebody else take advantage of him."

Her eyes met his. "All right, if you say so."

"Old pals, aren't we, with no nonsense between us."

"Yes." She gave him a faint smile.

"I'm going to strain your confidence in me to the utmost. Can your aunt hear me through that door?"

"She's fast asleep."

"May I shut the hall and bathroom doors?"

"Of course, if you want to." She watched him blankly as he did so. He came back, sat down, and leaned forward with his hands clasped between his knees. The chow dozed; quiet now reigned in the street outside, and a damp east wind suddenly fluttered the white curtains.

"I'm going to tell you something," said Gamadge. "I won't ask you any questions, and you needn't say a word. Just let me go through with it—no interruptions, if you can help it.

"On Thursday afternoon, at about twelve minutes to five, you drove Cameron Payne downtown as fast as you could, because he wanted to get to the old house before Mr. Vauregard took his afternoon stroll in the garden. He intended to get a picture of Miss Smith, if he could, and you were to wait in the car, around the corner.

"You had been very keen about the idea; in fact, you had tried to sell it to me. But a stranger would have had vast difficulties in getting a snapshot of Miss Smith, whereas Mr. Payne, a privileged party, could lurk in the arbor without fearing to lose reputation if he were discovered there; he could say that he was waiting for you. I refused the job—Payne took it on.

"You drove him down there, and parked in the neighborhood. It was obviously much less risky for one person to get into the arbor unseen, and to get out again, than for two, so he went alone. You saw him on his way between five fifteen and five thirty; I've doped out your route, and you could easily do it in the time, going in that direction at that time of day.

"He left cigarette ash on the arbor bench, which is not important; he also left the hole which his stick made in the ground, just to the left of the entrance. It's a damp corner, there'd been rain, and the impression is perfect. That stick has made impressions on my rug, and if you doubt my sense of dimensions, we can borrow it and go down there and fit it in again. We might even make a cast. I may add that the police haven't found anything in the arbor to interest them; they didn't hear your talk about photography.

"Payne returned to the car at about a quarter to six, in time for you to drive him uptown and leave him near his apartment house by six fifteen. He told you that he didn't get a picture; Miss Smith and Mr. Vauregard hadn't showed up, the day was clouding up again, and it was useless to wait. He said he must try it again.

"You dropped him, and went on for a drive yourself; but it wasn't the interminable drive you are so unsuccessfully trying to convince the police about; you left your car at the garage, parked Sun, and then walked home. You were a little bothered, and your troubles began at my tea party. You couldn't then understand why he had insisted on keeping the scheme from me, and why he was going out of his way to protest sympathy for Miss Smith. He seemed to be doing a lot of unnecessary storytelling, and you couldn't see why. Now, he had made you promise faithfully to say nothing to anybody about this abortive trip to Traders Row.

"When you reached home, or shortly afterwards, you heard that old Mr. Vauregard had been murdered between five and six o'clock, and that Miss Smith had disappeared. You didn't for one moment suspect Cameron Payne of poisoning the old gentleman; you knew why he had gone to Traders Row, and you knew that he wouldn't have taken you along if he had been planning anything worse than photography; besides, of course you knew that he wouldn't do such a thing. But he had been there on the spot, with his camera trained on the house, in full view of the side entrance and the garden door; he had been there during at least half of the crucial time, and probably at the fatal moment. If he didn't see the murderer come and go, if he didn't see Miss Smith go, it was almost a miracle. But he told you that he hadn't—that everything must have occurred before or after he was there.

"You choked on that, but you managed to swallow it. You had something else to swallow, too—he more than ever refused to let you tell about the trip to Traders Row. You wanted to tell, because you and he had valuable information—negative, but valuable—about times. He said it was impossible to hand out the story; you couldn't tell about photographing the zombi, because Mrs. Morton wouldn't release the arbor story; and the police knew that both of you had a motive for killing Mr. Vauregard. He's made you lie up and down to the police, and he expects you to go on the witness stand and perjure yourself.

"I understand your not letting him down; but since Thursday the affair has taken on a different aspect, and you don't like it at all. You have learned that Mr. Vauregard got the cyanide in his second cup of coffee; and you have learned that he could not have died much after half past five o'clock. You know that Payne saw something; but he won't own up, even to you. He won't own up, even though his evidence would clear you both. Why not?

"I don't pause for a reply; I venture the guess that he has told you he is keeping quiet to avoid scandal, and spare the feelings of the family and the memory of the dead."

Clara had been sitting motionless through all this, her face in shadow. She lifted it, and said: "He didn't see anything; but if he had, that's why he wouldn't tell."

"Won't burden even you with the awful truth; I guessed right. Well, I haven't gone into the thing to distress you, or to get information out of either of you; I have no questions. I simply told you the story in order to warn you—and him."

"Warn us?"

"He's taking a risk. That killer whom he's protecting knows that Payne has evidence—"

Clara looked at him in amazement. "He can't know!"

"Take my word for it." Gamadge returned her look with one of sad affection. "Whoever it was, knows."

"But how can he? It's impossible!"

"It's not for me to explain; just take my word for it. Payne's life is in danger. Don't cry!"

"I won't."

"Payne thinks he's safe enough; he isn't, not even for a night. Perhaps you can make him see reason. I don't want to discuss it with him at all—the less I know and say, the better."

"Cameron isn't afraid of anything."

"That's the trouble. If he won't climb aboard the raft with us, he won't; it's his own funeral; but I'm going to get you and Miss Vauregard out of this mess, and I'm not wasting sympathy on anybody else, I can tell you."

"Mr. Gamadge, he didn't see anything."

"All right, let it go at that. We'll drop the subject. My best regards to your aunt, and tell her not to worry; I'm suspect Number 1. My personnel is so ashamed of me that I can hardly get my meals, and I haven't laid eyes on Harold since yesterday. I haven't a soul to speak up for me except an insurance investigator named Schenck, who looks like a comedian in a variety show. Do you think that will bring a feeble smile to her lips? I hope so. It hasn't had that effect on yours."

He rose, and they faced each other. She said: "You can joke about it, but Aunt Rob and I are sick about your being dragged into it. She urged you and urged you, and now you're having all this trouble."

"Tell her to forget it; the case introduced us, and it's well worth my while. I might never have had the pleasure of her acquaintance."

"I'll tell her."

They shook hands solemnly, and Gamadge leaned over to rub the chow's enormous furry ears. Then he went downstairs, and sought Durfee until he found him in the little back room called the library.

CHAPTER EIGHTEEN

Dark Afternoon

DURFEE WAS SITTING at Mrs. Morton's desk, writing. He looked up. "Get that information?"

"I got some; too busy to bother about alibis."

Gamadge sat down and laid a slip of paper under Durfee's nose. "Here's a list of remedies, now accessible to us, supplied by Thorwald the druggist to this household during the past week. Mrs. Morton had Pyramidon, I don't know when, and Payne some sleeping medicine, prescribed by Doctor Schildmann and put up by Schumacher. Apart from those, we have:

Miss Vauregard: Fifty aspirin tablets, from Thorwald.
Miss Dawson: Eye ointment; Doctor Owen and
    Thorwald.
Mr. Richard Vauregard: Ephedrine (plain);
    Doctor Lestrange, Thorwald.
Mr. Duncannon; Chloretone Inhalant;
    Lestrange, Thorwald.

You know Thorwald and Schumacher?"

"Yes." Durfee stared.

"The Vauregard doctor, Lestrange? The oculist, Owen?"

"Lestrange was here for Duncannon. Owen I'm not acquainted with."

"I want to know whether any other drug or medicament of any kind was prescribed or put up for these six people during the past week; and I want to know whether any of these six people have a chronic disease or physical disability of any sort—apart from Cameron Payne's injury."

Durfee continued to stare.

"These doctors wouldn't supply information to me, and neither would Thorwald or Schumacher. Would they, to you?" asked Gamadge.

"Thorwald and Schumacher would. The doctors might tell me if the answer to the question was in the negative," said Durfee. "I might have trouble getting positive information out of them."

"But if they refused to answer, you might safely conclude that there was some disease or disability?"

"I might."

"Will you get in touch with them immediately—Owen is on West Fifty-ninth Street—and ask them the questions? I'll write them out for you."

Durfee leaned back, crossed his legs, folded his hands across his diaphragm, and lowered his head. He looked up at Gamadge from under knitted brows. Finally he said: "People can get drugs and remedies from other people besides their regular doctors and druggists."

"They can. I don't care if they did."

"We've seen all these things you mention, including Payne's tablets."

"Of course."

"The department can't work in the dark for anybody that wants information and won't say why."

"But my dear man, you asked me to assist; I'm doing it in my own way."

"I have to be the judge about whether your assistance is going to be worth anything to us, before I put department labor and money into it."

"I'll defray expenses."

"What I can't make out is, why you're doing all this."

"Not for excitement, I assure you. Will you get the information for me? I can get it myself, only it will take me so much longer. Do make up your mind—I'm starving."

Durfee, looking black, reached for the telephone.

"Blessings on thee." Gamadge rose. "I'll be at home all afternoon."

"You might have tried to get something from Miss Dawson."

"Forget about Miss Dawson."

Durfee's eyes followed him out of the room.

When he reached home, the expression on his usually amiable face was such that nobody dared comment on the hour—half past two o'clock. Athalie remained in her kitchen, and sent up a tremendous lunch; Theodore served it in silence. Gamadge was on his davenport smoking, and still scowling, when Harold appeared with an afternoon paper under his arm.

"Welcome, stranger," said Gamadge.

Harold laid the paper on a table. "Mr. Schenck called up," he said, in what the French would describe as a *voix blanche*.

"Did he?"

"Coming in this afternoon."

"Delighted to see him."

"Lady called up four times. Wouldn't give her name." Harold looked down at the headlines under his eyes. "I got an idea it was Miss—"

"No names."

"Miss. Glad she's still alive. I didn't more than think she would be—the whole story is out, now, Byron and all."

"Hope it reads well."

"A Mr. Payne called up, just before you got here. Coming in this afternoon."

"He and Schenck won't get on at all."

"I can keep one of 'em downstairs."

"Let 'em all come."

Theodore brought coffee, gave a sidelong, agonized look at the papers which Harold had laid on the desk, and went out quickly. The telephone rang. Gamadge swallowed some coffee, and went into his bedroom to answer it. A high, shaking voice said: "Mr. Gamadge?"

"Yes."

"Don't mention my name."

"No."

"Can we be overheard?"

"Not here; where are you?"

"In a booth, Mr. Gamadge—where is that book?"

"Don't worry about it; nobody will ever lay eyes on it again."

"Mr. Gamadge, if my name is ever brought into this, in any way—any way, Mr. Gamadge—I shall kill myself."

"You won't be brought into it."

"You believe me when I say I should kill myself?"

"I do. Absolutely. Please don't be so unhappy about it. Nobody will ever know."

"I couldn't live for one single day. Oh, what a fool I've been."

"You mustn't be hard on yourself. Why shouldn't you have a caller of an evening? Everybody else does."

"I shall never give anybody his name, whatever happens. You understand that? You understand that I should deny everything."

"Perfectly, Miss—er—look here; I must call you some-thing. Miss Flower. Perfectly, Miss Flower. You won't see the party again, though, I hope?"

"What?"

"You must never under any circumstances see the party again—privately. Not at all safe."

"As if I ever would!"

"Not safe in any way, I mean. The party seems very tough, and you may not realize it, but you are perhaps the only living soul who knows who he is. Without meaning to be sensational, I feel that I ought to call your attention…"

There was a pause. Then Miss Dykinck said in a different voice: "I'm not that sort of coward, really I'm not. I suppose you think I'm behaving very badly, Mr. Gamadge…"

"Who am I, to blame you?"

"I can't tell anybody!"

"Many civilized persons have preferred death to losing face. You are in good company."

Miss Dykinck's voice softened. "Would he tell, if they caught him, Mr. Gamadge?" she asked tremulously.

"Why should he give evidence against himself?"

"Just to be spiteful, perhaps."

"Not everybody prefers being spiteful to living, you know."

A faint, wavering ghost of Miss Dykinck's well-remembered giggle came over the wire, and Gamadge looked relieved. She said: "You and that book you were going to write!"

"I may write it yet."

"If you do, don't connect us in any way with that awful family! Imagine Mrs. Morton playing such a trick on that poor old man! Mamma isn't surprised."

Miss Dykinck was apparently quite herself again, and Garnadge felt that he might make an effort to terminate the conversation. He said: "Do please forgive me, but I'm fearfully rushed."

"Of course. Thank you. I—"

"Don't worry, now!"

As he turned away, Gamadge felt rather touched; even Miss Rose Dykinck thought it unnecessary to exact a vow from him, and that in spite of the fact that he had got her into her present state of tribulation.

He wandered about the library, and then stood looking

out of the window at a gray sky and wind-tossed branches. A chilly east gale was tearing at the leaves of his big tree. He reflected morosely that he might have to end by consulting Chandor for a message from the stars, if he had to throw out much more direct evidence.

A light, agreeable voice said: "Hope I'm not intruding. Your man let me bring myself up in the elevator."

Gamadge turned. "Oh. Good afternoon, Mr. Payne."

"Rotten afternoon it's going to be." Cameron Payne stood in the doorway, leaning on his stick. He smiled at Gamadge, and said in gentle protest: "Look here. I've heard of taking pennies from a blind beggar, but I never heard until now of anyone trying to take a cripple's girl away from him."

"Nor I. Won't you sit down?"

"What's all this you've been putting into Clara's head?"

"Nothing that wasn't there already; except the awful warning."

Payne laughed. "That be hanged. She telephoned me; I could hardly choke her off, and that boy at my switchboard must have got an earful." He made little marks on the rug with his cane, tapped them smilingly, and smiled at Gamadge. "Such rot. There are dozens of explanations for holes in a garden house."

"Oh? Such as?..."

"What do I know? Gardeners do all sorts of things."

"The gardener hadn't been in that arbor for a long time. Bench all dust and twigs, grass high. And I don't myself see why he, or anyone, should bore a hole in a corner."

"Fact remains, it's not evidence. And I can't see," continued Payne, in plaintive wonder, "why you didn't fill the thing up, while you were about it. If you're not going to give me away, why leave what you foolishly consider traces of my being there?"

Gamadge contemplated him with mild incredulity.

"You really are a kind of marvel, Payne; you really are."

"Am I?"

"You are. I don't propose to go about clearing up after you, my good fellow. I can leave evidence for the authorities to find or ignore, but I won't conceal it "

"Delicate distinction. You're concealing a good deal, so you think."

"More than I ought, and part of it I'm concealing from Clara."

Gamadge returned the bright-blue gaze fixed on him. After a pause, Payne said: "You're absolutely, hopelessly wrong. Do you know when a man's telling the truth, or don't you?"

"Yes. You really think I'm mistaken in one particular."

"The only one that counts, my boy!"

"The only one that counts with you. I assure you that I'm not mistaken, about that or about any of the rest of it."

"Why not explain, if you're as cocksure as all that?" Payne looked amused.

"Explain why you're in danger? Not on your life. You don't want the murderer caught."

"What has that to do with it?"

"Everything. But Clara Dawson doesn't want you caught by him—and killed. That killer you're shaking down isn't going to take it."

"Oh. Tell Clara that theory?" Payne studied him, still smiling.

"No, I didn't tell her. If she finds it out—"

"No reason why she should. But even if she did..." Payne gave him a dazzling smile. "I can't expect you to understand. If you'd seen her face, though, when she and that big filly she couldn't manage came down on top of me, you'd know what I mean. You simply can't do a thing about that."

"No; but you can."

"You're mistaken."

"She won't stand a racket, Payne. You didn't see her face when I talked to her."

"If it were all true, all this tosh of yours, nobody ought to blame me for saving her some of her money. She's been done out of a good big whack of it. Even Mrs. Morton wouldn't have been besotted enough to leave her will the way it was, after old Uncle Vauregard died. It's very annoying, you must admit."

"Very, indeed. Clara is sick of this money obsession."

"Noble of her. She'd be sicker yet, if she didn't have enough to spend about five dollars a day on a chow."

"I should say that it will come to your making a choice— easy dough or Clara Dawson."

"No advice wanted, thank you all the same. I can take care of myself, and I shall look out for Clara. I hear you're working with the law now."

"Yes; I prefer it."

"Private customers got rather out of hand, didn't they? I swear, I think you're responsible for the whole fiasco, deaths and all."

"I'm afraid I am. I may be said to have killed Mr. Vauregard and Mrs. Morton, in a negative kind of way."

"How were you going to prove that stuff about the book?"

"Photographs of the binding."

"I don't see what good they would do you. Are you keeping the evidence against a rainy day?"

"No, and that reminds me." He went into the hall, and lifted his voice: "Harold!"

Harold appeared, in the doorway of the elevator.

"Those pictures you took yesterday, and the enlargements. Bring them up here, will you?"

There was a short interval, during which Payne sat gently tapping the floor with his stick, and Gamadge leaned against the table. When Harold came in, he bestowed no glance on the visitor, but handed a folder to Gamadge, and stood waiting. He never did recognize the existence of callers, unless Gamadge introduced him; had been known, in fact, to step on their feet, so unsubstantial did they seem to be to him.

Gamadge took a couple of plates out of the folder, and gave them to Payne; they each showed a double row of irregular markings, not quite parallel; Payne inspected them, eyebrows raised.

"This plate, marked 1, doesn't continue on to 3," he said. "There's a gap; something ought to come between."

"Plate Number 2 didn't get enlarged; in fact, Picture Number 2 didn't get taken."

"And this is the evidence that made all the trouble, and caused two deaths?" Payne looked up at him, smiling.

"Two thirds of it. Harold, smash these up for me, will you, and destroy the photographs. We shan't be wanting them, after all."

"Smash them—in here?" Harold asked it stolidly.

"Here and now."

"Let's see the folder," said Payne, his eyes dancing. Gamadge picked it up and handed it to him. He read:

Exhibits A and C in the case of Vauregard vs. Smith, alias Wagoneur; and others.

"Thanks. Very amusing." Payne returned the folder. Harold slid the plates into it, took it over to the nearest window, and laid it on the stone sill. Having glanced about him, he picked up a large bronze paperweight, and cracked up the plates in their container very much as he might have cracked up a paper bag of nuts, or a towelful of ice. He then lifted the limp result upon a newspaper, and carried it out of the room.

"Impressive," said Payne, laughing. "I'm the witness, I suppose. I'll tell Clara that the case of Vauregard versus Smith is in ruins. Thanks for a very pleasant call."

He got up, and adjusted the crook of his stick comfortably to his hand.

"You go up there and see Durfee. Tell him all about it. I'll back you to come out of it without a blemish on your character," said Gamadge, watching him as he went to the doorway. He turned, and stood poised and graceful, a fine figure of a young man. No one would have guessed at an injury.

"Too late," he said. "Don't you worry yourself about me. You've got it all wrong—for once. I'm as safe as houses."

"I'm not worrying about you. You're too silly to worry about."

"I was rather expecting you to advise a short trip—for my health. You could look out for Clara while I was away."

"I was rather expecting a remark of that kind, sooner or later."

"At least, I haven't disappointed you there!" He laughed again, and went across the hall to the elevator. Gamadge did not press the button for him, or see him down to the door.

CHAPTER NINETEEN

Mr. Schenck Is Amused

WHEN THEODORE ANNOUNCED Mr. Schenck, that personage found Gamadge sitting in an armchair, his elbows on his knees, a highball glass in his hand.

"Hello," he said. "Schenck, you're an answer to prayer."

Mr. Schenck had a foxy cast of countenance, and sharp, humorous eyes. He said: "You look peaked. Where's the Souchong? Not getting this feller into bad habits, are you, Theodore?"

Theodore was tolerant of Mr. Schenck. He replied "Mr. Gamadge got a lot on his mind, today. He needs somethin' to hold him up."

Gamadge had not moved. He now took a swallow of whisky, and said: "Theodore is suffering from remorse."

"This mornin' I thought Mr. Gamadge had demeaned himself," explained Theodore. "Now I see by the paper Harold just brought in, police beginnin' to value him."

"We have Mr. Schenck to thank for that. Bring him a drink, and invite him to stay to dinner."

Schenck was nattily dressed in tropical worsteds, and carried a round straw hat. This he dropped upon the top of the celestial globe (from which Theodore instantly removed it), drew a newspaper from under his arm, and sat down.

"The Vauregard-Morton case is still up among the war news, this afternoon," he said. "Stay to dinner? I should say so. What good is Saturday, this weather? I was all set for the beaches, and instead of that I had to go to a movie."

Theodore brought another glass and more ice, moved a table to Schenck's elbow, and went out.

"Can't you relax?" asked Schenck, with a puzzled glance at his host. "Sit back in that chair, for goodness sake. I thought nothing ever disturbed the steely nerve. What's the matter with you?"

"I'm expecting a telephone call."

"Honestly, when I read the paper yesterday morning, I thought I'd die."

"Oh?"

"'Mr. Henry Gamadge, a caller at the Vauregard mansion on Traders Row, discovered the body. His statement was corroborated by the butler and he was allowed to leave.' I thought I'd die."

"So glad you were amused."

"I knew you were up to something."

"Lucky the police didn't come to that conclusion."

"Then the Morton case broke, with Mr. Gamadge involved. Thinking you must of course be hand in glove with the cops, as usual, and having Durfee on the wire about something else, I asked him for the lowdown."

"And found that he wanted it himself."

"He seemed to get such a jolt out of what I said that I was afraid I might have mixed things up for you, a little."

"On the contrary."

"Wait till some of these press men get around to digging up your past. You'll have a high old time. Theodore will get that private telephone wire at last."

"Fortunately, nobody has bothered me much yet; I hope they won't, for just a few hours more. Can you travel around with me, this evening?"

Schenck screwed up his eyes. "One of your wild parties?"

"Not so very."

"Because I didn't bring along my bullet-proof vest."

"I just want a witness."

The telephone rang in the hall, and Gamadge sprang out of his chair. Schenck listened, without shame.

"Durfee?...Oh, thanks...Just a second, I have a pencil and paper right here...Go ahead...No prescriptions except what I gave you, no drugs or medicaments. Payne gets his stuff only by prescription, and it's a private one of Schildmann's, and it's a very mild sedative...No illnesses or disabilities of any kind...No, I'm not a bit disappointed, just wanted to check up. I'll give you the whole thing either tonight or early tomorrow... No. I can't until then."

Schenck came up behind him and bawled into the mouthpiece: "Give him his head, Durfee, he can't be bossed." Durfee replied with a few words not entirely complimentary either to Schenck or to Gamadge, and rang off.

As they turned from the telephone they almost ran into Harold, who acknowledged Schenck's greeting with more than his accustomed taciturnity.

"And what's the matter with you?" inquired Schenck. "I never got into such a melancholy outfit. Don't know if I can stand it, if it lasts through dinner."

"Harold thinks I ought to be taking him on this ramble, instead of you. Matter of fact, he's got to stay home and wait for me to call him; I'm going to have to use the code."

"Mr. Schenck could do that."

"You think I'd give our code to Schenck, or anybody else?"

The code, Harold's invention, was dear to him. He said grudgingly, "Well..."

"And you'll have to keep the car at the door, ready to drive off at a moment's notice."

Schenck said: "It's one of your usuals, all right. I recognize the symptoms. Barometer's falling."

They went back to the library, and listened to soul-destroying news on the radio until Schenck turned it off and begged for a cocktail. They sat long over these, and had a leisurely dinner. At eight thirty Gamadge called the Morton house. A policeman answered, and Gamadge asked for Mr. Payne. When the officer inquired who wanted him, Gamadge said it was the Elmsport Gazette, in connection with the Vauregard case. Was not Mr. Payne engaged to be married to Miss Dawson? The policeman said: "Let the man have his evening in peace, can't you?" and rang off.

"All ready," said Gamadge. "Come on, Schenck and take one of my coats, if you haven't yours. You may want it."

Schenck, under protest, put on a light topcoat, and they sallied forth. The chill, cloudy twilight had come to an end, and lights were beginning to show in the high buildings; their towers were lost in iridescent mist. The street lamps went on. They took a cab to West Fifty-eighth Street, and walked down the block to a bleak, barrack-like structure, dating from the first decade of the century.

The lobby was deserted, except for a colored boy who slept in the elevator. Gamadge went softly past him. Schenck following on his toes. They climbed a flight of stairs, consulted all the cards on all the doors, and climbed to the next story. Here Gamadge stopped at a door marked "Payne." Instead of knocking, he turned and led the way softly down to the lobby again.

"Payne, eh?" whispered Schenck, greatly interested. "You thought he might leave his door open for us?"

"I wanted to find out whether anybody could call on him without being announced—or even seen."

This time Gamadge awakened the elevator boy: "Mr. Payne in?"

"No, Sir. He went out a half an hour ago."

"Can we wait?"

"Yes, Sir. I'll let you in."

They were borne slowly to the third floor, and the boy opened Cameron Payne's flat for them, and went down again. "Trustful guy," said Schenck, all eyes. "Nothing to hide. You going to wait for him, or was that a deception? Or am I indiscreet?"

"Far from it." Gamadge preceded him along a dark, narrow hall to a small room at the end of it. He found and turned a light switch.

The open window looked out on fire escapes and the brick walls of a courtyard. Schenck peered from it, and withdrew his head to glance in disparagement at disheartening brown walls and an imitation Oriental rug, at imitation tapestry chairs and a hard sofa, and at the radiator masquerading as a gas log in the fireplace. A gilt-framed picture hung over the mantelpiece, with its name on it—"Lake by Moonlight." Tennis and golf cups, with other trophies, stood on the shelf below. A large, comfortable chaise longue, nicely upholstered in chintz, crowded the rest of the deplorable furniture into a huddle.

Schenck said: "This place would give me the horrors."

"Payne isn't aesthetic."

"Neither am I aesthetic, but you ought to see my little flat. Chromium and red leather, glass-topped tables, geometric rugs, everything modern, built-in beds and a dinette."

Gamadge, with a slight shiver, said it must be fine. They went into the adjoining bathroom.

"My goodness, look at the tub and the plumbing! And peek in here at the brass bed and the stained-pine chiffonier!" Schenck had penetrated to a bedroom. "I thought Payne was a socialite."

"Oh, God, don't say that."

"Why not?" Schenck came back, surprised.

"No reason why not, except that I'm nervous. It's a word I don't much like."

"Nervous, are you?"

"Just a little. Excuse my manners." Gamadge had glanced among the usual assortment of objects on the shelf over the basin. He now opened a medicine cabinet badly in need of re-enameling and peered therein. He took out a small glass phial with a screw top. "Payne hasn't much money. That's why he can't have a dinette."

"I haven't any too much."

"You have an important job, you capitalist; Payne's a cripple, and can't earn."

"Are you ever going to tell me why we came here?"

"Just to look at this."

"It's the medicine you talked about on the telephone, isn't it? I see Schildmann's name on the label."

"Apparently." Gamadge put it in his pocket, and searched among the things on the other shelves. "No other medicines or drugs at all, even in powder form," he said.

"The police must have been all over his stuff."

"Yes."

"Are you going to take the feller's dope away from him?"

"I hope he won't need it tonight."

"I hope not, either. You have your nerve."

Gamadge said, smiling at him: "Do you feel like tasting one of the tablets, in the interests of science—or humanity?"

"No, I do not!" Schenck stepped back, negation in every inch of him.

"Even though the police must have been all over his stuff?"

"No, darn you."

"Quit criticizing me, then."

"Somebody out after the guy's life?"

"Might be."

Gamadge closed the cupboard, and they investigated two closets—one full of faultless clothes, the other, meant for a kitchenette, now used as a photographic darkroom. Schenck said: "You haven't really searched the place."

"No. No reason to."

They went back to the living room, and Gamadge found the telephone. After a short wait he got a sleepy response from the factotum below. He asked for his own number.

"That you, Harold? Got your green book? Take this down." He consulted the back of an envelope, and read out: "Prx, 6283, bjz …Of course I had it written out, all ready. Tubbing, crawl, flimsy pudge. ⍵ Got that? Hamburger. That's all." He waited until Harold had made some response, and rang off.

"Is 'Hamburger' part of the code, or were you ordering a snack?" asked Schenck.

"It means: 'Wait around the corner.'"

"Some code!"

"It certainly is."

Gamadge had his hand on the livingroom switch, when a very quiet knock came on the door of the flat. He paused. Schenck said: "That's not the colored boy. He hadn't time."

"No. Another visitor."

"I'll open it."

"Not on your life, you won't." Gamadge went down the hall and pushed the door open. He seemed to push the visitor with it, because the bare, gray, dimly lighted corridor showed no one. Presently, however, a figure moved forward and appeared in the entrance of the flat; and Schenck, with a considerable thrill, realized that the caller was Mr. Thomas Duncannon, whose picture, in and out of costume, had figured largely in the newspapers during the last twelve hours.

Gamadge said: "Come in, Mr. Duncannon." The actor walked slowly down the passage and into the sitting room, pulling off his gray gloves. He seemed to have recovered from his drugging, but his eyes were red-rimmed, and his skin yellow. Every line of his face had sagged; he looked exhausted.

"Payne at home?" he asked, as the other followed him.

"Sorry, he's not," said Gamadge. "So you did manage to lose your friend with the pink hair, Mr. Duncannon."

"He went to sleep. I don't suppose I can have been expected to sit and wait for him to wake up."

"You just walked out of the hotel?"

"By the back way, or one of them. It's quite a maze." He went over to the chaise longue, and sat down on it. "I wanted to talk this thing over with Payne. He's clever."

"Very."

"Thinks some prowler sneaked in and killed my wife." Duncannon's red-rimmed eyes looked up at Gamadge, but he did not lift his head.

"Not one of his more intelligent ideas, I think."

"I dare say that was for publication. He may have something else to suggest, when I've talked to him."

He took his hat off, dropped it on a chair, and leaned quietly back against the cushions of the chaise longue.

Gamadge said: "We were just going. Shall you wait for him?"

"Indefinitely." He closed his eyes.

Schenck followed Gamadge out of the flat, and down the concrete hall.

"Are you going to tip off the law?" asked Schenck, regarding his companion curiously.

"No."

"The widower had a smoldering eye, didn't you think so?"

"He has just awakened to harsh realities. We won't disturb the guardian of The Humbert; let's take the stairs."

"He's been disturbed." Schenck paused, and listened to the rising clank of the elevator. "Would that be Payne, I wonder? I have a kind of a sort of a feeling that I'd like to tell him he has a caller—with a smoldering eye."

"That wouldn't be Payne—not yet." But Gamadge also paused, and as the elevator came to a stop, hastily ducked down the stairs out of sight. Schenck joined him. The gate clashed, the cage descended, and heels tapped on the bare concrete. Gamadge and Schenck cautiously raised their eyes above the level of the floor.

A small, well-rounded figure in a very short-skirted dark suit and a black hat like a cup and saucer pattered along to Cameron Payne's apartment, knocked, turned the knob and walked in. As she closed the door behind her, Schenck asked blankly: "Was it unlocked all the time?"

"Certainly it was. Didn't you see the elevator boy open it?" Gamadge was already mounting the stairs again.

"Didn't notice." Schenck, alert and amused, followed Gamadge back down the corridor. Still more amused, if a trifle apprehensive, he watched his unpredictable friend gently turn the handle of Payne's door. Suddenly he seized Gamadge's elbow.

"Hey, look," he begged, in a whisper.

Gamadge looked over his shoulder, and met the gaze of two eyes, which peered at him above the level of the floor. Somebody else had come up the stairs, and now occupied the observation point which they had just abandoned.

CHAPTER TWENTY

Subhuman

"THAT'S ONLY CARRROTS," murmured Gamadge. "Duncannon's follower. Didn't have his sleep out, after all."

The plain-clothes man came up the rest of the stairs, and joined them. He appeared to accept their presence philosophically, allowed Gamadge to push the door quietly open, and gazed over their heads to the lighted sitting room beyond the dark passage.

Nothing could be seen of Duncannon but his legs, which were extended to the very foot of the chaise longue. Miss Garfield stood beside it. Unstimulated by cocktails, unembellished by make-up, and soberly clad, she looked like the careworn older sister of the lady in peppermint-stick pink whom Gamadge had met at the Brightstone Inn. Moreover, her gaiety had departed; she seemed not only anxious, but frightened. One would have said that she regarded Mr. Duncannon with a certain amount of apprehension.

"...shouldn't have asked me to come here," she was saying, in a thin voice.

"Absurd, m'dear girl. This dump is a sanctuary," replied Duncannon. "Did you get by the fellow downstairs all right?"

"He said it was against the rules, but anybody can call on Mr. Payne. You'll get me into trouble, and I don't know why I came. They'll be looking for you."

"I'm going quietly back, later, and that fellow will be asleep when I get there."

Schenck managed a hasty glance at the plain-clothes man, whose expression was one of mild irony.

"I don't like it at all," quavered Miss Garfield. "You ought to keep me out of it. If the papers get hold—"

"You'll be out of it from now on. That's one of the things I wanted to tell you. The play is off, for good. At least it is so far as we're concerned. Bridge may put it on, but he'll be coming to me for backing, now; and he won't have you in it, not even as an inmate of the House of Convertites."

"The what?"

"Didn't you ever read the thing?"

"I certainly did not, not beyond where I come in as the ghost and die from kissing your picture. Honestly, what the critics will do to that show!"

"They'll take it and like it. I wanted to reimburse you for all the trouble you took, learning those lines and rehearsing. Hope you don't object?"

Miss Garfield drew a step back. "So that's it."

"That's it."

"You don't have to pay me to keep quiet. Everybody except poor Mrs. Morton knew all about us, and your nephew won't protect you—not now."

Duncannon was silent for a moment. Then his voice came slowly, with a dryness in it: "You almost sound as if you thought I had committed two murders. What a brave little girl you are!"

"I'm not afraid of you, Tom Duncannon."

"That's why you've been jittering there; wouldn't even sit down. Well, that's very interesting. It never entered my head! Actually never entered it! I knew the police would have to keep an eye on me, ridiculous as it seemed, because of the money; and I knew the Vauregards would elect me, naturally; I'm the perfect fall guy. But I thought I could expect sympathy from everybody else, and most particularly from you. You knew better than anybody that I wouldn't even hurt Angela's feelings, if I could help it; didn't you?"

"I knew you had to keep in with her."

"Till I got a chance to kill the old gentleman, and then Angela herself? Thanks."

"Well, Tom, after all, it does look—"

"My heavens, a nice mob you must run around with! Or perhaps you've been getting too much Webster into your system. It's only a play, you know."

"Somebody did it," muttered Miss Garfield obstinately. "That Miss Smith business—the papers said you said she was really a refugee. I couldn't help laughing."

"I still think she was really a refugee, and I think somebody put her on a spot. That little girl—not an ounce of malice in her."

Miss Garfield said passionately, "You give me that money and let me out of here."

"Here it is, all I had in the bank. Mind you, there isn't any blackmail in the picture; as you reminded me, we have nothing to hide that the police won't find before we get it out of sight. It's a souvenir."

"I know all about that; so I'll tell everybody how fond you were of Mrs. Morton."

"Do that; and then I won't tell anybody that you weren't a bit fond of her. By the way, you got off some very peculiar cracks at the Brightstone yesterday, in front of Dick Vauregard and that detective, what-do-you-call-him—Gamadge. You probably don't remember, because you were on your fifth Daiquiri."

"I thought he was very attractive; nobody told me he was a detective," said Miss Garfield in a rising wail.

"He'll remember what you said, anyhow. I hope he got your type. I'd go on the stand and swear you wouldn't murder anybody, not even for money, and positively not for love. Too bad you can't do the same for me."

As Duncannon came into sight, a roll of bills in his hand, the three observers fell back. They all made for the stairs, and the plain-clothes man took it upon himself to watch, and report proceedings. This involved much ducking up and down, and a great deal of hoarse whispering.

"She's coming out. Stuffing the roll in her bag...Rung the elevator...Not a sign of him...She keeps lookin' over her shoulder, got the jumps...Elevator coming...She's gone down."

"Then we can go, too. I suppose you're staying on?" inquired Gamadge politely.

"You suppose right."

"Why don't you go on in there and get your nap? Payne won't be along for some time."

"This Duncannon might have a date with some other dame."

"So he might. Well, you have our prayers." Gamadge led the way down, passed the elevator without arousing the again somnolent operator, and strode rapidly to the corner of the street. Schenck, keeping up with him breathlessly, panted: "All over?"

"Just starting."

They got into a cab, and drove past garages and restaurants to Sixth Avenue. Here they turned north, followed Fifty-ninth Street, turned north again on Fifth, and stopped at Seventy-fourth Street.

Gamadge paid the driver, and he and Schenck walked eastward through wide, dark, quiet streets until they were opposite the Morton house. It loomed across the black, clean asphalt, its ornate facade in shadow, except where a thin yellow gleam issued from between the drawing-room curtains. Far up the block a street lamp glimmered through the branches of a tree.

The house in front of which they stood was boarded up, and its deep, old-fashioned area was a well of darkness. Gamadge descended into it, sat on a corner of one of the stone steps, and leaned forward to look out between the stout balustrades. Schenck, perching on the other end of the step, did the same.

"That the Morton house?" he asked, impressed.

"That's it."

"Quite a mansion."

"Quite."

"Who're you interested in?"

"All of them. Payne is calling there, as it happens."

"Police in there?"

"Three of them."

"Are we waiting for Payne to come out?"

"Can you stand it?"

"All right with me, only I'm glad you lent me the coat." Schenck arranged a double layer of it under him; cold brownstone had already struck chill through his tropical worsteds.

"Sorry you can't smoke."

"Don't mention it."

A shadow drifted past the area; Gamadge addressed it in a murmur, and Harold's short, square figure took form and descended the steps. It dematerialized again as footsteps echoed hollowly from the west. They approached. A policeman sauntered by, with a glance up at the Morton house; when he had passed, Harold came out of his dark retreat to whisper: "The car is around the corner, halfway to Seventy-third Street."

"Can you watch this block?"

"Yes. There's a doorway."

"Wait till you see us come out and follow somebody. If the party takes a cab, I'll have to depend on you. We'll come on as best we can."

"O.K."

Harold drifted back along the block, and disappeared.

Ten slow minutes passed, by Schenck's luminous, stream-lined dial, and then the front door of the Morton house opened, and two men emerged from it. One of them was blue-coated and brass-buttoned; the other, Schenck recognized as Cameron Payne—the light from the hall revealed smiling features which had often adorned the sporting pages of newspapers.

His cheerful good night came clearly across the street. The policeman asked him something, and he laughed, shook his head, and waved his stick. He came down the steps lightly and easily; the policeman went back into the house and shut the door.

Payne hesitated, glanced to right and left, and then came directly over to the south pavement. He reached it not two yards from the spot where the watchers crouched invisible, hung his stick over his arm, got out a cigarette case and a paper of matches, and lighted a cigarette. His fair, masklike face and bright hair sprang out for an instant against the dark; they disappeared, and the cigarette glowed. Payne threw away the match, took his stick in his hand, and walked at a leisurely pace up the street towards the west.

Schenck looked at Gamadge, but the latter was not preparing to rise and follow; he did not seem to be interested in Payne at all. His eyes were fixed on the facade of the Morton house, just below the open second-story bay, where masses of stone— foliage in high relief—divided into festoons and drooped to the drawing room windows.

Schenck, following his gaze, saw nothing to interest him in the fruit, flowers and immense curled leaves; but as he stared, he suddenly became aware that a portion of the stone-work had apparently detached itself from the rest, and was sliding downwards. The next moment he realized that a dark figure was lowering itself from one foothold to the next, moving slowly but with precision. It reached the drawing-room window ledge, then that of the basement, and dropped lightly to its feet on the flagstones of the area. It turned, crossed the street as Payne had done, but soundlessly; and was on the other's heels in a moment.

Payne swung about with a short, startled cry which changed into a laugh.

"Hello," he said. "How did you get here? Bribe a cop?"

A low voice answered briefly: "Give me that thing."

They faced each other, Payne's slight figure almost hidden behind the other's bulk. Payne stepped back.

"You can't stage a holdup here, with the house across the way full of cops," he said. "Don't be silly."

"Hand it over, you white rat."

"Nonsense. You won't risk a row."

"There won't be any row. Hand it over, or you'll find out why."

"Listen, Dick; have sense. One yell out of me—"

Vauregard closed up on him and put a hand on his shoulder. "You won't have time to yell. Just raise your voice, and you'll see. You won't get away with this, anyhow."

"Oh, go to the devil." Payne took something out of his pocket, and suddenly tossed it over Vauregard's shoulder. It fell to the sidewalk with a clatter. Vauregard whirled to pick it up, and as he did so footsteps again sounded, coming from the west. Payne, without a glance behind him, turned and limped quickly towards them.

Vauregard snatched up the object which lay on the flags, put it in his pocket, and walked eastward. He was almost at the corner before Gamadge, with Schenck at his side, came out of the area and followed him. The tall, bulky figure, in the old tweed suit and the felt hat with its brim turned low, crossed the avenue and proceeded along Seventy-fourth Street at a fast walk, hands in pockets and head down.

At the corner, Harold popped out of his doorway. After a word with Gamadge he got into the latter's car, and the pursuit divided itself into three; Gamadge on the south side of the street, Schenck (acquiescent and bewildered) on the north, and Harold crawling between, somewhere to the rear.

Vauregard went on, past brightly lighted avenues and along dark blocks of houses, keeping always to Seventy-fourth Street. He looked neither to right nor left, and he did not slacken his pace; he went like a man not pursued, but irresistibly drawn; his rubber-soled shoes carried him along as silently as if he had been a ghost. Schenck, not given to fancies, was conscious of a fatal quality in the atmosphere of this pursuit, as if the whole thing were settled, finished and foredoomed.

"It's Gamadge," he thought. "Feller knows what it's all about, he knew what was going to happen. He knows where Vauregard's going, I shouldn't wonder, and what's going to happen there."

They were nearing the river, and a cool easterly gust of air blew in their faces. This last block had been "reclaimed," and was a neat and trim oasis, with newly planted trees, three-story brick houses provided with dooryards or balconies, a good deal of bright paint on woodwork, and Venetian blinds behind clean, small-paned windows. Vauregard turned into the vestibule of a white-trimmed brick walk-up. The pursuit halted; Schenck and Gamadge arrived at the car together, and Harold leaned out of it.

"Now what?" Harold's eyes were burning, but his face remained properly impassive.

"Stay here. I'm going after him. He must have gone in. I'll have a look at the names in the vestibule."

Gamadge walked down the street, and also disappeared into the little house. Presently he returned. "There's evidently a superintendent in the basement," he said, "and six tenants. I have an idea that Jansen, top rear, is the party we want. The others seem more informative on their cards than Jansen does. All right, Harold; go on home. We're leaving."

"Listen." Schenck was unable to maintain his role of silent witness a moment longer. "There's nobody but us after this guy; aren't you going to tip off the police this time?"

"No. Come on, back to our hideout."

"We're going down the area again?"

"Certainly we are. We must see Mr. Richard Vauregard safely into his home."

Harold also protested. "Let me stay here and wait for him."

"Not you. Put the car and yourself to bed."

Harold turned, and drove away in dudgeon. Schenck, no longer amused, walked back to the area in silence, while Gamadge entertained him with a short dissertation on the rise, decline, fall and reclamation of small private dwellings in the city of New York.

They had not long to wait on the area steps. Vauregard came back within half an hour of their arrival, but this time he seemed nervous and wary. He took refuge twice in the areas— luckily, he kept to the north side of the street—and stopped several times between the corner and the Morton house to listen for approaching footsteps. Nobody came; he reached his own basement safely, and took a running jump to the broad window sill. Schenck, fascinated, followed his perilous upward course; it led him by ladderlike projections to the right of the drawing-room window, and thence to the bulbous foliage above. He climbed like a man who knows every inch of the way, quickly when the going was good, carefully when he had to straddle across a section of flat wall. He gained the scroll-work below the open second-story window, got a precarious hold on the sill with one hand, and stretched up his other arm. His hand just touched the ledge.

A shocking yell, sharp, earsplitting and inhuman, made Schenck leap to his feet; the great animal head and wrinkled face that surged from the blackness of the open window were like nothing he had ever seen but the mask of a Tibetan devil dancer. The sight and sound flung Vauregard back and out-wards; Schenck's cry was lost in an uproar of barking.

The front and basement doors flew open, and police poured out as Schenck dashed across the street. He heard Gamadge's voice loudly in his ear: "My God, the dog didn't know him."

CHAPTER TWENTY-ONE

Perfect Alibi

"MISS DAWSON SAYS the puppy was never in the house before, and Vauregard never laid eyes on him." Durfee, sitting beside a sphinx-legged table in the Morton drawing room, looked down at the amiably reclining chow whose ruff Gamadge was gently smoothing. "He's only a year old. She says Vauregard hadn't taken any interest in her dogs for over a year, and she was surprised when he went to see old Ching on Wednesday night."

Gamadge said: "I had completely forgotten that Miss Dawson had this friend staying with her."

"If we'd only known Vauregard was going to climb out tonight! We'd have let him go; glad to. We tried it on Duncannon, hoping he'd lead us to the Smith woman. All he did was what you two pests—" Durfee cast a baleful glance at Schenck, who sat modestly effacing himself in a corner—"saw him do. When that Garfield girl left, he went to sleep."

"What became of him?" asked Gamadge.

"Payne came back, and escorted him over to the Waldorf again. Our man got back into the room first, and they found him asleep, and had some trouble waking him up. We can try again; but if Vauregard had only got out of the house without getting killed, and one of these dumbbells I had on the job had only seen him go, he might have led us to the Smith woman himself. What's the matter with you?" He glared at Schenck, who was shuffling his feet.

"Nothing." Schenck cast an agonized glance at Gamadge, who said: "Schenck's civic loyalty is offended. He is afraid I won't tell you that Dick Vauregard was killed on his return trip."

Durfee stared.

"And that we saw him come out, followed him, and watched him in again—or as far in as he got," continued Gamadge amiably.

"You two happened by when he climbed out of this house?"

"Well—it wasn't exactly chance. I didn't know, of course, but I rather thought he would come out by the window."

Durfee said nothing, for a moment. Then he inquired, after a confounded look in Schenck's direction: "Why did you rather think he'd get out by the window?"

"Well, after all, this was the night of the perfect alibi—for Richard Vauregard. If he could get out, he would be able to get away with anything; and he had errands to do."

"Could you oblige me by saying why you thought of the window? We didn't, God knows why."

"Well, I learned the other day that he grew up without a latchkey. I wondered at the time whether he had really waited until he was out of college for one, looked at the footholds on the front of this preposterous house, and decided he hadn't. I mean, I knew what I should have done in his fix."

"Mind telling me why you thought he was the one that wanted to get away with something?"

"Not at all; that's what I'm still here for. It was on account of the information you were kind enough to get for me today."

"Those medicines?" Durfee looked incredulous.

"Oh, yes; they settled it. Closed the case."

Durfee said: "That's good. Actually closed it? No theorizing?"

"What I should call first-rate circumstantial evidence."

"I'd like to hear it; but what I want to hear now, is where Vauregard went tonight."

"You tell us first whether we're pests or not."

"No, you're not. Only we'd a little rather have your ideas, and dispense with all this amateur sleuthing. You let Vauregard get killed."

"So we did. Would you have stopped him before he climbed into the house?"

"I never had a chance to decide. Where did he go?"

"Do you very much mind hearing the other evidence first? We're quiet and peaceful here, with nobody to disturb us; I can't tell you anything if we're all traveling around in cars, and you ought to hear this tonight."

"You bet your life I'll hear it tonight."

"What I mean is, there's no hurry about that trip of Vauregard's—there really isn't."

Durfee looked at him, and then at Schenck, who said: "I don't know a thing."

"He was my witness," explained Gamadge. "Came along at great inconvenience to himself. We'll need him."

Schenck shuffled his feet, but said nothing.

"If you mean you want him to stay, all right with me. Let's get going," said Durfee.

"Let's. Old Mr. Vauregard got a dose of potassium cyanide—in solution—with his second cup of coffee. I wondered how a layman could get hold of such stuff "

"So did we."

"Of course," Gamadge went on, gazing innocently at Durfee, "Cameron Payne had once had the run of a chemical laboratory, and may have the run of it still. I suppose you knew he meant to be a metallurgical chemist?"

"I suppose we did." Durfee returned his look blandly.

"But you didn't have the advantage of knowing that Miss Dawson's old chow was given euthanasia on Wednesday evening, and that the whole family, including Payne, was present. The whole family except Mrs. Morton. The vet, Wadley, performed a slight operation on my cat, this morning, which the unfortunate beast didn't in the least require, and informed me that the hypodermic used on Miss Dawson's dog contained a solution of potassium cyanide."

Durfee jerked upright in his chair.

"The jar of cyanide," continued Gamadge, "was left in an accessible spot on Wednesday evening. Wadley ascertained, at my request, that it had lost nine minims of its contents."

"This vet—why didn't he come forward?"

"Because I promised him that I would tell you about it myself. We drew the logical inference, greatly to Wadley's discomfiture. Of course Wadley and I both realized that no visitor could count on finding a jar of cyanide ready to hand; but what Wadley didn't seem to realize at all was that if nobody expected to find it there, nobody would come provided with a container for it.

"But how difficult, how nearly impossible, to transfer this deadly and highly scented poison from one receptacle to another, secretly, at a moment's notice, and without spilling a drop! For the life of me, I couldn't imagine how it could have been done, except by means of a hypodermic syringe or a medicine dropper.

"I managed to dispose of the hypodermic syringe theory to my own satisfaction; nobody carries one about as a regular thing except a diabetic, let us say, who requires it for the self-administration of insulin, or a drug addict. I couldn't persuade myself that any of the principals in this affair was a drug addict—there were no signs of it; and if one of them had been suffering from an illness requiring self-administered hypodermics, you would have learned that fact yourself, or deduced it, from Schildmann, Lestrange, Schumacher or Thorwald."

Durfee said nothing. His eyes wandered to Schenck, and back to Gamadge; he gently rubbed the back of his head, gently tugged at his collar, and shrugged his shoulders as if his coat were too tight for him; but he said nothing.

"We pass," said Gamadge, "to the question of a medicine dropper. Why does one carry a medicine dropper about with one? Again, for the self-administration of a remedy of some kind; but a man would certainly never do it, unless he required treatment in the course of the day while he was away from home. Vauregard, of all the men concerned, was in an office; Vauregard had caught cold on Saturday, as I learned from Miss Dawson this morning, and Lestrange had prescribed ephedrine; five drops in each nostril, three times daily. None of the others had had any medicines prescribed that required a dropper; not within the week, anyhow; and we had no interest in secret medicinal supplies of any sort, because the theft of the cyanide was, as I said, unpremeditated. The thief used what he happened to be carrying with him."

Durfee interrupted, half rising from his chair. "That ephedrine of Vauregard's—"

"It's a new, nearly full bottle, and it doesn't smell of cyanide. Calm yourself."

Durfee sank back. "Thorwald said he'd had a repeat, but I thought nothing of it."

"Why should you think anything of it? You hadn't my information. There's another interesting little point in connection with the ephedrine; I have had plenty of experience with medicine droppers of that size. If you use extreme care, you can draw up ten minims at a time; if you hurry, you only draw up nine. Wadley having lost nine minims—"

"It's evidence, all right!"

"And it's evidence which accounts for the fact that the poisoner couldn't leave the container behind him in Traders Row."

"So you concentrated on Vauregard—"

"Oh, I had been concentrating on him from the first. It was pretty obvious to me that Miss Smith must have a heart interest in the business, or some close connection with the principals which assured her that her interests would be taken care of. But would she have the kind of confidence she required in a woman, or a married man, or an engaged man? I thought not, so I focussed my attention on the unattached man in the circle."

Durfee again leapt to his feet, and Schenck cowered in his chair. "Vauregard went to see the Smith woman tonight, and you said I wouldn't be interested! I think you're crazy, after all! What's the address?"

"What's the hurry? He just went to see her; there's no reason why she should run away—she's installed in a nice little walk-up, just along the street here; or I suppose she is. Name of Jansen."

"Of all the—come along in the car, and show me the place."

Durfee dashed out of the room. Schenck caught Gamadge's elbow as they followed, and hissed in his ear:

"You're giving me nervous prostration."

"Why, for goodness' sake?"

"You're holding out on this cop. If I get in wrong with the boys, I'm sunk. Why don't you tell him the rest of it?"

"What did I leave out?"

"You know what you left out. You left out about that thing Vauregard took away from Payne. You never said a word about Payne."

"Why should I?"

"Why should you? I thought Vauregard would kill the guy under our noses. I was on tenterhooks."

"He wouldn't kill him till he had the gadget off him, whatever it was; and then that pedestrian came along. You heard him, didn't you?"

"Yes. And I was never so relieved in my life. Vauregard

meant business. That thing may be important evidence. It looked to me—"

Gamadge interrupted him. "Did you see what it was?"

"No."

"Well, then! If it was on the body, the police have it; if he got rid of it, what can we do?"

This specious argument by no means satisfied Schenck, who favored Gamadge with a gimlet look. That individual tore away from him, however, and ran down the front steps. Schenck joined him in the back of the police car, where Durfee, fuming, awaited them; a uniformed man got in beside the driver, Gamadge supplied an address, and they rolled away.

The superintendent of the walk-up, a young Spaniard who carried his baby like a parcel under his arm, came up out of the basement and said it was a high-class house.

"Who's this Jansen, top rear?" asked Durfee.

"Nice lady. She came on a sublet, last April."

"Know anything about her references?"

"I don't know nothing about their references. Yes, I do; she's a friend of the agent's."

"Who's the agent?"

"Some relation of the landlord."

"Who's the landlord?" Durfee's patience was admirable.

"This is all Vauregard property, this whole row."

"I bet he sneaked her in—didn't even pay rent for her." Durfee threw this to Gamadge over his shoulder.

"I suppose Vauregard was the old gentleman's agent for these houses."

The superintendent and the superintendent's baby gazed at them mournfully, through sloe eyes. Gamadge asked: "Has she been away?"

"Since the third of May; only got back Thursday evening. First I knew about it, she rung down and sent me out for oranges and had me start the milk. And the paper."

"Furnished apartment?" asked Durfee.

"No, none of them is furnished. There was some things the other tenants left; they sold the lease, and they wanted to sell the furniture. She bought it."

"Just give me the keys. You stay down here."

The superintendent shifted the baby, got out his keys, detached one, and handed it over. Durfee pressed the Jansen bell, waited and pressed it again. He then crooked a finger impatiently at the superintendent, who unlocked the front door, a troubled look on his dark and sorrowful face.

Durfee, the uniformed policeman, Gamadge and Schenck climbed three flights of stairs, which were neatly carpeted in mouse color. When they at last stood beneath a skylight, facing a blank gray door, Durfee knocked hard.

After a pause, a voice asked: "Who is it?"

"Police."

The door opened. Durfee inquired: "Miss Lydia Smith?"

CHAPTER TWENTY-TWO

Gamadge Closes His Eyes

THE FASHIONABLE FIGURE which stood on the threshold gazing wildly at them was Miss Lydia Smith, transformed. She wore a short black dress with no sleeves, plenty of make-up, and a complicated array of curls, piled high on her head. She was very beautiful.

"I don't know what you mean, 'Smith,'" she said. "You got the wrong party. The name is Jansen."

Her voice, like her face, was almost unrecognizable; she spoke in a higher register than that which she had used at the old Vauregard house, and her words came faster. Her large eyes went past Durfee to the policeman, from him to Schenck, and then to Gamadge. They rested on him, and went blank.

"Mr. Gamadge," said Durfee, "can you positively identify this woman as the woman who passed under the name of Lydia Smith when you met her on Wednesday afternoon?"

"Yes, I can." Gamadge returned her gaze regretfully.

"Why didn't you take my tip, Miss Smith, and quit in time? I all but asked you to."

She moved her eyes from him. "What is all this? I'm Mrs. Jansen."

"Whoever you are," said Durfee, "you've been going under the name of Lydia Smith, and I have a warrant for your arrest. False pretenses."

He advanced, and Miss Smith backed before him into a sparsely furnished living room. She said: "I won't say a word, and I want my lawyer."

"Is your lawyer Richard Vauregard? Because if he is, you can't get him. He's dead."

"Dead!" She grasped the back of a chair. "You're making it up. I saw him—I know he's not dead."

"You saw him this evening, about an hour ago; but he's dead, just the same," said Durfee, watching her.

"What happened to him?" she screamed.

"Accident. Climbing into the Morton house window."

"Oh, God, he only did it to see me!" She staggered, recovered herself, and suddenly seemed to go mad. She turned, snatched a little boxlike object from behind a cushion, and hurled it to the floor. "Take it! The film's still in it. I wasn't going to throw it away! That Dawson girl can't have her man, if I can't have mine!"

Gamadge closed his eyes. Schenck, greatly puzzled, looked at him, bent, picked up the tiny moving-picture camera, and handed it to Durfee.

"What's all this?" demanded the latter.

Miss Smith sat down on the sofa, breathing heavily, but otherwise mistress of herself again. "Some refugee," thought Schenck. "I don't blame the old gentleman."

"What's this movie camera doing here?" asked Durfee, handling it carefully.

"That's what Cameron Payne has been blackmailing my husband with. He hid in the summerhouse, on Thursday; and he took a movie of Dick coming, and me going away, and Dick leaving. I hope it makes him an accessory, or whatever Dickie was always talking about. Poor Dickie did it all for me; he wouldn't have killed them, if it hadn't been to protect me," gasped Miss Smith, suddenly breaking into tears. "And then to have that awful, limping, grinning..." she sank down on the sofa, but she was far from collapsed.

"Now, Miss Smith—" Durfee was benevolent.

"Don't you call me that. I'm Mrs. Vauregard."

"Mrs. Vauregard; just tell us all the rest of it, and who got up this swindle, and then you won't have to go through it again tonight. We need the story right now. Was anybody else in the swindle?"

"Nobody but Mrs. Morton. He introduced us, and she taught me all about it, and what to say, and how to act."

"You are an actress, aren't you?"

"Yes."

"Name?"

"Lily Magnus."

"Where'd you know him?"

"Out in California. We've only been married a year, but I knew him before. He came out every summer. I was never East until this spring, when he—when he thought the money was going to some people called Chandor."

"How'd he think of the swindle?"

"He found that book—the second volume." Schenck saw Gamadge close his eyes again, and then open them when she went on: "I don't know where he picked it up. He showed it to Mrs. Morton, and they put me here, and she came and gave me lessons."

"How'd you get down to the Traders Row house in the first place?"

"Dick drove me down in his car, and I walked a few blocks."

"Where did the costume come from?"

"Mrs. Morton got the materials, and we made it ourselves."

"How did you communicate with Vauregard?"

"He used to stop on his way home from his office, and get notes I left for him, and leave others for me. We put them in a crack in the wall, to the left of the gates. There was nobody about, at that hour."

"What about Thursday afternoon?"

"I left a note for him on Wednesday, as soon as Miss Vauregard left with this man." Her fleeting glance at Gamadge was a frightened one. "I told Dick everything that was said; about the book, and that quotation from Byron, and that stuff about the arbor being hexagonal, and Mr. Vauregard asking him to come back on Thursday between six and seven. Dick stopped around the corner, on Wednesday, and waited till they left, and then came and got the note. Then he went home, and met this man, and thought everything was all over, because he was sure it would be found out about the other Byron. That night he got that stuff at the vet's. It was just an impulse."

"Killed old Mr. Vauregard and Mrs. Morton on an impulse?"

"He thought that if I left, old Mr. Vauregard would get some other fad. He just couldn't stand it. Dick wasn't a criminal. We didn't mean any harm. It was just Miss Vauregard insisting on a detective."

"I swear I don't know why Vauregard didn't kill the old gentleman at the start, and save himself and you all this trouble, and keep you out of it!"

"It was Mrs. Morton's scheme. Dick wouldn't have killed him then, for anything. He was driven to it, I tell you! He couldn't stand being found out. And then Mrs. Morton was going to go back on us!"

Durfee was unable to make any comment for some time. At last he said: "Just tell me how you made your getaway, Thursday."

Mrs. Richard Vauregard's courage was failing. She leaned back against the cushion, and the policeman brought her a glass of water. She drank some of it, and said: "Dick came up to my room on Thursday, a little before half past five. I had been asleep—I slept a lot, down there; it was all there was to do. He had a coat with him—he bought it for me on Fourteenth Street. He told me to put it on and run. I came up here by subway. I didn't know anything about what happened until I saw the papers. Dick telephoned me not to worry, and not to go out. I didn't see him until tonight, when he brought that camera, and told me to destroy the film. He had to get out of the house and get hold of it—Payne showed it to him after dinner tonight. Dick told me he was used to climbing in and out. Why did he fall? Oh, why did he fall?"

She burst into tears again. Durfee, gazing upon her as upon a portent, asked: "Why didn't you destroy the film, like he told you to?"

"Destroy it?" she almost screamed the question. "Destroy it? It shows me leaving the house, and shows Dick talking to Mr. Vauregard at the library window afterwards! I wasn't ever going to destroy it!"

As she buried her face in the cushion, Gamadge quietly left the room. Schenck followed him downstairs in silence. When they were in the street, and walking away, Schenck collected his wits:

"That girl has good nerve! You could see she was fond of the feller, and she wasn't going to turn him down because he'd committed a couple of atrocities; but she had her defense program all ready, and by gosh, she came right out with it, and no time lost!"

"Life is sweet to her."

"Payne's an accessory, all right; I don't see why he tried to blackmail Vauregard—he had Miss Dawson's money coming."

"I don't think a hundred thousand dollars looks like very big money to Cameron Payne."

"What would a feller like that do when he's found out? Kill himself?"

"Certainly not. Laugh it off."

"Laugh it off!"

"That's his system."

"Why were you trying to keep him out of it?"

"My dear man! I wasn't interested in the ramifications of the case. All I wanted was to get Miss Vauregard and her niece out of the mess for good."

"Pretty bad for them, having it come out about young Vauregard."

"It's all bad for them, but this isn't the worst that could have happened; not much affection there, I gathered; and besides, I was afraid he might try to do some framing. Things looked black for Duncannon, things didn't look too well for Payne, some mud might have stuck to Miss Vauregard, or Miss Dawson, or both. Vauregard had the means to plant what clues he liked."

"Miss Dawson won't like this business about Payne."

"There were so many things she mightn't like, one had to choose among them."

"You didn't like it, when that camera flew out from under the cushion and hit the floor."

"Forget it. What I like doesn't matter a damn." They had reached Lexington Avenue, where Schenck proposed to board a bus. "I'm greatly obliged to you," said Gamadge. "I had to have a witness."

"Only too glad; I always enjoy your parties."

Schenck stood on his corner, and watched Gamadge out of sight. His face was very thoughtful, and his sharp eyes glinted. Mr. Schenck was thinking furiously.

It had turned very raw and cold, with a slight drizzle; but Gamadge walked the half mile home. With his hat pulled low, his coat collar up, and his hands in his pockets, he was a dejected and forlorn sight as he mounted his own front steps. Within the hall, however, a pleasant odor greeted him, apparently wafted down from the second story. He cast his hat and topcoat on a chair, and took the elevator.

When he reached the library, he found that Harold had built a fire and was toasting muffins on the embers. A jug of chocolate—Harold's favorite beverage—stood keeping warm on the hearth; plates, cups and a dish of butter occupied a cleared space on the writing table, and Martin lay dozing among manuscripts. Harold had put on his white laboratory blouse to cook in; there was defiance in his eye when he looked up from his toasting operations, but Gamadge dispelled it.

"I like a man who knows when to disobey orders," he said. The largest chair had been pulled up in front of the fire; he sat back in it, and stretched out his legs.

"How'd you know when to start this collation?"

"Mr. Schenck telephoned, a few minutes ago."

"The deuce he did."

"From a drugstore. Said you looked as if you were going to walk it, and it was coming on to rain, and he thought I might as well make a fire."

"I'm touched. I don't know why he thought anybody would hear the telephone, at this hour."

"Mr. Schenck knew I wouldn't be in bed."

"Bound to hear the end of the story—that it?"

Harold said, stiffly, that that was it.

"Miss Smith is discovered—she was married to Dick Vauregard. He's dead. Fell getting in the window, and smashed himself."

Harold again reacted in his own peculiar way. He said, after buttering two muffins and handing them to Gamadge, "The Dykinck bird won't be sorry when she reads the papers."

"You forget the Dykinck bird! You never heard of her, remember!"

"I drove down there after I left you, and stuck around a while."

"No, did you?" Gamadge regarded him gravely over the rim of his chocolate cup. "What for?"

"We were responsible for her. There was a light in the third floor front. She was sitting up, all right, but I wasn't sure that it was only desperation. I thought she might be waiting to let the feller in."

"After he'd shaken us off and escaped over the rooftops. I see."

"The light went out after a while, and I came away."

"I wonder you didn't drive up to The Humbert and watch over the slumbers of Payne. You didn't know that he was comfortably dug in at the Waldorf."

"I wouldn't care who killed that guy, or when."

"You don't share Theodore's admiration for Mr. Payne, I gather."

"I feel about him," said Harold, sugaring his chocolate, "the way Miss Dawson does."

"Miss Dawson!" Gamadge sat up, thoroughly startled. "What are you talking about?"

"She's on the way to the booby-hatch," said Harold. "Didn't you notice that he gives her the creeps?"

"You must be crazy."

"I guess you never saw her look at him when he wasn't looking, and she thought they were alone."

"You need sleep, that's what you need. Leave this mess the way it is, and for goodness' sake go to bed."

CHAPTER TWENTY-THREE

"What About the Animals?"

"THE WHOLE TROUBLE WAS," said Gamadge, "that I never dreamed he'd go after Payne so early. I thought he'd wait until later, when things inside and outside the house looked safe. I thought he'd lead us to Miss Smith, and then go on down to The Humbert; I meant to telephone Durfee, or somebody, the minute I was sure I knew where Smith was. The police would have headed him off."

October sunlight flooded the library; Miss Vauregard, who sat beside an open window, lifted her pale but composed face to it, and pushed her veil back from her forehead.

"What happened," she said, "was the best thing for him, and for us all."

"But I never meant Schenck to know anything about Payne, and his moving pictures. I was doing my best to keep Payne out of it."

"Do you think Clara doesn't know that?"

"It looks as if I—"

"Clara isn't imagining horrors about you, Henry."

"Everything was going all right, it was only Smith's word against his that he was blackmailing Vauregard; and then Schenck had to get up on the witness stand and describe that scene in the street! I couldn't ask him to keep quiet about it; and the miserable fellow thought he was doing me a favor. He got on to me, somehow—confound those sharp wits of his."

"I'm glad I didn't have to be there in court, that day. From what I can gather, Cameron managed to come out of it all pretty well."

"He's magnificent in the witness box, and part of his story luckily happened to be true; all that about taking the picture of Miss Smith to save Clara's family's money. And then he was so frank and pathetic about the rest of it—how he had to suppress the evidence in order to spare the feelings of Miss Vauregard and Miss Dawson; I'm perfectly certain that half the people in the courtroom were convinced he never tried out the blackmail at all, and that he was the victim of a plot."

"People just think what they want to think."

"I suppose Clara will never get over it."

"Don't forget that she never was in love with Cameron Payne; and ever since that Thursday, she had been sure that there was something queer going on about the pictures. What exactly did he get?"

"He got a movie of Dick arriving, and going into the house by the garden door. Then he got a sequence—Miss Smith coming out in her seven-dollar coat, and dashing away; old Mr. Vauregard and Dick at the library window; and then Dick coming out and planting the ephedrine bottle in the fountain. He dug under the geraniums, you know, and shoved it down the old pipe. They had to tear the thing to pieces to get it out. Look here, Miss Vauregard, must you really talk it over? I'm not sure that you ought."

"I'm used to it, by this time."

"Payne swore that he had seen the error of his ways, and was going to hand the film over to the police that very night, and only gave it up to Vauregard because he would have been killed on the spot if he hadn't. There had been no time for him to develop the pictures, with cops all over his place at all hours. Of course he had brought it along with him to scare Vauregard. He thought he was perfectly safe while the Morton house was guarded, and I suppose he was going to put the camera in his safe-deposit box. I warned him that Vauregard could get out, but he chose to think that I was making a fool of myself, and that I was talking about Duncannon. He enjoyed our conversation very much."

"He's been a strange, desperate creature ever since his accident. Clara would have died, or gone mad, living with him; but it took this blackmail story to make her give him up."

"I bet lots of people will think she's very hard-hearted. I knew she'd never stand a racket."

"Well, she won't have to worry about him; he's getting a fresh start among the best people. Miss Dykinck met me on the street, the other day—very aloof and condescending. I don't need Rose Dykinck," said Miss Vauregard, faintly smiling, "to tell me that as a family we can never hold up our heads again."

"I must say I like her nerve! I ought to tell her that you hold her in the hollow of your hand!"

"Oh, don't, she'd make away with herself; I mean, she really might!"

"You bet she might. I had to go very easy with Miss Dykinck."

"She told me that people don't understand Cameron Payne, and that he's the most spiritual human being she ever knew."

"I do hope she isn't going to let him in of an evening by the area gate; he might dig up some information about Byron—I got Volumes I and III back to her, by the way; pasted the flyleaf in again. Nobody ever noticed them, down there in Traders Row. But I dare say Volume II is at the bottom of the East River."

"Even if Cameron Payne did find out about the Byrons, he can't very well blackmail the Dykincks, poor things."

"Well, I understand that they still have their Newport cottage."

"And Rose won't have to let him in by the area gate; he is received by Mrs. Dykinck."

"No!"

"He's teaching her to take moving pictures out of her front sitting-room window."

At this Gamadge laughed so uproariously that Miss Vauregard finally laughed a little, too. She said: "I do wish we knew what was in that letter of Cornelia's to Deken!"

"I have my unalterable opinion about that. It told Cornelia's dearest Dykinck all about Miss Wagoneur's elopement with your Great-grand-uncle Charles."

"There never was a single word of suspicion against Great-grand-uncle Charles!"

"No, he was in Albany. I bet you anything that Miss Lydia Wagoneur joined him there."

"That's a safe bet, I must say!"

"And that your respected ancestors, knowing Charles, and therefore knowing how the affair would be sure to turn out, kept it dark—for a hundred years, too. But they couldn't fool a Dykinck!"

"Poor Miss Wagoneur. I hope they're not going to be too hard on that Magnus girl, Mr. Gamadge."

"I doubt that they will be. She turned back into Miss Smith, in court, and got the benefit of the doubt every time. Now she's even appealing the criminal conspiracy charge; thought it was just a family game, to humor an old gentleman, and did what her husband asked her to. But you know all that." He glanced sharply at Miss Vauregard. "Who better?"

"Who better, Mr. Gamadge?"

"She had Loveman—the most expensive defense counsel now living. Who's paying for him?"

"Tom Duncannon; but that's a secret."

"It had better be!"

"He always liked her; and nobody thinks she knew anything about either of those murders." Miss Vauregard faced him, her eyes veiled.

"I bet you're financing her, or helping to."

"Nonsense."

"Of course you are! Duncannon isn't the sort to part with any such sum as that must be, even for his ideal woman."

"Mr. Gamadge, she was Dick's wife. And he heard nothing talked about but money, all his life. Angela tried to control him too much. His father…I knew he was going the wrong way, ever so long ago. He didn't care for any of us; I suppose that's why we couldn't care more for him. He was fond of that girl—it's the least I can do…Well, I must go. Clara will be waiting. She's going to drive me down to pick up those tickets for New Mexico."

"Isn't she coming up?" Gamadge looked horribly disappointed.

"I'll see. No, I won't have you going down. You know Theodore will be hovering."

Miss Vauregard stepped into the elevator. Gamadge returned to the library and stood facing the door, his hands in his pockets and a tenseness about his general attitude. There was a short interval of silence, and then a tremendous outburst of barking. A yellow animal resembling a cat, but with the tail of a raccoon, shot into the room and sprang from a table to the mantelpiece. A bronze jug and two ashtrays clattered to the floor.

Gamadge ignored all this. The barking ceased, and presently Clara came in, out of breath, her eyes wide and apprehensive.

"Mr. Gamadge," she asked, "What are we going to do about the animals?"

"Animals." Gamadge looked at her, for the moment completely stumped.

"Yes. We can't teach them to get on together—they're too old."

"Oh, I see. Er—I don't cart mine about with me, much. We could leave them at home."

"Yes; but I thought...sometimes...we might—"

Gamadge stepped forward and took her face between his hands. "We will, Clara! We will."

"I thought I could learn to help Harold in the laboratory." Clara did not seem to find Gamadge's gesture unusual.

"Or you could help Athalie in the kitchen."

"Or I could help you to detect."

"In the library. If I ever detect again, of course; I thought you and I might both have had enough of it, for a while."

"I know I'm awful."

"Ruthless; that's the way detectives ought to be. Well, you've detected me, all right; so let's tell Miss Vauregard to go down and get the tickets herself, and an extra one for me. I'm going too."